THE LAST BOHEMIAN

Also in the series

Daughter of Valdoro by Evelyn Stewart Armstrong
Vote for a Silk Gown by Jay Allerton
Rendezvous with Danger by Margaret Pemberton
A Dying in the Night by Jan Roffman
The Master Idol by Anthony Burton
The Seventeenth Stair by Barbara Paul
The Lady of Wildersley by Josephine Edgar

THE LAST BOHEMIAN

A Novel about Modigliani

ANTHONY WILMOT

A Troubadour
Edited by Lesley Saxby

MACDONALD AND JANE'S . LONDON

FOR SHELAGH

First published in Great Britain in 1975 by
Macdonald & Jane's,
(Macdonald & Co. Publishers) Ltd,
Paulton House,
8 Shepherdess Walk,
London N.1.

ISBN 0 356 082105

Printed and bound in Great Britain by
REDWOOD BURN LIMITED
Trowbridge & Esher

'Your duty is never to waste yourself in
sacrifice. Your *real* duty is to save your
dream. Beauty herself makes painful demands;
but these nevertheless bring forth the
most supreme efforts of the soul.'
Amedeo Modigliani

Prologue

The tiny *atelier* was lit by the yellow glow of a kerosene lamp. The wintry gale buffeted the house, rattling the wooden shutters and window frames. It was December, 1919, the dawning of France's second *belle époque*.

A girl was sitting at the window. She had a pale, ovaline face with delicate features, chestnut-brown hair to her waist in two plaits. A faint smile played on her mouth, reflecting an inner ecstasy and a haunting beauty.

A *pot-au-feu*, laced with garlic and marjoram, simmered on the stove in the kitchen. She went in and gave it a stir. It was hours since Amedeo had gone out to sell his drawings in the cafés, black felt hat at a characteristically rakish angle, portfolio under his arm, and a promise that he wouldn't be late.

She walked slowly into his studio. There were drawings and canvases everywhere. Portraits of little children with scrubbed faces and sad eyes; butcher-boys with cheeky grins; waifs, urchins, nuns, serving girls, bakers' wives, midinettes, laundry-girls, maids, *lorettes*, street buskers and society women. Leopold Zborowski*, Amedeo's Polish dealer with his melancholy Slavic face; Chaim Soutine, the young White Russian who painted putrefying meat from the abattoirs; Hanka Zborowska, aristocratic head reclining to one side; the Montparnasse models, Nina Stein, Gaby, Ruby Czechowska, Yvette, Aicha Goblet . . . and Elvira Lacrot, a Venus spawned in the liquor dens of Marseille. Amedeo's lustrous orange skin tones seemed to bring her to life on the wall.

But the girl had no jealousy; she accepted them for what they were. Fernande Barrey, Foujita's wife, had told her: 'You have to learn to share an artist with the women he paints. When a woman poses, he gives something of himself to her, and she to him. That's the way it is with artists. You

* *Sold at Sotheby's, London, for £85,000 in 1970.*

can never own them; they belong to Art.'

On his easel was a portrait of herself, half-finished. His bold strokes emphasized her ripening motherhood. 'There's no lovelier sight than woman with child, *cara*.' But her figure! she had protested as he worked; she was enormous! 'On the contrary – you look like a Dürer madonna. Or Leonardo's favourite model, Mona Lisa, the wife of Francesco del Gioconda, whom Vasari says took Leonardo four years to paint. Just think, *cara* – four years. One model!' He had run a hand through his thick, curling hair. 'If only my leaden hand could do justice to you!'

'It has. Many times. The proof is all around us.'

'Ah! The blind faith of the disciple.'

'No, Dedo. You taught me to open my eyes. To see beauty.'

He had scraped away the impasto with a palette knife, reworking the malleable pigments. '*Chiaroscuro, cara*. One of the first lessons I learned at Micheli's – light is everything. "Paint the light on things," Micheli used to tell us, "not the things themselves." Yes, old Gugliemo was no fool. He *knew*.'

She had trained herself to sit perfectly still whenever she posed for him; he hated her to move, even a fraction. Back and limbs like stone, she had watched him cross-hatching, as handsome as a Greek god.

Her thoughts turned to the present. On his work table was a telegram; she read it for the twentieth time.

PEASANT GIRL BOUGHT BY SACHEVERELL SITWELL STOP ALL CONVENT DRAWINGS SOLD ARNOLD BENNETT COMING TODAY STOP FAME AT LAST STOP REGARDS LEOPOLD

She returned to the window and stared out across the moonlit rooftops. It seemed an eternity since she had first attended life classes at the Colarossi Academy. Herr Schuler, the Austrian tutor, had told her parents: 'Your daughter has talent. She could become a fine artist.' Papa had been dubious; art was a pastime, a dalliance not a livelihood. But

Maman was thrilled and had somehow persuaded Papa to let her study for the entrance examination for the Ecole des Beaux-Arts. Then, one summer afternoon, her destiny had become irretrievably linked with the proud, penniless artist everyone called the 'Prince of Montparnasse'.

A knock came at the door. Her heart leapt. Who could be visiting at such a late hour? She stared at the door; her limbs seemed petrified. The knock came again.

'Madame Modigliani,' a familiar voice called from the hallway, 'I've been trying to find your husband. Would you know where he is?'

She opened the door a few inches. 'We have nothing to discuss, m'sieur; I explained all that to you yesterday.'

'Two minutes of your time, that's all I ask. Oh, I know your husband and I have – well, let's just say we have our differences. But I admire his talent and I'm willing to forgive and forget.'

'I have given you my answer, Monsieur Cheron. Now if you'll excuse me . . . it is late.'

'Just a minute of your time, madame,' said Emile Cheron, pushing his way inside and staring at the paintings festooning the walls. He ran his tongue over his thick lips. 'Do you know when M'sieur Modigliani will be home?'

'Soon. But he won't wish to discuss business, m'sieur – '

'These paintings – are they for sale?'

'You will have to ask him yourself.'

'I'm a busy man. I haven't time to comb the streets to find him.' He took out his wallet. 'You'll be needing money soon . . . for the baby. Two thousand francs, what do you say?'

'It's late, m'sieur, and I'm tired. And, as you know, Amedeo already has a dealer.'

'Yes, yes, the Pole, Zborowski. Oh, I admit he's a nice enough fellow, but can he *sell* paintings?'

She knew the Paris dealers thought Leopold gullible, prey to every sharp practice in the business, but she said: 'If he has a fault, it is being an honest man among thieves.'

'Look, I'm willing to promote Modigliani's work; get his

canvases exhibited in important galleries where they'll be seen by wealthy collectors – '

Oh, why didn't he go away and leave her alone? She was sick and tired of being pestered day after day.

'Two thousand francs, then. That's a generous offer,' Cheron said, transfixed by the paintings on the walls. 'What do you say, madame? Have we a deal?'

Why, why, why? The girl's head began to reel. What was inducing M. Cheron to part with two thousand francs when he'd never ever had a kind word for Amedeo's work? The dealer's eyes were huge orbs of greed; a film of perspiration had broken out on his coarse face. He waved the money at her, lips trembling with suppressed excitement. 'You accept then?'

The man's urgency made her blood run cold.

'I'm tired; please go now. I'm not well . . . ' She felt suddenly faint, unreal.

He glanced at her ripening figure. 'The baby. Of course . . . ' He began to back to the door, still unable to wrench his eyes from the paintings. 'You will speak to him?'

'All right,' she said wearily.

'The moment he comes home?'

'Yes, yes.' Anything to get rid of him.

'Here's my card. You can phone me here, day or night. I'll bring the money right away. Two thousand francs, tell him. Cash.'

Oh, why didn't he go! She began to close the door as he stepped out into the hallway, still reluctant to leave.

'Good night, madame. You can trust me; I only have your interest at heart. Take the money now – for the baby's sake.'

She closed the door, his words still echoing in her overwrought mind. Oh Amedeo, why don't you come home? Why must you walk the streets at night? What do you hope to find?

In her mind's eye she could still see Amedeo's face, tortured by fatigue . . . 'I'm sure to sell some drawings, *cara*. Saturday is the big night at the cafés.'

It was past midnight. She wrapped her shawl about her

shoulders. She would have to look for him round his old haunts.

The rue de la Grand-Chaumière was sombre, foreboding, the wind icy. The yellow haloes of the gas-lamps cast an eerie glow over the paving stones. She turned into the Boulevard du Montparnasse. The lights of the Café de la Rotonde seemed to beckon her.

She felt a stab of pain as her child began to kick protestingly; the doctor had warned her it might be a difficult birth.

There was no sign of Amedeo at the Rotonde or the Café du Dome. Nobody remembered seeing him at all that night. Perhaps he'd gone to Rosalie's for supper, somebody suggested.

She hurried through the dark streets to the little restaurant in the rue de la Campagne-Première, haunt of artists, musicians, models and writers. It was in darkness; closed for the night.

She walked the avenues of Montparnasse. Frost was gathering on the moonlit cobblestones, winking like tinselled confetti. The arching plane trees rustled in the night air.

Along the Boulevard Raspail she saw a familiar figure hunched on a bench; her heart leapt. He was lost in a private world. Propped up against one of the wrought-iron legs was his portfolio, crammed with sketches and drawings, some spilling on to the ground around his feet. Each had his masterly style and economy of line; character and personality were caught by a few sharp strokes of the pencil, revealing his superb draughtsmanship and unerring eye. How he loved to draw people in their unguarded moments. 'That's when they reveal their innermost thoughts,' he'd say, eyes burning, handsome as a Greek god, smiling at her in that roguish way she found irresistibly attractive.

'*Cara* Jeanne. It's late; are you very cross?' His voice was weary from rebuffs and gibes . . . Drawings? What do we need with drawings? Now, if you've got a pretty young sister . . .

He began to cough as the night air chilled his lungs. 'Ten

francs,' he said flatly. 'Hardly a treasure trove.'

'Your allowance from Leopold is due soon. We can manage.'

He smiled wryly and put a protective arm around her. '*Amor vincit omnia*. You still believe it?'

'Yes.'

He kissed her lightly on the forehead. 'Come on; let's go home.'

The fire was out when they arrived back at the *atelier*, but the *pot-au-feu* was still warm. Jeanne filled two soup bowls. As he sipped his, Amedeo stared unseeing at an unfinished portrait of her. 'Soup,' he murmured suddenly. 'That's what I need to keep him away.'

'Keep who away, Dedo?' she asked, trying to conceal her anxiety.

He said nothing, but dabbed lethargically at the canvas, eyes encircled by dark rings, pallid cheeks emphasizing the blue-black shadow of his beard.

Jeanne pressed her hand to his forehead.

'You've got a temperature.'

'It's nothing, *cara*; just the soup.'

'That cough's worse. You haven't slept properly for weeks.'

'Sleep?' He laughed hollowly. 'One day soon I'll sleep. The man in the hallway will see to that.'

One

The chisel flew off the cornice; the jagged block of marble seemed to have a life of its own, an inbuilt resistance to change. Amedeo wiped his brow. *Dio mio*! Being a sculptor was hard work. More hammering; he had no alternative. Again and again the marble deflected the chisel's steel blade until he felt his head would explode. Yet Constantine Brancusi, the bull-necked Roumanian sculptor, had warned him. 'Attack, attack, and when your chisel makes an impression, never retreat. Keep attacking, *mon ami*, or the marble will be the victor.' Ah, how true were Brancusi's words. The relentless tap-tap of the hammer echoed in his overwrought brain. Toulouse-Lautrec, at the tender age of twenty, had described himself as "a disillusioned old man". Amedeo now knew what the dwarf-legged genius had meant. Just turned thirty himself, he was despairing that his work would ever achieve recognition.

He laid down his hammer and chisel; he would have to postpone the Afro-Cubist head he was carving, though he had hoped to show it in the Salon d'Automne's next exhibition.

From outside his open window came the hearty cries of the street vendors. 'Ripe pimentos. Only two francs a kilo . . . Spanish navels, twenty centimes each.'

In the room below, Madame Velitch, once an opera star in Vienna, was putting her soprani students through their seemingly endless scales . . . *'Nein, nein, nein!* You must sink from ze diaphragm, not ze chest.'

Louis-the-Madman was leading his horse and cart through the street, begging for junk while the street urchins pelted him with apple cores, which prompted him to heap upon their tousled heads every Romany curse he could lay his tongue to.

Heavy boots clattered on the stairs: the Presle brothers were going off to their funeral parlour, troglodyte faces as ashen as their lifeless merchandise.

Amedeo smiled and opened his sketch-book at the drawing he had made earlier in the day. A laundry girl named Gaby had been squatting on her haunches outside the Vichy Laundry, puffing a cigarette during her morning break. He wished her to pose for five francs. *Certainement*. It was more than she earned in a day at her tubs.

He glanced at the clock: Gaby was due in fifteen minutes. He chose two hog's-hair brushes and began to prepare his palette: plenty of Flake White, Cobalt Blue, Vermilion, Yellow Ochre, Burnt Sienna and a touch of Magenta. His eye fell on the Botticelli reproduction pinned to the wall behind his easel. It seemed so long ago that Guglielmo Micheli had presented it to him, when he had left Livorno to study in Venice.

The once smooth matt paper was torn at the edges and yellowed with age. How well he remembered enrolling at Micheli's art school on his sixteenth birthday! The moment he had set foot in the bearded teacher's stone-built studio he had known art was his destiny. He had felt an affinity with the three-legged stools, models' dais, crucibles, brushes, charcoal-burner, linseed oil, turpentine and the reproductions of Bassano, Bartolommeo della Porta, Francesco Albani and Albertinelli.

Micheli had been impressed by Amedeo's burning ambition. But why did Amedeo wish to take up art? So easy to answer. 'I've been drawing ever since I was old enough to hold a pencil, *professore*. It's all I've ever wanted to do with my life.' Micheli had been encouraging, but not over-enthusiastic: art was a precarious profession. Only the very gifted could hope to earn a living. '*Wanting* to be an artist is commendable, my boy, but *becoming* an artist, ah! that's a very different matter.' Micheli had stressed that there was only one good reason why a man became an artist . . . 'Because he *must*. Because he cannot envisage earning his living any other way.'

It had not been easy, persuading his father. Flaminio Modigliani, with the dark eyes of his Jewish forefathers, had accused Amedeo of squandering his education. Why did he not become an engineer like his brother Umberto? Italy was famous for her engineers. Think of the Romans! Leonardo da Vinci! Galileo! Nobody made a living at painting: it was for the idle sons of the well-to-do. Did he want to hold the family name to ridicule? Were the Modiglianis not descended from the philosopher Spinoza? Had they not once been bankers to the Pope?

Only after weeks of argument and emotional outbursts did Flaminio reluctantly agree to let him study at Micheli's.

Amedeo set up his easel. On a wooden frame he stretched a piece of canvas which, the night before, he had primed with a white lead base. He was eager to paint Gaby; she was a handsome girl. She would be a fine nude to enter at the Salon d'Automne, along with *The Cellist*, a portrait of an out-of-work musician who lived in the apartment below.

He picked up the canvas and cast a critical eye over the cellist's lined, mahogany-like face, drooping shoulders and hollowed chest. Moise Kisling, the Polish artist who had studied in Cracow under the great Impressionist, Packiewicz, had urged Amedeo to show it. Jacques Lipchitz, the Russian sculptor, had been equally enthusiastic. 'It is in the finest tradition of the Siennese painters.'

At eleven o'clock sharp a tentative knock came at the door. He opened it. Gaby smiled shyly; her hair was piled up like a minaret and she wore a floral chiffon blouse and pleated skirt.

'*Bonjour*, m'sieur. You still wish me to pose for you?' she asked uncertainly.

'But of course!' He ushered her inside. 'You think I would forget such a pretty model?'

Gaby looked around at the latticed window which stretched up across the ceiling, walnut tallboy, horse-hair sofa sagging in the middle, chest of drawers, marble-topped table with ornate water jug and gate-legged table still littered with breakfast dishes.

'Is this the first time you've modelled, Gaby?' he asked, to put her at ease.

'Oui, m'sieur, I've never even been in an artist's studio before.'

'Well, don't worry. You'll soon get the hang of it.'

She watched him as he thinned the colours in his palette. 'Shall I undress, m'sieur?'

'When you're ready, Gaby.' She had a gamine's face: turned-up nose, lively eyes and well-scrubbed complexion. Her wrists and arms were coarse from the effect of the strong alkali in the laundry water.

Gaby began to undress. He softened his brushes in a jar of turpentine, catching glimpses of frilly petticoats and pantaloons. Her breasts were small but firm, thighs rounded and covered by a fine golden down. From this simple, warm-hearted laundress he would create a Modigliani woman; immortalize her in oils, as Toulouse-Lautrec had immortalized the cancan dancer, La Goulue, and the actress, Jane Avril. He selected a pencil with a needle-sharp point and opened his sketchbook. He began to draw.

Gaby gave him a puzzled look. 'You are not going to paint me?'

'Of course. But first some sketches. So that I can work on the portrait long after you've gone.'

'Ah, m'sieur is very clever.' And so handsome! She couldn't wait to tell all the girls at the laundry all about him.

Amedeo felt the canvas between his finger and thumb; yes, the primer was dry. He mixed Rose Pink and Burnt Sienna until it corresponded with Gaby's colouring. He squeezed Flake White directly on to the canvas and spread it with a palette knife. His boldness of execution increased with every stroke of the brush; his eyes instinctively rendered light and shade. Unhampered by the classic principles laid down by the Colarossi Academy, where he often attended life classes, his unique style began to emerge. His eyes flicked from Gaby to canvas, to palette to brush, to Gaby again . . . until he seemed almost a part of the portrait itself.

All too soon the hour was up.

'*Ecco*. You must be tired, Gaby.'

'Just a bit cold.' She smiled. 'At the tubs we stand ten

hours a day.'

'*Dio mio*, then you should leave!'

She shrugged. 'And do what? The laundry pays better than shop work.'

'Why, modelling of course! You could earn twenty francs a day. Maybe more.'

'You think I'm pretty enough, m'sieur?'

'Prettier than many who have modelled for me.'

'You have a favourite model, perhaps?'

'All models are my favourite.' He laughed. 'Now, it's time you were dressed.'

She pouted. 'I'm beginning to hate you.'

He smiled. 'That's a strong word.'

She stamped her foot on the bare boards. 'Now you are making fun of me.'

Amedeo merely smiled; he was used to the contentious, capricious nature of Parisian working girls. 'You haven't looked at the portrait yet. You may change your mind.'

She approached the easel, petulantly, stared at the canvas. Her eyes widened at the transluscent image illuminating the canvas with its rich golden hue, like a Normandy cornfield . . . her neck was like a swan's, graceful yet sensuous, limbs softly rounded like a Rodin sculpture, expression full of youthful *joie de vivre*.

'*Mais alors*, you're a real artist, m'sieur! Why, it's better than a photograph.'

'When it's shown at the Salon d'Automne, Gaby, you'll be the talk of Montparnasse. Every artist will be clamouring to paint you.'

'Me – famous?' Already she could hear the spitefully envious comments of the girls at the laundry, jealous of her success.

'You'll be as well known as Melba,' he said, suppressing a smile.

Gaby thought, then added eagerly: 'You'll want me to pose again?'

'Of course.'

She threw her arms round his neck. 'Cross your heart . . .

and hope to die?'

He drew his head back, laughing. 'I promise.'

Suddenly she began covering his face with kisses, her mouth hungrily finding his.

'Mademoiselle Gaby! You're a model – not a studio strumpet!'

'But I love you – '

'So soon?'

'Oh yes! Ever since that day outside the laundry I've thought of no one else. *Vraiment*.'

He shook his head. 'You should be thinking of marriage, Gaby. A nice young man with a steady job. Lots of babies.'

'You don't love me . . . just a little bit?'

'I hardly know you. Besides, what is love? Only poets can ever hope to define it.'

'I could clean for you. Do your washing. I wouldn't be a nuisance, honest.'

He took her face between his strong hands. 'I'm not the man for you, Gaby, believe me. An artist must be free. Free to experience life in all its capricious moods. You're a delightful girl. A wonderful model. Let's keep it that way, eh?'

Gaby began to dress, sniffing back the tears. 'But you will let me pose for you again?'

'*Mais oui*! Come whenever you like.'

He held out five francs. She stared.

'What's the matter, Gaby? Isn't it enough?'

'You really meant it?' she said. 'About paying me?'

'Of course.'

'Do all models get this much just for taking their clothes off?'

'Some earn much more.'

'What do I have to do? To become a model?'

'But you *are* one. I'll pass the word at the Rotonde. Good models are always in demand.'

'*Merci*.' She dropped her eyes. 'May I call you Amedeo?'

He laughed. 'But of course!' He was still smiling when she left, black boots clattering down the wooden stairs.

Whistling, he began to clean his brushes on a ball of rag. Love indeed! Whatever next?

The Boulevard du Montparnasse surged with people. Men in top hats, opera cloaks, twirling silver-knobbed canes; ladies with elegant coiffures and skirts that swept the ground; pretty midinettes with retroussé noses, ruby-red lips and mischievous eyes; leafy plane trees and boulevard cafés with striped umbrella sunshades; flower-sellers with wild violets; clanking motor-cars; horse-drawn omnibuses with their brass lamps gleaming; haughty Champs Elysées models staring from *fiacres*.

Amedeo's eyes absorbed the shapes, forms and colours. Paris! The Mecca of his dreams during four gruelling years at Guglielmo Micheli's art school . . . those back-breaking, head-reeling hours at the easel while his friends drank at the *bodegas* and flirted with the *signorinas*. Two further years of study at Venice's Institute of Fine Arts, every spare moment spent peering at statuary, frescoes, tapestries, busts, carvings and wood engravings . . . sketching beggars, washerwomen, waifs, tramps, midinettes in the Piazza di Marco, crinkly-faced crones and leathery artisans.

He took a deep breath. Ah, but you could almost taste the intoxicating air! He turned into the rue de la Grand-Chaumière and entered the Colarossi Academy through the heavy wooden street-doors; along a gloomy corridor to the life class. About thirty students, of both sexes, were scratching away with sticks of charcoal, gossiping and flirting with their eyes. A bosomy girl with large bold eyes and mousy hair cut in a fringe smiled as Amedeo passed her stool.

'*Bonjour*, Monsieur Modigliani.'

'*Bonjour* m'selle.'

He didn't pause in his stride; did she not realize he had more important things on his mind? Why, he still had four centuries of art to explore! From the pre-Raphaelites and the Florentine masters to the present-day Cubists and Surrealists . . . there was so much he had still to learn!

Herr Schuler peered at the class through pince-nez and made throat-rumblings. 'Silence, please!' Then he turned to a bored-looking girl who was sitting naked on a stool on the dais. She yawned and began filing her nails as Herr Schuler lectured the class on the rudiments of drawing the female anatomy. The girl's sole requirement was to sit still for an hour. Art? She had no idea what it was all about; cared even less. She was looking forward to joining her friends in the café.

Amedeo opened his sketchbook, sharpened his pencil until it had a needle-like point and began to draw the girl. He knew Herr Schuler's lecture inside out, but he was grateful for the opportunity to draw from life without having to pay the obligatory five francs, the price of a professional model. It was not every week he could afford a Gaby. Besides, the Academy had had famous alumni . . . Gauguin, Rodin and Whistler. It was something to put in his letters to Mama Modigliani back home in Livorno. It was a spur when things were not going well; a tradition to live up to, to be proud of.

An assistant at Vollard's Gallery had recommended he enrol, soon after he had arrived in Paris in 1906. He had been conspicuous then in his black cape, pressed Milanese suit, white starched shirt with its high, stiff collar, polished shoes, spats and cane . . . an attire he had believed befitted an up-and-coming young artist. He had considered the other students a bunch of ragged dilettantes in their faded denims, chequered shirts, patched trousers and *espadrilles*.

He found a seat next to his old friend, Foujita Tsugouharou, who was absorbed in one of his meticulously-drawn portraits. He glanced up, brown eyes twinkling intelligently.

'*Bonjour* Deo. Surprised to see me still slaving away?'

'Yes. You said you were leaving the last time I dropped in here. And that was weeks ago.'

'I still am. Maurice Vlaminck thinks I should become a *plein air* painter. Quit the Colarossi before it distorts my style. My father wants me to quit too – and go back to Yokohama to become a lawyer. In fact, he's stopped my allowance. But it won't make any difference. My girl friend

Fernande is going to manage my affairs. Wild horses couldn't drag me away from Montparnasse. As Nietzsche said. 'Paris is the only place for an artist.' He grinned. 'Fernande thinks I'm a crazy fool to stay with Cheron. She waltzed into his shop the other day and told him he was a rogue and a cheat – to his face! He almost had an apoplectic fit on the spot.'

'Bravo.' Amedeo laughed, visualizing the toad-like art dealer being chastised by the buxom Fernande. 'It's time someone struck a blow for artistic freedom.'

'You know Fernande! She doesn't stand any nonsense. Least of all from parasites like Cheron. So now she's taken charge of selling my work. She says it's her one great talent, because she's been selling herself ever since she came to Paris.'

'Fernande's one in a million.'

Foujita studied Amedeo thoughtfully. 'It's time you settled down, Deo. A good woman can do wonders for a man's career.'

'Oh, I can't afford to be tied down. There's too much to see. Too much to learn. Maybe one day.'

Frowning in concentration, Foujita sketched the model, cross-hatching in pencil. 'Have you found yourself a dealer yet?'

'No. I prefer to sell my own work.'

'It's better if you can. But dealers have their uses, *mon ami*. In case you ever decide to work for Cheron, let me give you a few tips.'

Amedeo listened gratefully to his friend's advice; it was hard to forget the past months . . . the exhausting, humiliating tramps around the pavement cafés, hoping to find a rare sympathizer . . . stomach rattling, hunger gnawing at his intestines. He walked the streets with hunger as his companion. Today. Tomorrow, the next day, eternally.

He asked himself honestly: was he bitter? No. Was he a martyr to the cause? Certainly not. Had he become a prey to self-pity? No. *Dio mio*, he was only just beginning! Paris could not be bludgeoned into yielding her accolades. She had to be wooed, flattered, enticed into surrender, like a beautiful woman. Why, Expressionism was only just coming into its full potential. He and Chaim Soutine had cleared the Impressionists' palette. They had rejected the past; only the new, the bold, the revolutionary mattered. Take shadow, for instance. Use black, said fools; so other fools painted academical black into their moribund canvases. But there was no black; it was non-existent. A shadow in nature comprised the colours of the spectrum. Its blackness was caused solely by the effect of light. Ah, but the fools were blind to truth.

'How *are* you making out, Deo?'

'Oh, I get by. A sale here and there.'

Foujita gave him a shrewd look. 'The market is in a depressed state. Picasso's finding Cubism hard to sell. Derain and Vlaminck do commercial art to make ends meet. People just aren't buying paintings. What do they care if artists starve? Ah, sometimes I think all artists are mad.'

'My father wanted me to be an engineer. By now I'd have a roly-poly wife and six kids.'

'As it is, *mon ami*, we're scratching a living in studios that leak rain and sway in the wind . . . at the mercy of pot-bellied dealers and their bourgeois idiot clients.'

Amedeo smiled. '*Vive la vie Bohème*!'

Herr Schuler bore down on them, peering myopically through precariously placed pince-nez. His brow furrowed. 'Ach, M'sieur Foujita, always you make with ze intricate designs. A woman should be elegant, m'sieur. Delicate like ze flowers, *hein*. You youngsters haf such strange ideas. Why, I'm told the Spaniard Picasso actually paints women with triangular heads and elliptical legs. Ach, I do not understand it. Perhaps I am getting old?'

Foujita looked at Amedeo and winked. To Herr Schuler he said solemnly: 'They ridiculed Gauguin. They crucified Van Gogh. And now they mock Foujita. Van Gogh painted more than two hundred canvases in his lifetime – and sold only one. Why? Because he painted truthfully – he painted real people involved in real life. He gave his life in pursuit of absolute truth. The ultimate idealist. And how did the world reward him? With a bullet through the head.'

'What's more,' Amedeo said, 'Gauguin had to die like a dog in Tahiti before the fools sat up.'

Baffled, Herr Schuler shook his shaggy head. 'Ach, you Modernists. Always you have your little joke, eh? Modernists,' he murmured, moving on to another group of students, 'will I ever understand them?'

The two friends sketched a while. Then Foujita said: 'Perhaps old Schuler's right, Deo. Maybe people don't understand our work. When they look at our paintings they see colours, shapes, ideas that contradict every law or concept they were ever taught.'

Amedeo nodded. 'People buy only what the Salon critics tell them to buy. They have few critical faculties of their own. Give them something new, they sigh for traditionalism. Give them traditionalism, they cry for originality.'

Foujita sighed. 'Ah, when I first came to Paris I was going to blaze new trails. Set the art world on its head. But the philistines don't want change, Deo. They want kippers, mandolins, bowls of fruit and vases of flowers.'

'*Ad nauseam,*' Amedeo added in agreement.

He studied his friend's drawing.

Foujita shrugged. 'I know what you're thinking: I'm pandering to popular taste. Cheron will pay twenty francs and sell it to some philistine for fifty. Don't think too badly of me, Deo. I've tried being original: it just kept me hungry.'

'Oh, don't think I'm criticizing what you're doing, Foujita. In many ways I envy you. I wish I could do the same. Don't misunderstand me . . . it's not that I consider being popular beneath my dignity. It's something else; something I hardly understand myself. It's as if there's a *sensation*, always just out of reach. I can't explain it; all I know is that there's a voice inside me which keeps telling me to keep on searching until I find it. Does that make sense, Foujita? Or am I chasing moonbeams?'

'It makes sense, Deo. It's a lonely path. Many have trodden it; few have reached the end.'

Amedeo felt an affinity with Foujita and valued his advice. He would never forget Foujita's kindness, or how he had loaned him canvas and oils and helped him to find a studio. Now, remembering his early years in Paris, Amedeo was appalled at the condescending attitude he had had to other artists. How shocked he had been to discover Foujita's impoverished circumstances and his austere attic studio. Aicha Goblet, a beautiful Negress with skin as smooth as ebony, had been posing nude for Foujita. Both she and Foujita had been amused by his fancy clothes. Ah, but what an insufferable prig he must have seemed to them. How naïve of him to imagine that artists would dress like aristocrats.

He had lost no time in exchanging his dandy's suit, cape, dress-shirt, spats and cane at Papa Lemey's rag-and-bone shop on the Boul' du Montparnasse.

He had emerged from the musty shop in a beige corduroy suit, scarlet cummerbund, yellow cretonne shirt, red cravat and a black felt hat with a wide Spanish-styled brim. As part of the transaction he had done a pastel portrait of the wizened old dealer. 'Something to show your grandchildren, *mon vieux*.'

He had sauntered self-consciously along the boulevard, a little deflated that his appearance didn't bring the expected curious glances from passers-by. To complete the metamorphosis he had rented a creaky old attic studio near the Bateau Lavoir, the derelict laundry inhabited by Picasso's coterie. It had been a rude awakening, after months of living off capital, browsing in the Louvre and fashionable galleries in the rue Laffitte, buying materials in the snobbish Avenue Frochot: 'My sketch-book is the place for private rehearsals' (or) 'I'll take a dozen of your best graphite pencils.'

Every night he had climbed the steps of the Sacré-Coeur. Ah, how superior he had felt! He had scorned the struggling artists who congregated on the Butte of Montmartre. From the top of the high basilica he had gazed across the luminous sea of twinkling lights, convinced he was on the verge of greatness. Ah, but how quickly Paris had shattered his illusions!

'Moise Kisling says you've got a patron, Deo.'

'Père Angely? He's just a dabbler. He really deals in junk

and bric-à-brac. He buys paintings as a sideline.'

'So? One of my best customers is a fat old crone from Neuilly. Wouldn't know a Millet from a Canaletto – but her money's good.'

'But old man Angely's almost blind; he has no idea what he's buying. A carved African head might just as well be a *bidet*. He arrived one day saying he was looking for picture frames. Well, after a lot of humming and hawing, he admitted he had a client who collected Italian paintings. I showed him a portrait of Beatrice Hastings. I'd re-worked it so many times I was sick of it. Blow me down if he didn't offer twenty francs. What's more, he said he'd take one a month like it.'

Foujita studied Amedeo's ruggedly handsome profile; with his dark brooding eyes and olive skin, it was easy to see why girls threw themselves at him.

'Who's this ravishing flaxen-haired model you've been seen with? The gang say she's like a Renoir barmaid: voluptuous and willing. You lucky devil. How do you do it?'

'Gaby? She's just a girl from the laundry.'

Foujita grinned. 'Don't be so modest, you paint-stained Casanova. She's crazy about you. Like all the others.'

Amedeo laughed. 'As a matter of fact I'm entering a nude of her at next week's Salon exhibition.'

'*Mon Dieu*! Are you mad? You know what those stuffed-shirts think of realism. They'll have you barred for life.'

'Times have changed, Foujita. The Salon is more liberal-minded now.'

Foujita snorted. 'Liberal – *merde*! Armand Avenne and his gang of sycophants will always be die-hard conservatives.'

Grinning, Amedeo closed his sketch-book. 'Come on, I'll buy you a coffee at the Rotonde. I know you're dying to tell me what you're going to show at the Salon.'

Two

The Fauve Group's fourth Salon d'Automne Exhibition of 1917 caused a stir of excitement throughout Paris. As the outstanding event on the social calendar, it would be patronized by society hostesses, wealthy dowagers, exiled princes, debutantes hopeful of finding eligible bachelors, young men-about-town, poets, merchants, representatives of provincial art galleries, hangers-on and charlatans in a variety of guises.

Inside the gallery's main hall Amedeo and Foujita watched the arrival of blasé connoisseurs, speculators and beady-eyed dealers.

'A formidable bunch, Deo.'

'Don't worry, my friend. Our work is as good as any here.' Amedeo appraised the Sunday painters' exhibits: decorative but lacking in style and originality. 'Already I can smell our red seals of merit.'

'Spoken like an optimistic idiot,' Foujita said wryly.

'You're just a born cynic, Foujita. Where are your hopes, your dreams?'

'The Salon buried them years ago!'

Amedeo had high hopes of *The Cellist, Etude de Tête*, two Afro-Cubist stone carvings and the Gaby nude. Hadn't Augustus John, the bearded, velvet-waistcoated Welsh painter, and the American sculptor, Jacob Epstein, praised his work? John had bought two stone heads for three hundred francs. 'You have a feeling for stone, young man. A rare talent.' No matter that his studio was a jumble of canvases, stone heads, paint pots, tins, picture frames; no matter that his corduroy suit was paint-stained and creased, or that his cretonne shirts were frayed at the collars. They had recognized his ability. He was finding himself as an artist. That was what mattered.

The Salon's coterie of critics who were to judge the exhibits arrived in morning coats, pin-striped trousers, carnation buttonholes, cravats, chequered waistcoats and ornate watch-chains. Their leader was a tall, cadaverous-looking man who twirled a silver-knobbed cane.

'Armand Avenne,' Foujita sniffed. 'He thinks he's the greatest art critic ever. But I think he's a pompous ass. That red-faced one is Arsène Alexandre; he's an even bigger ass. Next is André Salmon. And now Gustave Coquiot. The rest are sycophants. Salmon's the only one with any real critical ability. That's why Picasso, Derain, Vlaminck and the Cubists won't show here. Only the traditionalists are favoured by the Salon. So don't build your hopes too high, Deo.'

But Amedeo was unperturbed; the Salon critics could not afford to dismiss good work. They had their reputations to think of. He and Foujita would fare well, he was convinced.

The Salon's custodians of artistic merit stopped at Foujita's and Amedeo's exhibits, coughed, cleared their throats in unison, adjusted their monocles and lorgnettes. Then their eyes alighted on the Gaby nude.

Nobody spoke.

Amedeo shot Foujita an enquiring glance, but his friend's face was as bland as ever. Not by a flicker of an eyelid did Foujita betray his awareness of the critics' scrutiny.

'Unusual,' M. Avenne said at length. The others took that as their cue. 'Oh, quite,' they chorused. 'Most unusual.'

'Who's the artist?' somebody piped up.

Amedeo's heart began to pound. If the nude earned a Press mention it was certain to find a buyer. Catalogues rustled, eyes scanned pages, but nobody spoke his name. Would they never find it? He longed to tell them, but he knew Salon etiquette forbade painters to fraternize with judges; there could be no hint of collusion. The Salon prided itself on its long history of impartiality.

'Modigli, or some-such-name,' M. Salmon said. 'Probably Spanish.'

Amedeo stepped forward; this was no time to observe Salon etiquette. How dare they liken him to a Spaniard! Didn't they know a Tuscan's eye for colour when it was before them?

'Italian, m'sieur. And it's Modigliani.'

'*Sans blague*!' M. Avenne gave Amedeo's crumpled suit a withering glance. 'We should have guessed, *mes amis*,' he said to his colleagues. 'He had too much spaghetti on his palette.'

Amedeo flushed as the critics sniggered. He stepped back, controlling his urge to retaliate as he remembered Foujita's warning.

M. Avenne turned his attention to Foujita's water-colours. 'Hmm. I thought Japanese gardens went out of fashion years ago. Seems I was wrong,' he added scathingly. 'Here they are, as gaudy as ever. Why can't we have something original?' He shook his head in feigned incomprehension.

'What would you know of originality, m'sieur? Your eyes are blinded by prejudice.' Amedeo had uttered the words before he realized it was his own voice speaking.

M. Avenne glowered. 'You have a sharp tongue, m'sieur. A pity your paint brush is not as lucid.'

'At least do Foujita's work justice,' Amedeo said hotly.

'I've seen your work, m'sieur. And your friend's. I can't see that looking again would serve any useful purpose. Now, if you'll excuse us . . . there are other exhibits to see.'

Amedeo was about to retaliate, but Foujita cautioned him.

'Let them go, Deo,' he murmured. 'It's only what I expected. For two hundred years the Salon judges have ridiculed foreign artists. Even the Salon d'Apollon in the Louvre used to bar painters of whom it did not approve. The moral is obvious: to succeed in Paris, one must first be French.'

'I'm sorry, Foujita. I spoiled your chances, didn't I?'

Foujita's solemn face broke into a broad grin.

'So what! It was worth it – wasn't it? – just to see their pompous faces!'

A ripple of excitement suddenly ran through the gathering.

'It's Degas,' somebody shouted.

The critics hurried towards the group already forming around the ageing Impressionist. Edgar Degas, stooping, grey-haired, straggly beard, blind in one eye, a recluse in his seventy-eighth year, a living legend who rarely exhibited or visited galleries. An artistic giant whose pastel drawings of the Paris Opera ballet commanded thousands of francs; who said, when told his *Dancers At The Bar* had been bought for ninety thousand dollars: 'I'm like the horse that wins the Grand Prix and is given a bag of oats.'

Foujita began to pack his water-colours. 'We may as well go, Deo. It's just our bad luck Degas should choose today to visit the Salon. Come on, let the old fellow have his glory. Who knows, one day they could be mobbing us the same.'

'I still can't get over those critics,' Amedeo said. 'Their intolerance. The way they dismissed our work. Art, surely, is universal, transcending such mundane considerations as one's birthplace, one's nationality? What matters, surely, is what one puts on to canvas?'

'You're an idealist, my friend. Critics are motivated like all other narrow-minded men: by petty ambitions and social snobbery. But there will be other exhibitions. Next month it's the Salon des Indépendants. We'll get a fair showing there.'

'I hope you're right, Foujita. These bigoted popinjays shouldn't be allowed to stifle progress. And one day I'll prove them wrong.'

Foujita gave him a shrewd glance. 'You really mean it, don't you?'

'Every word.'

It was evening. The studio was airless, claustrophobic. Amedeo cleaned his brushes. He needed a change of atmosphere. He picked up his portfolio; he would try his luck in the cafés.

As he strolled to the Rotonde, he reviewed the past weeks. He had been driving himself harder and harder, trying to find his way, discover his 'sensation'. Always it seemed to elude him. Just when he was convinced he had found it, it slipped away like will-o'-the-wisp. But his unique vision was developing. Each portrait of a laundry-girl, *femme de chambre*, midinette, milliner's assistant or pastry cook increased his confidence. Money, as always, was scarce; but there were commissions from butchers, bakers or merchants. It was an unwritten law among the Rotonde fraternity that artists charged twenty francs a sitting, taking care to stretch out the number of sittings. Not entirely ethical, perhaps, but it was either that or starve.

He entered the café. Foujita and Chaim Soutine were already at the zinc. At a nearby table Picasso and his disciples were arguing and debating theories, new techniques, clay pipes glowing like portable stoves.

Chaim's battered Talmudic features widened into a toothy grin.

'*Shalom*,' he greeted.

Amedeo shook hands with his friends.

'You look under the weather, Deo. Anything wrong?'

'Nothing.'

'Not still brooding about the Salon?'

'No. Just a headache.'

'Ha, a glass of wine will cure that!' Foujita poured out some Médoc.

'Those Salon critics are a bunch of fools,' Chaim growled. 'They wouldn't know a good painting from a dollop of horse manure.'

In Montparnasse everybody knew that if an artist had not studied at the Establishment-run Ecole des Beaux-Arts he had little chance of having his work recognized at the Salon d'Automne. Most of the modern artists had utter contempt for the Ecole because it had once refused entry to Rodin.

'I've definitely decided,' Foujita announced. 'I'm quitting the Colarossi. I'm joining Raymond Duncan's art group. He has some exciting ideas.'

Isadora Duncan's eccentric brother was a familiar figure in the Boul' du Montparnasse, with his flowing Grecian robes, rope sandals and white hair worn shoulder-length.

Amedeo nodded approvingly. 'I'm sure you'll make out,' he told the dapper Japanese. 'The Colarossi is useful occasionally. Helps you keep your eye in for anatomy. Old Schuler doesn't mind. In fact, I do believe he's quite flattered when a former student drops in.'

The smoky café was beginning to fill up with artists, poets, models, *grisettes*, sculptors, theatricals, assorted flotsam and fugitives from Tzarist Russia. The noise rose to an almost deafening crescendo. Lenin and Trotsky, their fanatical eyes glowing above dark beards, talked of the Revolution; Honegger and Milhaud scribbled music. Vlaminck told his shaggy companions: 'Paint with pure Vermilion. Pure Veronese Green, pure Cobalt Blue; that's the only truth, *mes amis*.'

Picasso was telling Chagall: 'I've a new theory for portraits, Marc. When you paint the head and shoulders, you place the limbs alongside the body, as though dismembered.'

The poet Max Jacob inhaled a marijuana cigarette. 'That's interesting, Pablo. I'll include that in my next piece for *Le Moniteur des Arts*.' Ferret-nosed, waxen-faced, Max was the son of a Jewish tailor in Brittany; though only in his twenty-ninth year, his drug-ravaged face looked twenty years older.

'Hallo, Max.' Amedeo waved; the wiry poet had been a good friend in the past, loaning him money to buy art materials, always trying to promote his work.

Ruby Czechowska, a willowy blonde infatuated with Amedeo, pushed her way to the zinc. 'Like me to pose for you, Amedeo?'

'Sorry. I'm broke.'

'You can pay me in kind,' she said, fluttering her long eyelashes.

Amedeo merely smiled.

'Well, if you change your mind, handsome, let me know . . . '

A ripple of excitement swept through the café. A beautiful dusky-skinned girl with jet black hair, wearing a figure-hugging silk blouse and skirt, sauntered in on the arm of Adolphe Basler, a miserly Polish émigré who had set himself up as a dealer. She walked with a rhythmic swing of the hips, delighting in the covetous glances men gave her. They sat at a table and Basler self-consciously ordered drinks.

'Who does she think she is?' Ruby said. 'Queen of Montparnasse?'

'It's Elvira Lacrot,' somebody said. 'She's singing at the Gaiety Theatre.'

'Singer, my eye,' Ruby sneered.

Amedeo opened his sketch-book. 'Basler doesn't know it yet, Foujita, but he's about to treat us to dinner.'

He approached their table. The girl looked at him with sultry arrogance.

'A portrait, m'sieur?' Amedeo addressed Basler. 'For the lady?'

Basler shook his head.

'I'd *love* a portrait,' she said huskily.

'Café artists are ten a penny,' Basler growled. 'We came here for a drink, remember?'

'Don't be tiresome, *chéri*,' she retorted, gazing into Amedeo's eyes.

Basler nodded to Amedeo reluctantly.

The girl watched, intrigued, as Amedeo, with quick, clear lines, captured her high cheekbones and wide mouth with its hint of cruelty.

'I'm Elvira Lacrot. The actress. You've heard of me?'

'You're at the Gaiety.' *Dio mio*, how could she bear to be pawed by that cod-eyed, fungoid-moustachioed idiot? True, Basler ran a successful business in antiques and objets d'art, but in appearance he resembled a cantankerous walrus.

'Only until the end of the week,' she said into his eyes. 'Then the company goes to Lyon. But I'm going to be a model. Aren't I, Adolphe?'

Basler just grunted, jealous of the way she was looking at Amedeo.

Amedeo signed the drawing and handed it to her.

'You draw very well . . . ' She looked at the signature. 'M'sieur Modigliani.'

Basler took out his wallet. 'What's the price? Five francs?'

'*Chéri*,' Elvira protested seductively, 'that's not nearly enough. Fifty would be better.' She gazed into Basler's eyes. 'It *is* a lovely drawing . . . and I adore it,' she added, smiling up at Amedeo.

Amedeo bowed; dinner was now a distinct possibility.

'Twenty-five,' Basler muttered.

'Don't be mean, Adolphe. Give him fifty.'

Basler, fuming, handed over the money.

Amedeo kissed her hand and expressed his appreciation. She smiled, her dark eyes devouring him.

Amedeo rejoined his friends. 'Drink up. And let's eat.'

Gastric juices stirring, they strode out of the Rotonde. Fifteen minutes later they were entering Chez Rosalie's, in the rue de la Campagne-Première, savouring the spicy aromas emanating from her mouth-watering kitchen.

Moise Kisling, the Polish Impressionist, was at a corner table, eating *pasta asciotta*. He waved. '*Bon soir*. Pull up some chairs.'

Mama Rosalie, red neckerchief flapping, bulged in the kitchen doorway. 'Who's making that racket?' She was brandishing a wooden soup ladle. 'This is a respectable establishment, not a bawdy house.'

'Mama Rosalie, my Bellini cherub,' Amedeo laughed. 'You get prettier every day. Tonight we'd like *pâté de foie gras, moules marinières*, caviar, champagne – '

'*Madonna mia*! You think I run a place for the idle rich?'

Amedeo grinned. 'A bottle of your best chianti, Mama.'

Luigi, Rosalie's son, rushed to their table with a bottle all ready. Amedeo poured it out. 'Chianti is Italy's finest wine. From Tuscany. It must be drunk while *frizzante* – prickly on the tongue.'

Suddenly the café door burst open and a buxom young woman with roguish eyes came in.

'What did I tell you?' she said, marching up to Foujita. 'I've sold every one of the paintings you gave me. Here – ninety francs.' Her cheeks glowed like the ruby-red wine from her native Moselle Valley.

Amedeo drew up a chair for her. Foujita had tried to keep it a secret, but everybody knew Fernande Barrey was his mistress.

'*Voilà*,' she said, putting the money on the table. 'Didn't I tell you I had a talent for selling?'

'I must repay you,' Foujita said, crimson-faced.

'I don't want payment,' she cried. 'Just marry me.'

'Bravo!' Amedeo laughed. 'More chianti, Mama Rosalie.'

Rosalie poked her head round the kitchen door, scowling. '*Basta*, or I call the *flics*!' But her eyes were twinkling and she told Luigi to open a fresh bottle. As his friends ate, drank and exchanged gossip Amedeo's thoughts were occupied with the rebuffs he'd received at the galleries in the rue Lafitte. After Augustus John's visit, he had taken the Gaby nude to Vollard's. They had been sympathetic. But why did he not paint a still life? Their customers wanted guitars, apples and pears, landscapes, flowers, mandolins . . . Yes, they knew Augustus John's work. And Epstein's. But neither of them was a big name in Paris.

Rosenburg's gallery had been less kind; a sale to Augustus John meant nothing to them. He was hardly in the class of Renoir or Seurat, was he? Monsieur should paint more fashionable subjects . . .

The salesmen at Druet's had been equally patronizing. 'M'sieur's work has a certain panache, but nudes are hardly suitable for our clientèle.' The doubts returned. Was he just a talented dilettante? Never to rise above mediocrity? Was his quest for his 'sensation' self-delusion? Degas would know. Degas had seen the greatness in Gauguin when the stock-broker-turned-artist had been starving in a garret, scorned by critics and public alike. Who would know Degas' whereabouts? His old friend, Maurice Utrillo.

'Drink up, Deo.' Foujita poured out more chianti. 'Fernande and I are engaged.'

'That's wonderful, Foujita. I'm delighted for you.'

Amedeo joined in the toast.

The next morning he took the Métro to Montmartre. Under his arm were a portrait of Gaby, another of a girl in a blue dress, and one of Max Jacob; a fair representation to show Degas. If Degas would see him . . .

Finding Maurice wouldn't be easy either. Amedeo hadn't seen him for several months. He began at Pigalle, searching cafés and *brasseries*. He ended up at the Lapin Agile Café in the rue Saint-Vincent, haunt of drug-addicts, apaches, *grisettes*, thieves, pimps, tourists and artists. Over the entrance was the legend: *Man's first duty is to have good digestion*.

Inside the air was thick, blue haze; everything was bathed in the ghoulish light of yellow lamps hanging from the rafters. He caught glimpses of voluptuous bosoms inside low-cut blouses, roguish expanses of thigh between black silk stockings and frilly pantaloons. The ladies of the house might almost have stepped down from the Moulin Rouge cancan posters that festooned the walls. Maurice was slumped over a table; beside him was a wine-stained sketch-book. He raised his eyes when Amedeo spoke his name.

'Deo.' Maurice wiped his drooping moustache on his hand. 'Long time no see. Have a drink.'

Maurice's bony hands shook as though palsied when he reached for the wine bottle. His face was sallow, eyes sunken and bloodshot. He had been drinking heavily.

Amedeo sat at the table. Poor Maurice. Drink had been his downfall since the age of fifteen. He was the illegitimate son of the artist Suzanne Valadon, and for years had been in and out of institutions, yet never cured of his craving for liquor. Art dealers called him a *peintre maudit*, a painter cursed. People ridiculed him when he sat in the streets of Montmartre painting white-stucco walls and crumbling masonry. They saw a shambling wreck whose haunted face was prematurely old. Amedeo knew that loneliness and despair drove Maurice to seek oblivion in liquor. He appreciated the melancholy beauty of the street scenes Maurice painted in white impasto. He too had known loneliness and despair; he understood Maurice's problems. Suzanne Valadon was an artist of distinction. *The Dress-maker*, one of her best known paintings, hung in the Musée de l'Art; it was she who had encouraged her tormented son to take up painting.

'How goes it, Maurice?'

'Oh, a sale here, a sale there. You know how it is.' Maurice's eyes were glazing over; his lantern jaw sunk on to his hollowed chest.

'Suzanne's arranging an exhibition for me. Wonderful woman, my mother. André Utter wants to marry her.' He began to sway like a hollyhock. 'Let's have another bottle of wine.'

'Some other time, Maurice. Just tell me where I can find Degas.'

'Degas?' Maurice looked round vaguely. 'He's here? Buy him a drink. Great artist. Used to paint my mother. Lives like a hermit. Going blind, they say. Let's drink – to Degas.'

'Just tell me where can I find him.'

Maurice cocked one eye open. 'If I tell you . . . you'll drink with me later?'

Amedeo agreed.

Maurice fumbled in his pockets and produced a wad of crumpled scraps of paper; the remnants of an address book. '*Voici*. Eight, rue Victor-Masse.'

Amedeo carried his canvases through the winding streets of the Butte. Maurice had deteriorated. Liquor was destroying him, but there was no stopping him. Hospitalization had failed. Cures had failed. Only painting provided him with the will to live; but it was a thin shred of hope. Something had to be done. But what? In 1914 he and Maurice had volunteered for Army service, within days of the outbreak of war. What a summer that had been! Temperatures in the nineties; cafés buzzing with rumours. A fat archduke assassinated? Served him right! The Kaiser didn't want war; he would rather fill himself with *Schnitzel*. Even when German troops had marched into Austria and Belgium, Parisians had gone on talking about Pavlova, Nijinsky and Diaghilev's *Ballets Russes*. The Kaiser wouldn't dare set foot in France. When the Government was evacuated to Bordeaux, Parisians smiled cynically. Wasn't that just like politicians?

But Gallic pride rose. Maurice went to enlist. Amedeo too: France was his adopted country. The artists rallied round the flag. Ortiz de Zarate, Ferdinand Léger, André Utter, Moise Kisling, Blaise Cendrars. They sang the *Marseillaise* outside the Hôtel des Invalides. Maurice was rejected because of delirium tremens; Amedeo because of 'chronic bronchitis'. Nonsense, he had told the medical officer. It's just a cough.

More tests. Same result.

But he was as strong as a horse; they couldn't fail him. Fail him they had.

Amedeo turned into the rue Victor-Masse. Number eight was a gaunt, three-storey, terraced house with dark windows, peeling paint and chipped white stucco. He was tempted to walk away. Degas might think him a novice masquerading in artist's clothing. He knocked at the door. No answer. He knocked again.

'Who the devil's there?' a voice growled from inside.

Amedeo gave his name.

'Dealer or creditor?'

'Artist.'

'*Mon Dieu*! That's worse than either.'

Yes, it had been a mistake to come. Degas hadn't the time or inclination to receive uninvited callers. He should have obeyed his instinct and gone. He descended the steps to the pavement.

Suddenly the door creaked open. A grizzly rust-coloured face peered out. 'You're going?' it asked Amedeo.

He nodded.

But – hadn't he said he was an artist?

He had.

'Well, don't stand outside. Come in. Come in.'

The inside of the rambling old house was a workshop, studio and art gallery in one. Pastels, gouaches, lithographs, paintings, busts . . . portraits of ballerinas, *chanteuses*, laundry women, girls on horseback, jockeys, women in bath-tubs and chic Parisiennes with cheeky faces and upturned noses.

Amedeo was overwhelmed. How could he show Degas his work after seeing all this? But suddenly, warming to the old artist's rough charm, he was pouring out his ambitions, telling of his humble beginning at Micheli's, of his two years at art school in Venice, his search for a unique vision. 'I want to paint the patina of colour rather than colour itself. The cloudy gold of mellowing varnish. The sun-bleached blue of a Tuscany wall.'

'Ah, Tuscany! Wonderful place. Was there myself as a young man. Yes – follow the Italian masters, without imitating them. Purity of line; that's the secret. I learned it from the early *quattrocento*. But style, personal expression, ah! that comes from within. That's the way, my boy. Breathe life into your work. Show people's suffering. Their hopes, dreams, vices, pride, pretentions, dignity.'

He studied Amedeo's canvases.

'As yet, undisciplined. Needs more control, but shows great promise. Remember: drawing is not form, but only a way of expressing form. Art doesn't expand; it repeats itself. As for what you seek . . . it's here, in Paris. In the scrubbed face of a washerwoman. The bold eye of a *lorette*. The smile of a child.'

'But the critics, m'sieur. They dismiss my work. And my friends, Utrillo, Soutine, Foujita – '

'Did you say Utrillo?'

'Suzanne Valadon's son, m'sieur. A great artist.'

'Ah, Suzanne Valadon! What a woman! And what a figure! She used to model for me. Wonderful woman. Fine painter too. What times we had at the Café Guerbois! Manet, Renoir, Pissaro, Zola, Maupassant, Whistler, Oscar Wilde. Ah yes – golden days! But all gone, all gone. And that bearded dwarf, Lautrec. What a drinker! *Mon Dieu* – absinthe, campari, cognac, champagne – anything! A miracle he lived as long as he did. See that?' Degas pointed to a collection of yellowing photographs on a wall. 'That's me. In the middle. With Lautrec, Van Gogh, Bonnard and Gauguin.'

He shook his head at the memory. 'What was that you were saying about critics?'

'The Salon d'Automne – '

'Hah, those parasites! They feed off the success of artists. They are the same the world over. Ignore them, my boy.

Trust your own judgement. The public will decide for itself what is art. Until then, paint, paint, paint. Go deeper into yourself. Find out what you have in you.' Degas closed his eyes and leaned back in his armchair. 'What nights we had! Bal Tabarin, Moulin Rouge, Lapin Agile, Deux Magots, Moulin de la Galette . . . ' He yawned. 'So tired these days.' Degas's chin slumped on to his chest.

Amedeo collected up his canvases. 'A thousand thanks, *mon vieux*. You have given me hope; something to strive for. A *raison d'être*.'

Degas began to snore gently. Amedeo tip-toed to the door.

'Sleep well, *mon vieux*.'

He retraced his steps to the Lapin Agile. Degas believed he had promise. That was something, wasn't it? Worth more than all the Salon's accolades. He couldn't wait to break the news to Maurice.

He entered the café. Maurice was slumped in a corner, breathing stertorously. Dead to the world. Ah, perhaps it was just as well: Maurice had no faith in anybody, save Suzanne.

'Maurice?' Oblivion. He scribbled a note and tucked it into Maurice's top pocket. *Au revoir*, old friend.

There was a visitor waiting when Amedeo arrived at his studio – Père Angely, the dealer in bric-à-brac. He greeted Amedeo warmly, squinting through cracked spectacles. 'You have more canvases, m'sieur?' he said, following Amedeo to the stairs.

Amedeo took the old man's arm and helped him up. First, praise from Degas; next, a potential buyer. His lucky day. Once inside the studio Père Angely got down to business. He wanted two portraits, preferably of young women. Amedeo selected a head-and-shoulder portrait of Gaby; another of a baker's wife. Both skilfully painted, but not his best work. But, then, Père Angely was not paying best prices.

The old man peered at them. 'Good canvas?'

'The finest. It's the one thing an artist doesn't economize on.'

'Eh, *bien*. Er, um, twenty francs?'

'Each?'

Père Angely hummed and hawed, but agreed. Amedeo handed over the canvases; a sale was a sale. A gift horse should not be looked in the mouth.

'You, um, *are* Italian, m'sieur?'

'Born and bred,' Amedeo replied. 'You have asked me that before.'

'Um, so I did. Tuscany, wasn't it?'

'Livorno. It's a seaport.'

'Sea port, um. Tuscany.'

Amedeo nodded, amused. Eccentric, but a nice old fellow.

Père Angely tucked the canvases under his arm and reached for his walking-stick. Amedeo helped him down the stairs to the street.

'*Merci*,' he wheezed. 'Not as young as I was. Fine country, Italy. *Au revoir*.'

Amedeo rushed back to the studio. There was no time to lose. He had colours to mix, visions to paint, ideas to develop, sketches to do. Ah, life was good. Degas thought his work showed promise. Père Angely had bought two portraits. He was forty francs richer. Recognition couldn't be far away; it was just a matter of time.

He set up his easel, singing a Neapolitan song from sheer *joie de vivre*. An artist. In Paris. Yes, that was the life. He had been right to defy his father. Engineering wasn't for him. Why, the colours in his palette were glowing. Glowing!

He applied Yellow Ochre in happy abandon.

'*La donne e mobile*,' he sang.

Three

The early autumn sunshine was warm on Amedeo's cheeks. Leaves scurried like russet starfish along the boulevard. He passed the news kiosk, pausing momentarily to read the headlines in the Italian newspapers. The human flotsam of Montparnasse was beginning to wake on wooden benches, yawning, scratching, stretching, hoping, already hungry for a bowl of soup from the nuns at the Couvent Les Dames de la Visitation.

He decided to breakfast in the corner *brasserie*. Behind the zinc an antiquated phonograph ground out the war-time propaganda song *Over There*. Enrico Caruso's powerful tenor made him suddenly homesick for the luscious, rolling hills of Tuscany.

'Black coffee. And two croissants.'

'*Tout suite*, m'sieur. You believe that?' The barman jerked his head towards the phonograph. 'The Yanks are coming?'

'Why not? The war will end that much sooner.' Blaise, André, Moise and the others would be back in Paris; the art market would improve. Yes, the end of the war could not come soon enough.

'I'll believe it when it happens,' the barman said, serving up Amedeo's breakfast. 'Three francs, please.'

Amedeo sat by the window. For the past few months he had been following Degas's advice, using bolder, more sensuous colours, solidly modelled like Cézanne's. He felt he was near to realizing his dream. He had been wise to leave Venice; the Institute of Fine Arts clung too rigidly to classical principles. Paris offered challenge, stimulation, the opportunity to discuss new ideas, new techniques with other artists who, like himself, had come to Paris seeking the same inspiration. Foujita, who was developing his infinitely meticulous style which blended Western art with Far Eastern; Chaim Soutine, conjuring up fantastic colours from his rotting carcasses of meat; the Roumanian sculptor,

Constantine Brancusi, who had taken an interest in Amedeo's own sculpture. 'Be wary of stone, *mon ami*. It must be controlled. Until it is, it is the very devil. But nothing else has its expressive hardness. So master it you must,' the thick-set Roumanian had impressed upon him. 'Otherwise stone will be your master.' Ferdinand Léger was using cones, cylinders, cogged wheels, pistons to extend Cubism. Chagall, the wiry little Russian, was exploring the dream-world of Yiddish folklore on canvas . . . surrealistic animals and young lovers floating above the roof-tops, hands clasped. And Van Dongen, the Dutch artist who, like himself, had absorbed the spirit of Paris into his blood, depicting *grandes dames, demi-mondaines*, serving girls in vivid Fauvist hues.

Amedeo spent the day going from café to café.

'A pencil portrait, madame, m'sieur? Five francs.'

He charmed dowdy wives, flattered mutton-faced husbands.

At the end of the day he sat at a table outside the Closerie des Lilas, grateful for a coffee laced with cognac. *Dio mio*, but it was a wretched existence. In Venice, as a young student, he had believed Paris would welcome him with open arms, hug him to her bosom and offer him fame and fortune. He must have been greener than a carob tree.

'M'sieur Modigliani . . . may I join you?'

Adolphe Basler, the shady Polish refugee with artistic pretentions, doffed his pork-pie hat, and sat at Amedeo's table. 'Such weather. Why doesn't it make up its mind? I can't stand this greyness, *hein*.' When Amedeo went on drinking his coffee, Basler added: 'M'sieur Cheron has been asking after you. He's always interested in new talent. As a matter of fact he, er, just happens to be needing another artist . . . '

'I didn't come to Paris to do commercial art.'

'He pays well; it's better than hawking your work round the cafés, no?'

'No.'

Basler shrugged. 'Well, suit yourself, but the offer still stands.'

Amedeo stood up and left two francs in his saucer.

'You're leaving so soon?'

'*Adieu*.' Amedeo tipped his hat and headed for the Rotonde. Work for Cheron indeed; that day was a long way off!

He went into the Rotonde. Chaim Soutine was at the zinc. '*Shalom*.'

Amedeo shook hands and sat on the next stool.

'What are you drinking, Deo?'

'My treat. I've just sold six drawings.'

'So many! I haven't sold one in days.'

Amedeo ordered *marc*. Across the café he caught sight of Elvira Lacrot. She was surrounded by seedy theatricals and bar-flies. Her husky voice carried across ' . . . so I said to Mistinguet and Chevalier . . . '

Chaim raised his glass. '*Prosit*! Some meat I have,' he enthused in his almost incoherent French. 'From the abattoir. Putrefying and eaten by flies. But such beautiful colours!'

' . . . oh, yes, I've played in Feydeau farces. And Molière, Jean Cocteau . . . '

Suddenly Elvira was approaching the zinc. 'Amedeo Modigliani, *le peintre*. We meet again.' She gave Chaim a withering glance, her nostrils twitching. '*Mon Dieu*, you smell like a farmyard.'

The tousled-haired Russian grinned toothily; he was used to being the butt of ribald humour, but he didn't concern himself with what people thought of him, only of what they thought of his work as an artist.

The tenth of eleven children born to a Jewish tailor in Smilovitchi, he had been obsessed with drawing from childhood. While other children were chasing a ball, he had been drawing pictures on any bit of paper he could find; when he ran out of paper, he chalked on walls. Even as a baby he'd crowed at the coloured patterns sunlight made on the plaster wall by his crib. He'd been brought up on the legends of Baba Yaga the Witch and Rousalka the Water Sprite. Since coming to Paris he had roamed the abattoirs, fascinated by the sight of beef and lamb carcasses hanging from roof hooks, dripping blood. He lived in a private world of his imagination, ekeing out a meagre existence on the few francs he earned from selling his moribund paintings. He would paint until he collapsed from exhaustion, often going days without food; he survived on raw vegetables he scavenged from Les Halles and *pastas* he ate at Rosalie's, on credit.

'What's that mess on your shirt?' Elvira asked him, grimacing.

The Russian stared dumbly at his filthy overalls; what was wrong with his shirt? It looked fine.

'Raw meat stains,' Amedeo elucidated. 'Chaim gets unwanted carcasses from the abattoir at La Ruche – and paints them.'

'Ugh!'

Chaim nodded vigorously. What did she find so terrible about such reds? Richer than any man-made pigment.

'You were just off to the slipper baths – isn't that so, Chaim?' Amedeo said, pressing a five-franc piece into the Russian's gnarled hand.

Chaim blinked. Slipper baths? Was Amedeo having a little joke?

'A friend of yours?' she asked as Chaim sauntered off, shaking his head.

He nodded.

'*Mais alors*, I wouldn't befriend him if he were the last man on earth!'

'He's a gifted painter. One day he'll be famous.'

'*Sans blague*! Well, no girl in her right mind would pose for him. They'd suffocate from the fumes.'

He laughed.

'I've been playing the Gaiety Theatre in Montparnasse,' she went on, pleased by his interest. 'The rest of the cast have moved on to Lyon, but I didn't fancy it. Too provincial. A girl has to broaden her horizons, if you take my meaning?'

He nodded. His painter's eye was assessing her. The coffee-coloured skin of the South; eyes almost black; as voluptuous as the Venus di Milo; a gipsy wildness with a hint of arrogance.

'I've decided to do some modelling. Here, in Montparnasse. For artists like Picasso, Chagall, Renoir, Degas. I'm told they pay well.'

'An impressive list.' He knew she was reciting names she had heard in the Rotonde.

'And you, Amedeo . . . do you use live models? Or do you paint, how do you say it, still-life?'

'Models.'

'I still have your drawing. Everybody says what a good likeness it is.'

'I'm flattered.'

'That girl you were with . . . the one you were talking to when I came in with M'sieur Basler.' She was looking at him over the rim of her glass; her eyes narrowed. 'Is she a friend of yours too?'

'I'm afraid I don't remember.' An earthy, primitive beauty and eyes like orbs of exigency. A nude study at the Salon d'Automne would be sensational . . .

'Fibber,' she pouted. 'Blonde with an anaemic face, legs like bean poles and a sack for a dress. She kept gazing into your eyes – '

'Ruby Czechowska.' He laughed, remembering the incident.

'What's so special about this Ruby?'

'Nothing. She's just a model.'

'That scarecrow? I don't believe it.'

He shrugged. 'You want to do some modelling?'

Her eyes gleamed opulently.

'Is that an invitation?'

He found himself looking into her eyes, dark pools of sensuality; he was attracted and she knew it. 'If you want to take it that way.'

She smiled. 'I do.'

'When are you free?'

'Whenever you are.'

'I'm free tonight.'

'So am I.'

At his *atelier* Amedeo lit the kerosene lamp; the shadows heightened Elvira's gypsy features. He sketched her head and shoulders while she told him of her life in the theatre. As she talked her face was a carnival of pouts, sighs, smiles, frowns. She moved closer to him. 'Why don't you paint me, *chéri*?'

She sat on the bed, her cat-like eyes watching him, and crossed her long slender legs. Then she unhooked her suspenders. Inch by inch she rolled down the black silk stockings, languidly stretching out a smooth sienna leg; then peeled off the other stocking. She stood up, unhooked her skirt, stepping out of it when it dropped to the floor. Underneath blouse and skirt was a flimsy chemise. She pulled it over her head, revealing coffee-coloured skin, she looked like a voluptuary of Ancient Rome, a Messalina.

He squeezed a tube of Vermilion on to his palette, thinned it with turpentine, added a dab of Yellow Ochre. He studied her perfect figure. 'You have a pelvis like Goya's *Maja*.'

'What's that?'

'A painting. By the Spanish master, Francisco Goya.'

'Never heard of him.'

Time passed. Only Elvira's wanton body was reality; all else illusion. He worked with savage intensity, gripped by a compulsion that consumed his being.

'I'm bored, *chéri*.' Elvira yawned after an hour. 'Isn't it finished?'

'Rome wasn't built in a day.'

'Let me see.' Her breath caressed his cheek; her warm lissom body pressed against him. 'What do you think of, Amedeo, when you paint a woman . . . that you would like to make love to her?'

Suddenly her lips were seeking his; the *atelier* was alive with the ghosts of her past . . . cellar clubs, fairground barkers, harlequins, slit-eyed apache dancers, music hall jugglers . . . the sweet smell of her perfume caught in his throat.

'*Chéri* . . . I've wanted you from that first moment in the Rotonde.' She pulled him to the bed, eyes hooded, hair cascading across the sheets, a hydra-head of sensuality. Her mouth closed on his; a raging desire stirred in him as her tongue flicked like a libidinous whip, 'Make love to me, *chéri*,' she breathed.

Amedeo awoke in darkness. Elvira was sleeping beside him. He slipped into his dressing-gown and lit the lamp. He felt the canvas with the tips of his fingers; yes, the oils were dry. He studied the effect. Somehow the colours lacked depth, essence. Something was missing . . . an elusive quality, an atmosphere, a *sensation*. But he was getting nearer to what he sought. Degas said colour came from an artist's emotion. Degas was right. His eyes were beginning to open! The voluptuous nude of Elvira stared out of the canvas at him, the black hair offset by the green cushion under the shoulders; thighs splayed, breasts thrusting . . . eyes dark chasms of promised ecstasies.

He felt a strange, exciting affinity with the wanton body. Hardly aware of what he was doing he began painting the final flesh tones, blood pounding through his veins like molten lava, sweat trickling down his back. This was a Modigliani woman, a woman like no other, belonging to no school of painting, no artistic style.

An hour passed. Then two. Finally he was finished, his hair damp, arms aching . . . consumed by an exhaustion that comes from parturition.

He collapsed in a chair. The groping and stumbling was over, he thought; he was beginning to find a way through the labyrinth.

'*Chéri*,' Elvira said from the bed. 'I'm so hungry I could eat a horse. Making love always has that effect.'

He found some French bread and Camembert and a bottle of claret. The work had given him an appetite too. They ate and drank ravenously. Then she sat close to him, lips parting.

'Now we make love again, *chéri*.'

Elvira proved an excellent model, but was easy prey to boredom. To revive her flagging interest while she posed he questioned her about her stage career, closing his ears to the endless stream of banalities and platitudes she had gleaned from penny novelettes. He learned to contain his irritation when he found stockings in his paint-box, or when she used his brushes to make-up her face. She was untidy, selfish, capricious and lazy; and often his exasperation drove him to the Rotonde. He should throw her out, he thought. There were dozens of models who understood a painter's work, and took pride in their role as model. But none fascinated him like Elvira. Her bold eyes conjured up visions of the Provençal gipsies who once roamed the Camargue and scorched plains of Andalusia. His finer instincts were appalled, but the flesh was weak. She was a Bacchante whose nubile body knew a hundred ways to delight. He was amused by her frothy chatter and the way she boasted about him to his Rotonde cronies. 'Amedeo's going to be rich any day now. Mark my words.'

Their nights were whirlpools of sensuality. 'Nobody has loved me like you do, *chéri*.' Her voice would be husky with desire. 'Tell me you love me.' She knew he did, he lied. Ah, those worn words of illusion. Love . . . what did it mean to her? Lust? Possession? Refuge?

'*Bonne nuit, chéri.*'

Good night. Soon she would enter a dreamless sleep; happy like a child.

One day a middle-aged man called at the studio. His clothes were well tailored and he had the respectful aloofness of a butler or major domo.

He handed Amedeo his card. 'I represent Madame la Baronne Hertzog,' he said. 'She wishes you to paint her portrait.'

'I've heard of her,' Elvira said tartly. 'Used to be on the stage. Singer. Called herself something else in those days. Madame la Baronne indeed!'

The visitor dismissed her remarks with the merest raising of his eyebrow. 'Five o'clock this evening, m'sieur.'

'Tell Madame I'll be there,' Amedeo said as the man took his leave.

He closed the door. 'You fool. You could have lost me a commission.'

Elvira's face began to crumple. 'I'm sorry, *chéri*. I was jealous – that you'll be painting another woman instead of me.' She put her arms round his neck and kissed him. 'Forgive me?'

Ah, were not women the very devil? How could he be angry with her?

He looked at the address on the card the man had left. An apartment house in the fashionable Boulevard Haussmann. Madame la Baronne could afford to pay well.

'Only fifty francs?' Elvira shrieked when he returned. 'And you've been gone ages. You must have spent hours painting the old cow. You should have asked a hundred.' She made up her eyes with kohl, observing the result in the mirror. 'You're not hard enough,' she said. 'That's your trouble. Give me some drawings.'

He selected a dozen. She took them without even a cursory glance.

After she'd gone, Amedeo settled down to read a chapter of Dante's *Divine Comedy*. At 2 am she had not returned. Finally he went to bed. Elvira did not return until noon the next day. Triumphant, she handed him two hundred francs.

'I stayed the night with a girl friend. This morning I sold your drawings. At that little art gallery in the rue de Boiete.'

'Basler's? But he's the biggest shark in the business.'

'Maybe. But his money's good.'

She coiled her arms round him. 'Miss me?' He kissed her and went on working at the canvas on his easel, a portrait of Elvira which he was calling *The Reclining Nude*.*

'Can't we go out somewhere? The Tuileries, or the Bois de Boulogne. We can afford it now.'

'When this is finished. One more sitting; that's all.'

'Must I?' She sighed and studied her face in the mirror.

* Gianni Mattioli Collection, Milan.

'Ugh, I look awful.' Out came her make-up. He watched the ritual, amused, as she applied kohl with a thin brush, pursing her lips as though blowing a kiss. Then she slipped out of her clothes and draped herself on the couch. 'I'm ready, my lord and master.'

He knew he must work quickly: boredom would soon reduce her to yawns and irritability. Within half an hour he had completed it.

'I'm tired, *chéri*. Let's not go out. We've got some wine. We can have a party here. Just the two of us.'

While he was cleaning his brushes Elvira poured two glasses of red Macon. Then, sipping hers, she sat cross-legged on the bed. He drank slowly, feeling himself beginning to relax. He only half-listened when she told him how she had haggled with Basler.

The room was beginning to move. Dio mio, he had been working too hard! As he raised his wine glass he noticed his arm was weightless; it wouldn't go where he wanted it. *The Reclining Nude* was glowing, lit from within; the colours separated as though he were seeing them through a prism. What curious *tenebroso*; the tactile values had changed too.

Elvira was laughing, but no sound came from her. He tried to speak; his tongue was choking him.

Elvira began to strut around like a drum majorette. The studio walls began to swim like a field of corn in the wind. His arms were floating up to the ceiling.

'*Capelli biondi*,' he sang. Why should he suddenly think of a popular Italian song? '*Vestita bianca*.' The words were excruciatingly funny. He was a *Kapellmeister* conducting a German brass band.

'Let yourself go, *chéri. Ach, du liebe Augustine*,' she sang in a ridiculous falsetto, marching round, faster and faster until she collapsed on the bed in shrieks of laughter.

Amedeo fell down beside her. His head was hammering. He was consumed by thirst. He staggered to the sink and gulped cold water. Elvira was pedalling her legs in the air. '*Dieu* . . . wasn't that fantastic?'

His head began to clear. 'What was it you put in the wine?'

She looked askance at him. 'If I tell you, promise me you won't be angry. Please, *chéri*.'

'All right.'

'Hashish pellets. But only two. I only did it because you looked so tired and miserable. You're not angry with your little Elvira, are you?'

He smiled. 'Cunning bitch.' He lay back, a delicious lethargy stealing over him.

Elvira laughed and ruffled his hair. 'My friend Solange gets them. From a man in the rue St. Sulpice. She gets Mexican cigarettes, too.' She tipped out her bag. 'Here – look. Try one. They're even better than pellets. Go on. There's nothing to be frightened of. Everybody in Montparnasse smokes them.' She lit two and handed one to him. He smoked it for a while; he didn't feel any different.

'You're sure these are reefers?'

'Just keep puffing.' She grinned. 'Soon you'll be in heaven.'

He inhaled again. He began to notice a subtle change. A gentle lassitude stole over him, then a euphoric sense of well-being. The fatigue he had experienced while painting was evaporating. The effect of the drug was opening up a fantastic new world, a world he had never dreamed existed. Vibrant colours and shapes writhed before his eyes.

Elvira snaked her arms around him and pulled him back on to the bed. 'My handsome lover.'

Soft, moist lips pressed on to his mouth. An insistent hand slipped inside his shirt. 'It's even better with a reefer, *chéri* . . . '

Desire surged through him. He ripped her blouse off her shoulders and kissed the honeyed swell of her breasts. Talon-like fingernails dug into his back as Elvira bit his lip.

'*Ti voglio bene*,' he said hoarsely.

The days passed in an orgy of marijuana, drinking and love-making. They ate whenever they had money; when they didn't, they lived on wine. Amedeo hawked his drawings around the cafés. Elvira sang *chansonnettes* in grubby little restaurants. What money they earned immediately went over the bar counter. They made love and slept, woke and made love again. They argued and fought. Their thirst for liquor was insatiable. Their escapades became the talk of Montparnasse. They danced in the Boulevard Raspail and got thrown out of Rosalie's. They took to smoking Mexican reefers and drinking absinthe at the same time. But though Elvira gave herself to him with a frequency bordering on nymphomania she had a fatalistic urge to arouse his jealousy. She flirted with the Rotonde crowd, encouraging any man who found her attractive.

He knew that to let her see he was annoyed would only encourage her to do it all the more. He began to drink absinthe with *marc*. In the brief periods of lucidity he realized he was sinking deeper into a vortex of self-destruction. In his hallucinated state it was impossible to paint a canvas. His working day was reduced to a few hasty sketches in the Rotonde; even those were only to get money for more liquor. Chain-smoking had induced a cough which plagued him night and day.

One night he sold six drawings to a group of tourists. They wanted to know if the Rotonde was the place where the artists hung out. It was, he said. Was he the one they called 'Modi'? He was indeed. But his name was Modigliani – and they were not to forget it. Alcohol made him boastful. 'I'll be famous one day. Those sketches will be worth a thousand francs a time.'

Elvira dragged him away: Ortiz de Zarate wanted them to join his party. 'And how much did you get for those drawings?'

'Enough to buy champagne.'

'Half's mine.'

'Nonsense. I've just earned it.'

'We live together, don't we?'

'What's that got to do with it?' Her face seemed blurred. He tossed back another glass of absinthe. Nothing mattered any more.

'Give me ten francs, damn you.'

Through the alcoholic haze he was vaguely aware that people were staring at them. The noise had subsided. Faces he couldn't distinguish were turned in his direction.

'Sit down, Elvira, and have a drink.'

He closed his ears to her curses and threats. The café was slowly revolving.

Elvira was in the middle of the floor; she shouted to the accordionist, then turned her electric eyes on Amedeo at the zinc.

'I spit on you, Modigliani.' Her hair fell over her flushed face; she laughed defiantly at him. 'I'm Elvira, the gypsy dancer,' she shouted. 'I'm not owned by Modigliani – or anybody else.' The accordionist played a slow number. Elvira began to gyrate like a Turkish belly-dancer. She threw back her head, laughing. 'Hold on to your glasses, boys. Elvira's going to do a striptease.'

The crowd whistled and clapped. '*Vive*, Elvira!'

'Listen to them, Modigliani. At least *they* appreciate me.'

Her naked breasts gleamed in the smoky light; her features were animal-like as she unhooked her skirt. The café was in a fever of excitement. One group began to chant her name.

The blood drained from Amedeo's face. Everything was spinning: a nauseating carousel of colour and noise. He groped for the door. Elvira's mocking laughter rang in his ears like the diabolical shrieks of a banshee. Outside was a black abyss . . . like something imagined in the inky depths of Dante's *Inferno*.

He woke. He looked round the *atelier* with a curious sense of disorientation. The studio looked as though it had been a battleground. Dirty crockery was strewn everywhere. The floor was littered with bottles, cigarette ends, glasses, sketches and Elvira's junk. But of her there was no sign. The air reeked of stale food and reefer smoke.

The angelus bell at the Dames Augustines convent began to ring. Sunday? Could it be? The last clear memory he had was Elvira stripping in the Rotonde. That had been Thursday. *Dio mio* – two days a complete blank! He held his head under the cold tap. His legs were leaden. In the mirror a greyish face with dark circles round the eyes stared back at him. His hands were trembling; he had an irresistible desire for a reefer. He searched through Elvira's things, turned out drawers, went through his clothes in the tallboy. His head began to pound. One smoke would end the pain.

He forced himself to sit on the bed; reason began to prevail. One refer . . . or twenty? . . . or a hundred? For one horrifying moment he saw where the craving was leading him. He was like a lemming racing toward the edge of the precipice. Drugs had helped to anaesthetize the effects of poverty and loneliness. In that artificial paradise he had been able to scorn the man in the corridor and the daggers of the mind lurking in every dark corner, in every sleepless night. There had to be an end to it. Soon hashish wouldn't be enough. Soon he'd want cocaine or heroin. The promised ecstasies would turn into a saturnalia from which there would be no escape.

When Elvira arrived back he was washed and shaved. She wore her irrepressible smile like a mask; under one arm she carried a bottle of champagne.

'*Buon giorno, chéri*. Veuve Clicquot. With the compliments of M'sieur Basler. He's bought some more of your drawings.' She flung her bag on the bed. '*Mon Dieu*, but how you slept! Nearly twenty-four hours. I just couldn't rouse you. You must have drunk the Rotonde dry.'

So he had slept through Saturday, he thought. 'What happened on Friday?'

'Don't you remember? We drank and drank and drank. We had a marvellous time.'

'Where?'

'Here of course. Where do you think?'

He stared at her: he felt nothing. Her body aroused not a vestige of desire. There was a time when he'd have danced her round the studio, thrilled with her success. Now he could barely bring himself to meet her eyes. It was as though she were a complete stranger. Two days, he thought. Lost in an alcoholic cloud.

'Why so long-faced, *chéri*?'

'It's over, Elvira.'

She began to uncork the bottle. 'A glass of this will make you feel better. I've got something else. Solange says it's fantastic. Beats hashish all ends up.'

'You and me, Elvira – '

'What about us?'

'We're finished.' He was drained of emotion. He just wanted her to go. He was disgusted with himself for having succumbed to her carnal nature. Now, more than ever, he knew he should have broken with her weeks ago. The dissolute life they were leading was undermining his health, destroying his self-control.

She began to plead and grovel, kneeling on the floor and hugging his knees. 'It's the hang-over talking, Modi. You'll feel better when you've had a drink.'

'You had better pack your things.'

'No, *chéri*. Please don't send me away. I'll cook for you properly; and wash your things and pose whenever you want me to – '

'No.' He should have known it would come to this. She was irresponsible, self-destructive, hedonistic, an exotic butterfly who flitted from man to man, neither seeking nor wanting permanence. He had been a fool to think she was anything else. She had been a diversion. He had allowed it to get out of hand. He had only himself to blame.

'All right, Modigliani – see if I care. If that's the way you want it. *Je vous enmerde*,' she spat. 'I'm sick of this flea pit. I'm sick of artists. Always smelling of paint and never having the price of a coffee between them. Go and sell your precious drawings yourself and see how far it gets you. Yes, you need to ask yourself a few questions, Modigliani, Prince of Montparnasse. Why do you think M. Basler bought them?' She threw back her head and laughed.

A cold knot tightened in his stomach.

'Yes, that's right.' Her face was contorted by hatred and vindictiveness. 'Don't look so surprised, Modigliani. Why else would he pay two hundred francs for some tatty old drawings? Put that in your palette and stir it, damn you.' She swung her bag over her shoulder and grabbed the champagne bottle. 'I'm glad I didn't waste good champagne on you. Basler may be an ugly old goat but at least he doesn't expect a girl to live in a pigsty. He's going to get me an apartment to myself. In the rue de Chateaudun. Miles away from this dump.'

'Get out.'

He felt sick with humiliation. He should have known Basler would not have parted with so much money so easily. She had twisted Basler around her little finger until he had become infatuated.

She flounced to the door. '*Je vous enmerde*, Modigliani,' she shouted, slamming the door in his face. He was shaking. *Dio mio*. He would go to the Rotonde and get drunk. Never had he wanted oblivion so much.

'Amedeo. Wake up.' The voice penetrated his numbed brain. A fist drummed on the *atelier* door. He rolled out of bed; his head was like a sap bucket. He vaguely remembered the night before; he had no recollection of getting home from the Rotonde. He opened the door. It was Moise Kisling.

'Amedeo – it's about your friend Maurice Utrillo. His mother Suzanne Valadon phoned me.'

'What's wrong with Maurice?' His head began to clear.

'He's running around the streets. He's gone berserk. Suzanne thinks Maurice might listen to you.'

As Amedeo dressed, Moise told him something of what had happened, of how Maurice had been arrested for causing a breach of the peace, then had escaped from the police cell to go on an almighty binge.

'Like me to go with you?' Moise volunteered.

'Thanks, but I can manage.'

Amedeo took the Métro to Montmartre. At Suzanne's studio in the rue Cortot he was met by André Utter, blond hair tousled, his normally florid face deathly pale. From inside the old house came animal noises and screams, the clatter of boots on floor-boards.

'Thank God you could come,' André whispered hoarsely, ushering Amedeo inside. He closed the door and bolted it. 'In the studio.'

Amedeo followed André into Suzanne's high-ceilinged *atelier*. Two uniformed men were holding Maurice down on a narrow iron-legged bed; he was snarling, foaming at the mouth, and kicking out at his captors. Suzanne was crying.

'How long has he been like this?' Amedeo asked.

'Days. We've tried to stop him drinking – ' André shrugged hopelessly.

'If we lock him in his room, he climbs out of the window. When we manage to keep him at home, he drinks turps or eats oil paints.'

Amedeo tried to reason with Maurice; it was hopeless. Maurice cursed and snarled, his glazed eyes unseeing.

'It's no use,' an orderly panted. 'We'll have to use the strait-jacket. He'll have to go away.'

'Oh, no, not Villejuif. Maurice isn't insane,' Suzanne cried.

'He can't stay here, madame. He's violent.'

She appealed to the family doctor with an anguished: 'Must they – ?'

He nodded gravely. He had treated Maurice for alcoholism from the age of fifteen; he had long despaired of a cure. Institutionalizing Maurice was the only hope, in his opinion. But then he was approaching retirement, he was tired: he had given enough of his life to medicine.

'It's for the best, Madame Valadon,' he murmured.

The two orderlies forced Maurice into the strait-jacket and carried him, struggling, down to the street. They thrust him into a decrepit wagon with an iron grille over the rear window. A crowd had gathered outside. 'It's Maurice Utrillo,' somebody said. 'I saw him outside the Lapin Agile. Barking like a dog and screaming obscenities.'

André took Amedeo's arm. 'There's nothing we can do. Let's go inside. I can't bear the way these fools just stand and stare.'

André comforted Suzanne while their doctor wrote a prescription. 'Something to make you sleep,' he told her.

'What's going to happen to Maurice?' André asked the doctor.

'As soon as the sanatorium authorities say he can have visitors, I'll let you know.'

'Is he as bad . . . as people are saying?'

The doctor shrugged. 'I won't lie to you. Maurice is very ill. How ill we don't know yet. He isn't insane, if that's what's worrying you. He has a serious paranoid condition. But, with proper care, rest, and no alcohol . . . he should recover.' He picked up his medical bag. 'I'll see myself out.'

Nobody spoke as the doctor's footsteps echoed away.

Suzanne's voice was a whisper. 'Amedeo . . . I'm afraid for Maurice.'

'Maurice will be all right,' Amedeo said, trying to sound convincing; but the memory of Maurice's imbecilic face wouldn't recede; it had given him a shock.

'Will you come with me, Amedeo, when I visit him?'

'Of course.'

'Maurice takes notice of you. He's always talking about you. Only recently he said he'd given some of your paintings to Laura Wylda, to exhibit in her art shop. You've been a good friend to him.'

'Madame Wylda,' André broke in. 'That reminds me.' He crossed to a mahogany writing desk. He took out an envelope and handed it to Amedeo. 'Two hundred francs. Maurice was going to bring it to your studio.'

'I don't understand. Where . . . ?'

André smiled. 'Your paintings. In Madame Wylda's shop. She sold one – a laundry girl – to a collector named Dr Paul Alexandre. You see, people *are* beginning to notice your work. Dr Alexandre is a discerning collector.'

Amedeo blinked as tears stung his eyes. What torment and agony of mind André and Suzanne must have endured because of Maurice's drinking. 'How can I thank you . . . ?'

André gripped his shoulder. 'We understand.'

Four

Amedeo shivered. He was painting in the background of a nude study of Elvira. He stood up and walked round the studio; the cold seemed to strike at the very marrow of his bones. He lit a cigarette and studied the canvas. Three weeks . . . and he hadn't missed her at all; even this painting of her he'd finished from memory. *Dio mio*, but it was cold! He poked the stove; the dying coals sparked feebly. Only fifteen francs between himself and the poorhouse! Père Angely wasn't due for another week; in any case, the old man's payment of twenty francs wouldn't go far. There was the rent, groceries, laundry, oils, canvas . . . Of course, as a last resort, he could work for Cheron. Basler could arrange it. No! He thrust the thought from his mind. But Foujita worked for Cheron . . .

A knock at the door broke into his thoughts.

'*Entrez*.'

It was Fernande and Foujita. He rose to greet them, but before he had a chance to utter a word Fernande voiced good-natured disapproval. Just look at the state of the place! How could he neglect himself? Why hadn't he been to see them? Was he deserting his friends? What were friends for if not to confide in? ' . . . and just look at yourself, white as a sheet.' She looked at the Elvira nude. 'Has that hussy still got her claws in you?'

'We've parted.'

'You mean you've finally had the good sense to chuck her out. And not before time. *Grisettes* like her are no good to an artist. Just look at the place!' she went on. 'Going to rack and ruin.'

'I've been working hard. It just hadn't occurred to me . . . '

'You look as though you've been at death's door. You want to join Maurice Utrillo at Villejuif?' Fernande began to tidy up the studio, muttering a tirade against trollops who pursued any man who would buy them a drink.

Foujita shrugged hopelessly. 'When Fernande gets one of her pious moods, Deo, there's nothing to do but let it run its course.'

Fernande addressed them both. 'Every man needs a woman. But a good woman, one who'll look after him, not drag him into the gutter. Elvira Lacrot is a no-good little tart who should have stayed on the stage where she belongs.'

Foujita squinted at the Elvira nude, nodding. 'You are finding your style. It's more mature.'

'You really think so?'

'It's better than anything you've done. But you really should look for another studio. This place is riddled with damp.'

'I will. Just as soon as I put some money by. I'm thinking of going to work for Cheron. I was wondering about terms.' It was time he swallowed his pride, he thought. If working for Cheron was all right for Foujita, it was all right for him too.

'Take whatever he offers you,' Fernande broke in. 'But don't take less than twenty francs a day.'

'Feminine logic,' Foujita grinned. 'Twenty is what he pays me.'

Foujita began to study the Elvira nudes. 'Magnificent. I've rarely seen colour used so penetratingly. Truly, you've found your way.'

'I'm trying to paint the patina of colour. Cézanne, Van Gogh, Gauguin – they've shown us the way, Foujita. Now I must develop my style, discover my *vision*. Paint the very essence of flesh.'

'You're seeking the impossible. It's just a dream – '

'Yes – a dream. But not a pipe-dream: a vision of the Absolute.'

'It just isn't possible, *mon ami*. It can't be done.'

'It can. And I must find it.' Amedeo ran his fingers through his thick black hair. 'The colours are here, in my head, it's just a matter of finding *how*. It's as if there's a door in the mind. If only one could find the key . . . all would be revealed.'

'Talk, talk,' Fernande interrupted. 'Don't you artists ever do anything else?'

'They also eat,' Foujita grinned. 'Come on. Let's all go to Rosalie's. My treat.'

Inside the tiny restaurant in the rue de la Campagne-Première the warm air was impregnated with paprika, pimentoes, garlic and aromatic herbs; for what Chez Rosalie's lacked in culinary *finesse* it made up in gusto and spice.

Rosalie fussed at their table like a mother hen. 'Tonight I cook you something special. *Courgettes à la provençale* and *risotto Bologna*.' She waddled off to her kitchen and began to slice up fresh juicy marrows laced with marjoram and rosemary from her majolica jars. A native of Tuscany herself, Rosalie felt a matriarchal affection for Amedeo. 'He's like a son to me,' she would tell people.

As they ate, Amedeo explained his theories to Foujita; that he had to keep searching for a *sensation*, a fusion of mind and paint. 'Words can't really explain it. But find it I will.'

'Ah, my friend, you are beginning to suffer for your art. Degas says no man can paint until he can truly see. And he cannot truly see until he has known suffering.'

'Poppycock,' Fernande interposed. 'Shut up about art – and let's have some more chianti.'

'Forgive me,' Amedeo apologized. 'Shop-talk is no substitute for chianti!'

The next day Amedeo went to La Maison Cheron in the rue de Boiete. It was a narrow-fronted, dirty grey shop sandwiched between a *patisserie* and an auctioneer's. He peered through the grubby window; among the framed paintings were water-colours of Japanese gardens. The subtle harmony and delicate handling was unmistakably Foujita's. With what consummate ease his friend balanced his compositions. They were price-tagged at fifty francs, but he knew Cheron had paid Foujita only fifteen each. It saddened him that his friend was exploited by a dealer whose only attribute was an eye for a quick sale. Now it's my turn, he thought. But beggars could not be choosers. He went in.

Cheron enthused: 'Ah M'sieur Modigliani. Foujita said you might be coming to see me.' He smiled unctuously and extended a limp hand. Amedeo took it; it was like shaking a mackerel. Cheron's head was a curious egg shape and his rheumy eyes peered myopically through thick-lensed spectacles. Stiff, arthritic joints caused him to move like a marionette. His mottled, puffy face was covered with a film of greasy perspiration.

'Is this a social call or . . . ?' Cheron began, rubbing his hands.

'Business.'

'Of course, of course. Sit down, m'sieur.' He ushered Amedeo into a threadbare armchair. 'Cigarette?' Amedeo took one, lit it.

'I understand you're looking for artists.'

'Yes, yes. I'm always looking for good artists. You, er, wish to discuss terms, of course.' Already he was calculating how much profit there would be in one of Amedeo's paintings.

'Of course.'

'These are difficult times, you understand. What with the war, rationing, shortages, the price of oils and canvas . . . My, um, terms are fifteen francs a day. Um, generous in the circumstances.' He looked at Amedeo, smiling benevolently.

'The daily rate is twenty I believe.'

'Er, twenty?' Cheron's benevolence evaporated. 'Times are difficult – '

Amedeo rose. Prostituting his talent for twenty francs was bad enough, but fifteen!

'Wait.' Cheron's expression hovered between a grimace and a plea. 'Er, um, twenty you said?'

'Yes.'

'Agreed,' Cheron said miserably. 'Two paintings daily. I supply the materials. When, um, could you start?'

Amedeo considered. No point in delaying the inevitable. Twenty francs was twenty francs. 'Right away.'

'Fine, fine – I'll show you the studio.' Amedeo followed

Cheron down some stone steps into the shop's basement. In a corner was a battered easel and two paint-spattered orange boxes on which perched numerous dirty bottles and tins containing straggly rat-tailed brushes. The sole source of light was from a small high window covered by a metal grille. The air was cold and dank. In the centre of the room was a wooden table on which was a bowl of wizened fruit.

'My clientèle go crazy over apples and pears,' Cheron explained. 'In the style of Renoir, Courbet. I used to have a Portuguese painter who could do apples just like Courbet's. Sold like hot cakes. Alas, he died of pneumonia,' Cheron sighed, as though the artist had done him an injustice. 'And just as I was building up a good trade, *hein*.' He set up the easel and turned to Amedeo. 'You paint apples?'

'Not since my student days, but I expect I can.' Apples? Was this what he was reduced to? But, he told himself, it was only until his own work began to sell. As Foujita had said, it was just a means to an end.

'*Dio mio*, but it's cold down here. Could I have the stove lit?'

Cheron's eyes became wary; already he could see the profits being eroded. 'I, um, can't feel the cold. You'll soon accustom yourself to it.'

'I think not. A painter must work in an even temperature.' He picked up an emaciated apple. 'You see how the skin has lost its lustre? It needs warmth. Just as an artist's colours require warmth.'

'An apple is just an apple,' Cheron said dubiously.

'Ah, but your apples are not just *any* apples, m'sieur. Yours must look like Courbet's. Warm, glowing, pulsating! Why, it's one of the first principles: warmth means lifelike colours.'

Cheron's eyes widened. 'Is that so? Well, um, perhaps I'd better order some coke.'

'What would you like me to paint first? A portrait perhaps?'

'Apples, m'sieur. Like Courbet's. Never mind what the apples really look like. Paint them with a red and gold sheen.

That's how my customers expect them to look.'

Half an hour later Amedeo stood back from the easel and peered at the canvas through narrowed eyes. Apples like Courbet's? Hmmm, perhaps a little more yellow ochre to heighten the effect. Yes, that should satisfy Cheron's bourgeoisie clientèle. *Dio mio*, but already he was sick of the sight of apples!

Ten minutes later it was finished. He stood his brush in a jar. He shivered; dampness was enveloping him like an invisible cloak. He went to the foot of the steps. 'M'sieur Cheron! What about the stove? Don't forget what I said about warm colours.'

Footsteps sounded above. Cheron came down the steps in alarm, fingers on his lips. 'Keep your voice down, m'sieur. Madame Cheron . . . she doesn't approve of artists. I'm having some coke sent down this afternoon.' His eyes fell on the apples Amedeo had painted. 'Delicious, delicious. Ah, my customers will love them.' He hopped from one foot to another. 'Truly delicious.'

'What do I paint next?' Amedeo lit a cigarette, smiling.

'Apples, m'sieur.'

The days fled by in a kaleidoscope of red, green, yellow. He painted apples and pears until he saw them in his dreams. *Dio mio*, was Paris a city of apple-lovers? Heavy of heart, he gave birth to more and more fruit on canvas: pomegranates, cherries, grapefruit, peaches, persimmons, bananas.

Then, his patience exhausted, he flung down his brushes. Enough! He would quit; he had painted his last bowl of fruit. An artist could tolerate only so much . . .

'But you can't,' Cheron cried when Amedeo went into the dealer's cubby-hole office in the shop and announced his decision. 'We have a contract.'

Amedeo shrugged; he knew their agreement would not be considered legally binding. 'Twenty francs, m'sieur. Then we're paid up.'

'I'll increase your pay. Twenty five francs a day,' Cheron pleaded, knowing he would not get another artist of Amedeo's talent easily. Had not Mme Pommet raved over his apples? Had not M. Chevalier, the banker, declared his pears more mouth-watering than the real thing? *Hein*, he must be bribed to stay. 'That's a generous offer. What do you say?'

'I'm an artist, not a fruiterer. Find someone else to imitate Courbet.'

Cheron thought quickly. 'As a matter of fact, I've been thinking of promoting you. Artist-in-chief. No more bowls of fruit . . . '

Amedeo was listening; twenty five francs a day was not to be scorned.

'I'll hire models. There's a steady demand for portraits. Not as profitable as fruit, of course, but a good selling line nevertheless.'

Amedeo returned to the studio-basement, richer by five francs a day, happy that in portraiture he would be able to develop his own ideas.

The following day Cheron brought a forlorn-looking girl, aged about twelve, into the studio. She had sad blue eyes, chapped hands and a shapeless blue dress. Amedeo's heart immediately went out to her. He guessed that Cheron was paying her a pittance.

'Just head and shoulders,' Cheron murmured. 'And for God's sake paint her smiling.'

'Very likely she has nothing to smile about.'

'Maybe so, but my customers like smiles.'

As he painted the girl Amedeo gently encouraged her to overcome her shyness and tell him about her home life. Her mother had died in childbirth; her father was in the Army and she hadn't seen him since the war began. She was being looked after by a widowed aunt. They had little money and she had to do odd jobs as soon as school finished.

Amedeo took the finished portrait off the easel.

'Can I go home now?' Her voice was a plaintive appeal.

'Will you stay a little longer, m'selle? This time, to pose for me?' Something about her wistful smile and sombre expression stirred his emotions. Her whole life ahead of her and already she had a world-weariness! He had seen urchins in Livorno with the same air of defeat; denied the joys of childhood, old before their time.

'But Auntie will be wondering where I've got to.'

'I won't keep you long, *mia piccola*. I promise you.'

He set up another piece of canvas and mixed his colours, instinctively, working with total absorption. Soon he had outlined a full-length portrait of the girl with her hands clasped in front of her, in delicate blues, greens and greys . . . the title suggested itself. *Girl in Blue*.* He was pleased with the result; it was one of those rare occasions when artist and model had a special affinity of mutual sympathy and understanding.

He pressed a five-franc coin into her hand. 'Tell your auntie you earned it posing for Modigliani.'

'*Merci*, m'sieur.'

'Be careful not to lose it.'

'*Oui*, m'sieur.' The girl ran up the steps, pausing a moment to give him a shy smile. '*Au revoir*, m'sieur.'

Amedeo cleaned his brushes and dried them. He put on his hat and coat and took the portrait off the easel, propping it against the wall to dry. The head and shoulders portrait he'd done first he took upstairs to Cheron's cubby-hole. He lit a cigarette while Cheron made noises befitting a dealer who had an expert eye.

'Quite lifelike, m'sieur. And you got the little brat to smile too! Good, good.' He rubbed his horny hands with relish. Modigliani was exceeding his expectations. He would offer the painting to Mme Pommet for fifty – no, seventy-five francs. 'Very good.' He gave Amedeo an obsequious smile of dismissal.

'My pay,' Amedeo reminded him. Having to be subservient to the miserly dealer brought a flush of humiliation.

'Ah, yes.' Cheron counted out twenty-five francs. '*Bon soir*.'

Amedeo strode out of the shop, somehow resisting the urge to tell Cheron to go to hell; it seemed grossly unjust that he, Foujita, Maurice and Chaim should be compelled to

* This famous canvas is in a private collection in Paris.

peddle their wares in this fashion. Artists had to be realistic . . . yet, because they dealt in abstracts, imagination and intellectual concepts they were totally ill-equipped to think like businessmen. Ah, life was full of such contradictions! But he had created a satisfying work of art . . . *Girl in Blue*. That, at least, was something to celebrate.

He went into the Rotonde and ordered *marc*.

'On the slate?' Papa Libion, the *patron*, asked.

'No. Today I got paid. I'm a working artist these days,' he added ironically. He sipped the drink. A group of students caught his attention: girls from the Colarossi. He was amused when they kept looking across at him and giggling shyly. He was used to curious glances; he knew people found his style of dress daringly unconventional, but he was indifferent to their opinion of him. He was an artist, not a banker.

One girl caught his eye. She wasn't giggling like the others. Chestnut-brown hair plaited to her waist, eyes like blue velvet. Not more than twenty, yet her oval-shaped face had an almost ethereal aura . . . like one of St. Ursula's virgins. Her smile had a secretive quality, reminiscent of Botticelli or the Siennese Trecento and possessing Bellini's timeless beauty. A strange emotion overcame him as her eyes locked with his; he felt he had known her all his life.

He took out his sketch-book and began to sketch. The girl with the almond-shaped eyes kept looking across, smiling shyly. Those eyes, such a delicate shade of blue! What a subject for a portrait.

On an impulse he approached their table, a strange sensation in his throat. Who was she? He was hardly aware of her companions who stared at him with awe as though he were Svengali or Rasputin. Her eyes were fathomless, like the azure-blue Mediterranean. He offered her the sketch, murmuring an introduction but scarcely able to recognize his own voice. *Dio mio*, he was behaving like a gauche youth!

'You are a student, m'selle? At the Colarossi?'

She nodded, deeply conscious of his intense, burning eyes; he was even more handsome than people said. 'Yes, m'sieur. I'm in the life-class.' The other girls giggled and she was annoyed with herself for blushing.

'It's time we were going, Jeanne,' they said.

Amedeo was suddenly aware that he was staring at her with unusual familiarity. He stepped back. 'Please, m'selle, don't be late on my account.' His heart began to pound. Jeanne . . . A stanza of Dante's *Divine Comedy* came to mind . . .

Ma Beatrice si'bella e ridente
mi si mustro, che tra quelle vedute
si vuol lesciar che non sequir la mente

Amedeo followed the students with his eyes as they left the café. *Beatrice showed herself to me so beauteous and smiling* . . . Was this blue-eyed girl the Beatrice of his dreams? Was it possible?

'Excuse me, m'sieur – '

Amedeo turned his head. The newcomer was a young man with a black beard and moustache, homburg hat and brown melancholy eyes. Amedeo was used to the freaks, eccentrics and tourists in the cafés of Montparnasse who hoped to catch a glimpse of 'the wild artists' . . . but this man was not a curious bystander. There was an air about him that suggested urgency.

'You are M'sieur Modigliani, the artist?' The young man doffed his hat, clearing his throat nervously.

Amedeo nodded, amused by the other's awe.

'Ah,' the other said, dropping his hat, stooping to retrieve it and apologizing profusely. 'My nerves are somewhat shattered.' His voice seemed to have an integral note of self-effacement. 'It's what comes of being an alien in a foreign country.'

'You are Russian, m'sieur?' Amedeo felt himself warming to the man.

'Polish.'

'You'll join me in a drink? Brandy?'

'Please, no, it's rather too early in the day for me . . . '

Amedeo insisted, smiling.

'Well, perhaps a coffee.'

As they drank the young man shyly handed Amedeo a

small hand-printed card.

Amedeo read: *Leopold Zborowski, dealer in rare books and fine arts, 8 rue Joseph-Bara, Montparnasse.*

'A difficult business these days,' Leopold said. 'What with the war and everything.'

'It is indeed,' Amedeo agreed, wondering what the man was leading up to.

'That girl you drew.' Leopold lowered his eyes. 'She was very beautiful. Is she a friend?'

'I saw her for the first time today.'

'Oh. Well, please don't think I'm prying, m'sieur, but I couldn't help seeing what you did. A fine drawing, m'sieur. Swift and sure, yet with perfect economy of line. You have a fine talent. And please,' he added hastily, 'don't think I'm patronizing you. I've been following your career for months. As a matter of fact, I own one of your pastel portraits. Of an old gentleman who runs a second-hand shop in the Boul' Montparnasse.'

'Ah, Papa Lemeye!'

'Yes, that's him. He drove a very hard bargain, the old fellow did. Fifty francs. I remember it clearly, for I was extremely impoverished at the time.' He gave a wry smile. 'My wife and I lived on *haricots rouges* for a whole week.'

Papa Libion leaned across the zinc and addressed Leopold in a voice that did not invite contradiction. 'Amedeo is a great artist. More than that, he's a genius.'

'Oh, indubitably, m'sieur.'

'And what's more,' Libion said, 'the art galleries don't appreciate him. No eye for real art – that's their trouble.' He shot Leopold a significant glance, then resumed cleaning his glasses.

Amedeo laughed; all this acclaim! It was positively embarrassing.

'Oh, but it's true,' Leopold said earnestly. 'I've seen your work. It's unique, m'sieur. Which brings me to the point of my introducing myself. I was hoping . . . I'd be honoured, that is, if you would consent to paint my wife's portrait. As a commission, of course. Just as soon as you are free.'

'Delighted,' Amedeo replied. 'I'm available whenever you like.'

'Capital, capital. Will fifty francs be all right?'

Amedeo protested; the rate was twenty.

'Fifty it is then,' Leopold smiled, rising.

Amedeo watched Leopold leave. Fifty francs! It was his lucky day.

'Did I hear correctly?' asked Libion who never missed even a syllable of any conversation at the zinc. 'Fifty?'

'You did.'

'*Mon Dieu*! Who is he – Baron Rothschild?'

'He says he's a dealer in fine arts.'

Libion snorted. 'Do you believe he's honest?'

'Oddly enough I do.'

Amedeo read Leopold Zborowski's card again. He would soon know for certain.

Five

Amedeo turned into the rue de la Grand-Chaumière and stopped outside the Colarossi Academy. The huge wooden doors were ajar; a thin shaft of sunlight pierced the black shadows inside. A few students, hurrying to join the afternoon life-class, gave him curious glances, whispering among themselves.

He smiled and followed them inside. Ah, how well he remembered his early life in Paris. The months he had spent as a Colarossi student with Foujita when, with all the confidence of youth, he had expected to find the streets of Paris paved with proverbial gold. He looked around at the musty, cobwebbed ceiling, whitewashed walls stained with paint; the reproductions of the French masters and Italian lithographs and mezzotints which festooned the corridor walls . . . the undulating, creaking floorboards, the odour of sandalwood and pastel crayons. Yes, it brought back memories. And that last day as a student . . . he could almost hear Herr Schuler's guttural voice struggling to pronounce French with a good accent. 'Ach, but you haf a fine future, my boy. I haf nossink I can teach you now. Nurse your gift. Make it flower, *hein*.'

He entered the life-class just as the students were settling down to begin work, chairs scraping, paper rustling, conversation being hastily concluded. He sat on a stool at the back of the class, searching with his eyes. Perhaps she wasn't attending today's class? Ever since that first moment in the Rotonde he had thought of nothing else; those velvet-blue eyes and chestnut hair had haunted him.

He couldn't concentrate on his work at Cheron's. One still life – a bowl of pears – had ended up resembling wizened crab apples. Cheron had ranted and raved about the wastage of good oils and canvas. Was that what he paid Amedeo for? Who would buy pears that resembled dried-up crones? On another occasion he had been painting a vase of flowers and, unconsciously, he'd worked in the deep blue tones of her eyes; but instead of the expected reprimand, Cheron had lavished praise. 'Ah, that is much better. That has the Gauguin influence.'

Amedeo studied the model, a tall willowy girl with lank hair and a pasty complexion. How he loathed professional models who lacked the very essence of life; how much more satisfying to sketch a washerwoman or pastry cook or cheeky-faced urchins on the streets. His hand moved over the coarse cartridge paper on his drawing board. With a few precise lines he caught the girl's innate boredom. Suddenly he sensed he was being watched. He raised his eyes.

It was her – four rows in front of him. She turned away quickly when she saw him looking. Was this the face which had inspired Dante to write of Beatrice in Florence all those years ago? Had Dante experienced that throat-constricting, pulse-surging excitement when *he* had first set eyes on the girl of his dreams? *Ma Beatrice si'bella e ridente*. What strange compulsion had urged him to seek her out?

His thoughts and emotions were suddenly confused. He turned over the piece of cartridge paper and pinned it to the board; then he moved his stool further round the room, ignoring the stifled giggles his surreptitious movements caused. Now he could see her from profile. He began to draw her, pouring his heart into creating a drawing worthy of her. The sketched pencil and crayon lines sprang to life beneath his facile hand; he shaded in her pink gingham blouse, mauve shawl and fashionable ankle-length pleated skirt.

'Ach, M'sieur Modigliani. Is it really you? After all this time, *hein*?' Herr Schuler, pince-nez sliding down his aquiline nose, pumped Amedeo's hand. 'You haf not changed, my boy. Perhaps a little fuller in ze cheeks. But the same. Well well, ziss iz a surprise,' he enthused, his face glowing like an autumn sunset. 'Ah, such a lifelike drawing.' The old Austrian tutor squinted at Amedeo's drawing board. 'But this iz not ze model?'

Amedeo shrugged, suddenly overcome by shyness.

'I recognize ze young woman you haf drawn,' Herr Schuler

said, squeezing Amedeo's shoulder with fatherly affection. 'You haf lost none of your talent, my boy. You draw superbly. You are acquainted with M'selle Hébuterne, *ja*?'

Amedeo shook his head, his heart pounding like a youth attending his first dance.

'No? Then I must introduce you. Jeanne has just joined my classes. Already she iz one of my best pupils,' he said to Amedeo. Herr Schuler approached Jeanne's stool. 'But she is so modest. Always she belittles her work. Don't you, Jeanne?'

'M'sieur is very flattering.' Spots of pink tinged Jeanne's cheeks.

'This iz Amedeo Modigliani, Jeanne. He was one of my best students. And I know he's dying to meet you.'

Amedeo took her soft, warm hand in his and bowed, looking deeply into her eyes. '*Enchanté*.'

'It is an honour to meet you, M'sieur Modigliani. I have heard so much about your work.' Her voice was full of subtle inflections.

'He has done your portrait,' Herr Schuler said, showing her the sketch. '*Mais alors*, but look at the clock. It's five minutes past time, *hein*. Class dismiss.'

Jeanne began to put her things into a satchel.

'Would you have coffee with me, m'selle?' Her innocence enchanted him.

'I'd love to . . . if you don't mind my brother coming too? He always meets me from classes. I'm afraid my Papa is rather old-fashioned. He insists André accompanies me home.' A smile crossed her face. 'Papa thinks Montparnasse is full of depravity. Especially the Rotonde, which he thinks is a den of iniquity!'

Outside, a tall blond man, a few years younger than Amedeo, was waiting on the step. He raised his hat when Jeanne and Amedeo appeared, then gave Amedeo an enquiring glance. Shyly Jeanne explained who he was.

'I've heard of you, m'sieur,' André said, impressed at the pencil portrait Amedeo had done of his sister. 'You exhibited at the *Salon des Indépendants*. An old man playing the 'cello.'

'*The Cellist*,' Amedeo elucidated.

'It earned an honourable mention,' André added.

They walked to a little café in the rue Notre-Dame du Champs. Jeanne listened intently as Amedeo reminisced about his student days. When she asked a question, it was thoughtful and intelligent. They discussed Gauguin, Van Gogh, Bonnard, Seurat, Renoir, Chagall, Picasso, Derain, Canaletto, Watteau, Rubens, Turner, Sisley, Constable, Goya, Rodin, Degas, Toulouse-Lautrec. Jeanne was for this one or that; he defended some, criticized others. So engrossed were they in each other they completely forgot André. After half an hour André said with amused desperation: 'Papa will be expecting us home, Jeanne.'

Amedeo sprang up. '*Mea culpa*,' he apologized. 'When I start talking art I forget everything.' But he knew Jeanne had enjoyed herself: regret that she had to leave showed in her expression.

'Tomorrow?' he whispered. 'Same time?' She nodded. He watched her and André until they turned the corner. Her hand had been like warm silk in his.

The next afternoon he sat at the same table outside the café. Four o'clock. The life-class had finished; soon she would arrive. His day at Cheron's had passed as though in a dream. He had thought of nothing else but seeing her again. He hardly believed it of himself . . . waiting for a girl he had spoken to only twice – and then always in the company of others.

He glanced at his watch. A quarter past four. He looked up the dusty street. There was no sign of Jeanne or her brother.

Across the road he recognized some of the other students, satchels swinging, gossiping, their afternoon class finished. Perhaps she had been detained by Herr Schuler? Perhaps she had decided not to come after all? He pushed the thought from his mind and took out his pocket edition of the *Divine Comedy*. He flicked through the pages. *Quel sol che pria d'amor mi scaldo 'l petto* . . . "that sun which first warmed my bosom with love . . . " But, for once, Dante's immortal lines failed to capture his interest. Four-thirty. Obviously she was not coming. He finished his coffee, disappointed. It was the weekend; he would have to wait until Monday now.

At his *atelier* he lit the stove and plunged himself into sculpturing a female head in Afro-Cubist style, hammering the steel chisel until the floor was covered in stone fragments. He coughed as the fine abrasive dust caught in his throat. Brancusi had warned him sculpture would pay havoc with his lungs. His mouth was dry, his throat sore. *Dio mio*, he needed a drink!

As he put on his jacket he wondered whether Jeanne had had second thoughts. Perhaps her Papa had learned of their rendezvous? Perhaps her brother secretly disapproved? He thrust the doubts aside: idle conjecture was self-destructive.

The evening air was crisp. The street traders were taking down their stalls and packing. A sudden whiff of wet fish evoked memories of the quayside at Livorno in Italy.

As a boy he had sketched the offshore fishermen at their winches, hauling their gaily-painted boats up the chalk-white beach, surf sucking at their gumboots . . . crusty-red weather-beaten faces pleased by the kilos of sardines, turbot and whiting . . . barrel-chests swelling, muscles rippling. Then the foghorn reverberated through the port. The housewives came running, baskets swinging, black shawls flapping, eager eyes assessing the quality of the catch. 'Ten *lire* a kilo for those tiddlers, *basta*, you make a joke, no? . . . call those newts sardines! *Dio mio*, we wouldn't feed them to the cat.' How his young hand had loved to draw that scene! Endeavouring to make his sketches like living, breathing images; then walking home through the cobbled Via Roma, past the *duomo* and the *carabinieri* in their high-necked policemen's tunics, swords swinging at their sides, past the Villa Baciocchi where Guglielmo Micheli had his studio. Yes, so long ago . . .

He stopped by a chestnut-seller's brazier, savouring the bitter-sweet tang of burnt nuts, but smiled a polite refusal when the old lady proffered a bag. He was in need of a more substantial meal. Whistling, he made his way past the Colarossi, into the Boul' Montparnasse, then down the rue de la Campagne-Première to Chez Rosalie's.

Foujita waved to him from a corner table. 'Join me. The *lasagne* is excellent.' He sat at his friend's table. Foujita imparted the news of the day in amusing fashion, but Amedeo was unable to give his friend his undivided attention. Why did he think of no one else but Jeanne Hébuterne? What was happening to him? Could it be the birth-pangs of love? That elusive emotion which came in so many different guises, consuming mind and body, more urgent than hunger or thirst. If not love, then what? Never before had his emotions been in such a turmoil.

'What's this I hear about you and a pretty young student at the Colarossi?' Foujita's tone was one of amused curiosity. 'Jeanne Hébuterne.'

Amedeo felt himself reddening.

'I've met her. She is attractive, like a madonna,' Foujita said, amused by Amedeo's confusion. 'And a very talented artist. I've seen some of her work in the Colarossi exhibitions.'

Suddenly Amedeo heard himself blurting out the story of how he'd first met her in the Rotonde.

'She's obviously had a profound effect on you,' Foujita said soberly.

'*Mama mia*,' Amedeo sighed. 'But I've never felt this way about a girl before.'

Foujita shook his head, bemused. 'I never expected to see the day you were brought to heel by an affair of the heart. Haven't you always said a woman has no place in an artist's life, other than as model or mistress?'

Amedeo conceded the point with a smile. 'There's a flaw in every argument.'

Foujita ate the last of his *lasagne*. 'Ah, the pangs of unrequited love. *Mon ami*, until I met Fernande, I used to eat my heart out for a milliner's assistant in the Boul' Raspail. I pursued her for weeks, but all I got was a polite snub. Then one day I went in the shop for a final showdown . . . and discovered she had eloped with the milliner's husband.'

Amedeo laughed; already he felt better.

'That's more like the old Amedeo. Come, I know the perfect remedy for affairs of the heart. Mama Rosalie, a bottle of your best chianti.'

It was Monday. Amedeo entered the basement studio at La Maison Cheron. He couldn't wait for four o'clock! He was surprised to find a blond youth in a sculptor's apron working at a new bench on which was a pile of modelling clay. For weeks Cheron had been talking of taking on a new apprentice.

Amedeo inspected the youth's model of a church. 'Not bad. Not bad at all. What's your name, *mon ami*?'

'Pierre Moncrief. And you're Amedeo Modigliani,' he gushed. 'Monsieur Cheron has told me about you.'

'Don't believe anything that artistic desert tells you, Pierre. What he knows about art can be painted on a postage stamp.' He pointed to a drawing of a bowl of flowers on the scabby, whitewashed wall. 'That's Cheron's conception of art. Or, if his aesthetic sensibilities are especially roused, perhaps a bowl of fruit.'

'But I don't want to be a painter, Monsieur Modigliani. With respect, I want to be a sculptor.'

'You're wise to have made the decision so early, Pierre. Some never learn. I spent years with stone and chisel before I began to develop my skills with oils.'

'I'm supposed to be apprenticed here. Making sculptures which Monsieur Cheron can sell in his shop. But I'm only doing it to pay for my studies at art school. One day I hope to take the entrance examination to l'Ecole des Beaux-Arts. Rodin studied there.'

'Indeed he did. Auguste was a fine artist and an entertaining companion.'

'You actually *knew* him?'

'A little. When I first came to Paris he and Odile Redon frequented one of the cafés on the Butte. I used to eavesdrop on their conversations with the Montmartre artists. Sometimes I even plucked up enough courage to join in.'

He smiled at the memory. What a dilettante the two great artists must have considered him dressed, as he had been then, in a suit of finest Italian cloth, black cape and silver-nobbed cane. What pretentious twaddle he must have talked; but how patient and indulgent they had been with him. It seemed decades since he himself had been apprenticed at Micheli's, in Livorno. How he had wrestled with those soggy lumps of clay! Moulding and prodding that malleable but capricious material, trying to get a likeness of a horse. Micheli had impressed upon him: 'Clay modelling is excellent for developing one's visual memory; it will help you become a fine painter.'

Cheron came into the studio. 'Ah, I see you've met my new assistant,' he said to Amedeo. 'I've told him to watch you work; he'll learn more from you than from all those high falutin' theories they teach at art school.'

Amedeo winked at Pierre. 'What is today's assignment, m'sieur? A portrait from life, or an abstract?'

Cheron threw up his crab-like hands. 'Must we always have this pantomime? You know very well my customers like – '

'Flowers and fruit bowls,' Amedeo cut in, grinning. '*Dio mio*, but there can't be a house left in Montparnasse that doesn't have a Cheron still-life.'

'Dozens,' Cheron said, taking Amedeo seriously. He scurried upstairs to the shop and came back with a bunch of mixed flowers. 'A nice bouquet, please, for Mme Beniot; she's coming for it this afternoon.'

'But it won't be dry in time.'

Cheron shrugged. 'She was most insistent. And she wants them to look like Renoir's flowers.'

'Then I suggest she commissions Renoir to paint them.'

'Please bear with me, m'sieur. She is my best customer.'

Cheron turned to leave, paused, then said to Pierre: 'Be sure to study Monsieur Modigliani's technique, young fellow. I want you to be painting flowers soon, too.'

Pierre proved a willing and talented pupil; but watching Amedeo paint and listening to his reminiscences about his student days in Livorno and Venice made him yearn for the same experience. He took out a letter and showed it to Amedeo. He had been offered an apprenticeship at a sculptor's studio in Montmartre.

'Would I be doing the right thing in accepting, Monsieur Modigliani? I mean, suppose I discover I have no talent; suppose he – '

'You have talent, Pierre.'

'You really think I can be an artist?'

'*Dio mio*, boy, would I be encouraging you if I thought not? Get going – before you change your mind. Drop me a postcard some time. And don't let those Lapin Agile *cocottes* get their claws into you.'

That afternoon he was at the café near the Colarossi when the students' life-class finished. His eyes flitted from girl to girl. Jeanne had to be there. She couldn't have dropped out of the class; she would have told him when he'd last seen her. He recognized two girls who had been with Jeanne at the Rotonde. They passed by, giggling, giving him shy glances. He heard one say: 'He's waiting for Coco le Noix.' He smiled after them. The tables began to fill up. Had he missed her somehow? Impossible. He'd scrutinized everybody who passed.

Suddenly she was standing at his table, smiling, eyes like the Mediterranean at Livorno.

'You waited,' she said simply.

'Of course . . . Coco le Noix.'

She blushed. 'Where . . . ? How did you – ?'

'That's what they call you at the Colarossi – Coconut, because of your brown hair. It suits you.'

'It's just a silly name the girls thought up.' She drew a circle on the table with her forefinger.

'Do you have an *atelier* near here?' she asked then, not looking up.

'Quite near.'

She gave him a mysterious smile, then said: 'There's André. I must go now. I have to visit some relatives with

Maman.' She opened her satchel and took out a sheet of drawing paper. 'I did it in class. I'm afraid it isn't up to your standard.'

A pencil drawing. Of himself. And a good likeness too. He was on the point of telling her so when he saw that curious smile again. And then he understood.

'I'll meet you in the Luxembourg Gardens. Noon. Next Sunday,' she said and went to join André.

The work at Cheron's became more and more tedious and soul-destroying. He had enjoyed instructing Pierre; it had relieved the monotony. It was doing nothing to advance his career or develop his art; but it enabled him to survive.

On his day off he visited the Louvre. He felt a need to look at the works of the Old Masters, absorb their colours, go back to the grass roots of painting. He marvelled at the emotional intensity of Van Gogh's gnarled olive trees and sensuous cypresses growing out of the scorched *terra-cotta* earth of Provence; he studied Cézanne's mastery of light and form, his ability to achieve perspective with only shades of colour; and admired again Leonardo's wonderful Venus di Milo.

He emerged, head reeling with a hundred impressions, a kaleidoscope of colour and lines dancing in front of his eyes like midges in a honeysuckle garden. He had an urge to share the ideas that bubbled up from his imagination.

The Rotonde was crowded. The artists were assembled around two tables. Soon Amedeo joined in the discussion about Cubism, Dadaism, Expressionism. Their babel grew louder when Fernand Léger, in a huge Army greatcoat, joined them.

'I'm on a week's furlough, friends, so the drinks are on me.' He produced two bottles of cognac from his voluminous pockets and gouged them open with his combat knife.

'I sold a portrait to a woman at the Flea Market,' Chaim Soutine crowed. 'Twenty-five francs.' He slapped it on the table. The others cheered and dug into their pockets.

Léger ruffled the potato-faced Russian's hair. 'You have

the gods on your side; you must have been born in a caul.'

'What's a caul?' asked Aicha Goblet.

'Russian and Polish Jews have a saying,' Amedeo explained, 'that to be born in a covering inside the mother's womb brings good fortune.'

'An old wives' tale,' Aicha scoffed.

'I've heard Freud was born in one – and is he not eminent?' Léger asked rhetorically; the Austrian psychoanalyst proved the theory's validity, did he not?

Amedeo joined in their good-humoured banter, but his thoughts kept returning to the girl with the blue eyes. *Ma Beatrice si'bella e ridente.* Jeanne Hébuterne, he thought. The very name was like sunlight filtering through the chestnut trees in blossom. But he was an artist, not a poet; his job was to translate emotions into colour and shapes. Yes . . . he would paint his vision of her on canvas.

He worked long into the night. To achieve his artistic Nirvana, he thought, he must paint until he dropped. Paint, paint, paint! That was the only way to discover his dream. Gauguin, Van Gogh, Toulouse-Lautrec, Degas, Rodin . . . all the artists he most admired had dedicated themselves to Art to the exclusion of all else. There were no short cuts. Art demanded one, body and soul. There was no room for compromise: to compromise was to accept mediocrity. It was all or nothing and no turning back once one began to tread the path. Banal philosophy? Of course, he thought; but wasn't banal philosophy always right? That was why it survived when lofty ideologies sank beneath the weight of contradiction and cant.

It was dawn when he finished. He collapsed happily into an armchair and quickly fell asleep.

When he arrived at La Maison Cheron next morning, the street outside the shop was crowded. People were pointing at the windows of houses and shops.

'Didn't you hear them during the night?' Cheron was saying.

'Hear what?' replied a sour-faced biddy, clutching a tow-haired urchin to her side.

'The explosions! They say it's Big Bertha, an enormous cannon the Boches have. They're firing shells on Paris.'

'*Mon Dieu*!' the biddy screamed, dragging the urchin off up the street. 'We'll all be killed in our beds.'

Cheron rushed across and grasped Amedeo's arm. '*Regardez*. See what the Kaiser's done to my lovely window.' He began to wring his hands. 'Where's the money coming from to buy a new pane of glass that size?'

Amedeo stared. The window resembled a huge cobweb.

'When I phoned the War Department this morning,' Cheron added miserably, 'they said how could I be sure it wasn't boys with catapults? *Mon Dieu*, as if business isn't bad enough. First this,' he wailed, 'and now the model hasn't turned up. And I paid her in advance, fool that I am.'

'But there's an air raid on. Didn't you hear the siren? I nearly didn't come myself. The poor girl's probably frightened to leave home.'

'I'll get my money back,' Cheron said, talking to himself. 'I wasn't keen on having that girl anyway. Madame Desmaison wants a posy of flowers painting for her new town house. I'll send my assistant to the florist's.'

Amedeo went down to the basement studio. He set up the easel and began mixing colours for the inevitable vase of flowers. Presently Cheron came clattering down the steps, followed by his wife. 'There's been a change of plan. My mother-in-law wants a portrait of my wife, doesn't she, dear?' Mme Cheron's mouth hardened in acquiescence; her eyes remained bleak.

Cheron looked from one to the other. 'Well, I'll be up in the shop . . . if you need anything.' He gave Amedeo an apprehensive glance and scurried off upstairs.

Madame Cheron stared suspiciously at Amedeo. 'I'm ready when you are. Head and shoulders, painted nicely. None of that arty-crafty nonsense. Mother is very particular.'

Amedeo changed the colours of his palette. How could he be expected to paint a flattering portrait? Sallow complexion, flat-chested, hawk-like nose, beady eyes, lifeless hair done up in a tight bun, dowdy dress buttoned up to the neck. *Dio mio*, she looked like a scrawny chicken!

He felt her hostile eyes on him as he selected a suitable hog's-hair brush and dipped it in turpentine.

'This is Mother's idea, understand,' said Mme Cheron. 'Don't think I approve of you modern painters and your nudes. And as for that man Renoir and those *brasserie* hussies of his! Why, they ought to be burned.'

Amedeo smiled. 'Renoir's paintings hang in the Louvre. There's no finer accolade.'

He began to paint, closing his ears to her tirade against artists, models and cheeky shop assistants, but she was stretching his patience to the limit. Gardenias for Mme Grunnier . . . a bunch of bananas for Mme Jules . . . a kipper on a plate for M. Clouziot . . . was it for this he had come to Paris? To work for a pittance as a galley slave for Cheron and his scarecrow wife?

'Is it finished?' she demanded. 'I have better things to do than sit here.'

'*Voilà*, madame.' Amedeo stepped back; he had endeavoured to produce a flattering likeness, but was he to blame for her ugliness?

She approached the easel as though fearing he might assault her. Then she gazed aghast at the canvas. '*Nom de Dieu* . . . I look like a witch!' Blood rushed to her face. 'You monster, you Borgia! Just wait till Monsieur Cheron hears about this.'

Amedeo shrugged – and waited for the inevitable.

Cheron came down the steps. 'What is it? What's happened?'

Mme Cheron poked a horny finger towards the easel. 'Look what this scallywag has done. I've never been so insulted.'

Cheron took his wife's arm appeasingly. 'Oh, I don't know, my dear . . . it's not an unreasonable portrait. Your mother will – '

'What? You're as bad as he is.' She seized the canvas and

thrust it into his hands. 'Burn it. This instant.'

'But it's still wet.'

'Put it on the stove. Immediately. Do you hear?'

'*Mais alors*, good canvas is expensive,' her husband wailed.

Amedeo packed his paint-box; this was the last straw. Cheron could go to hell.

'Wait,' Cheron implored. 'I'm sure Madame Cheron didn't mean what she said.'

'Every word of it,' she snapped. 'Burn it. This minute.'

Amedeo started up the stairs.

'But we have a contract,' Cheron cried, running after him.

'We *had*, m'sieur.' He tipped his hat rakishly. '*Adieu*.'

An hour to kill. *Dio mio*, would it never pass? Amedeo was at the little café in the Luxembourg Gardens. He went through his pockets: thirty francs. So little! Perhaps he had been too hasty, quitting Cheron's. Cheron would take him back; but it would mean having to apologize to Mme Cheron. Apologize to that shrew? Never. Something would turn up; it usually did.

'What would m'sieur like?'

'Coffee. Black; and very strong.'

A horse-drawn brewer's dray rumbled past the wrought-iron entrance gates to the Gardens. Sunlight filtered through the trembling plane trees, forming a shadowy mosaic on the patio. An urchin came up to Amedeo's table.

'Want an errand running, m'sieur? Cigarettes? Newspaper?'

He ruffled the lad's hair. 'No. But I do need a model. *Ecco*.' He opened his sketch-book and sharpened a pencil. 'A portrait. For a sherbet fizz. Agreed?'

'*Oui*.' The lad combed his hair with his fingers and posed self-consciously. Amedeo bought him a sherbet and told him to start. The boy sucked on a straw. He made several sketches. Later, he would paint the scene from memory. He gave the lad fifty centimes, laughing when he tore off to find a sweetshop.

He looked across the lawns and flower-beds. Perhaps

Jeanne would not come. Then his heart leapt as he saw her enter the gates. He waved.

He rose to greet her and ordered two coffees. Jeanne, overcome by a sudden shyness, looked away. How enchanting she was, he thought.

He persuaded her to tell about her day at the Colarossi.

'The students have a special name for you,' she said.

'Oh?'

'They call you the Prince of Montparnasse.'

He laughed. 'Well, tell them their prince hasn't a sou to his name. And you should see what effect he has on the good citizens of Montparnasse. Why, women cross the street when they see me coming; and tell their children to hide in case I gobble them up.' She laughed. He pointed to a book she was carrying. 'Your sketch-book?'

She nodded. 'Herr Schuler tells us to carry it with us wherever we go. So we will be ready if we see something worth sketching.'

'Good advice. May I see?'

Jeanne demurred. 'Oh, there's nothing worth showing. Just doodlings.'

'Such modesty,' he teased. 'Please?'

'You won't think much of them,' she said, handing it to him. 'I'm always having to rub out and start again. *Repentir*. It's my middle name.'

He studied her work, impressed by her clear line, imaginative use of shading and cross-hatching. 'You have an eye for detail. That's good.'

'Now you're just being kind,' she protested; but he knew she was pleased.

'Are you still working for Cheron?' she went on quickly, to hide her confusion.

Amedeo explained what had happened, that he had met another dealer.

'His name's Leopold Zborowski. He's Polish. And next week I'm painting a portrait of his wife. He's offered me fifty francs.'

'That's a lot, isn't it?'

'More than twice what I'm usually paid.'

'You'll soon be as famous as Picasso.'

He shrugged. 'There's only one Pablo.'

'And only one Amedeo Modigliani,' she added, blushing. 'Oh, but just look at the time! I must go.'

'So soon?'

'I don't want to go. Honestly. But my mother hasn't been well – '

'I understand. When will I see you again?'

'Here. After classes next week. I go this way on my way home.'

He watched her as she crossed the Gardens; he waved when she glanced back. Her eyes had told him what he wanted to know.

As he climbed the stairs to his studio he noticed an odour; it was vaguely familiar. A fish dish that someone was cooking. Mme Velitch? No, she rarely did any cooking. He opened his door. There, standing over a casserole on the stove, was Elvira. He was stunned.

Dio Mio, would he never be rid of her?

'Hallo, *chéri*,' she said breezily. 'I'm cooking you a Provençal *bouillabaise*. It's got conger eel, rascasse, whiting, mackerel, spiny lobsters, prawns . . . you'll love it. But you've no idea what trouble I had to go to get all the ingredients. These Parisian shopkeepers – *merde*! – they have no imagination.'

He looked round. The studio was transformed. The bed was made, the floor scrubbed, the stove was shining, the dishes washed up. And she had laid her things out on the bed. Her old leather case lay open on the floor.

She was behaving as though she had never been away. It was over between them: dead. Yet here she was acting like a wife.

'I've decided to forgive and forget, *chéri*. Anyway, I never really cared about Adolphe Basler. He was a skinflint. I only went with him to make you jealous.'

'I don't want you here, Elvira. I thought I made that clear.'

'Oh please, lover, let me stay. I won't be a nuisance. I

won't get in the way. I promise. You don't have to say you love me . . . just tell me you want me now and again . . .'

His dismay turned to pity. She was like a crumpled rag doll left out in the rain. Used, exploited, tossed away. The leather case conjured up forgotten lovers, shoddy boarding houses, waterfront cellar dives, dingy theatres in provincial towns.

'Can I stay, Amedeo?' Her voice was pathetic.

'No.'

'Please – '

'We belong to different worlds.'

'I promise I won't be a burden – ' She broke off, eyes on the portrait of Jeanne on his easel. 'That's her, isn't it? That art student you've been going around with? Don't think I haven't heard how you make cow-eyes at her in that Colarossi place. Well, she doesn't impress me, Modigliani.' She picked up a palette knife and went toward the easel. He seized her arm as she raised the knife.

'Let me go, damn you!'

He wrestled the knife from her grasp.

'Take your things and get out.' Her vicious little mouth and spiteful eyes sickened him. He wished he had never ever laid eyes on her. He cursed his lonely craving for human companionship which had driven him into her arms.

She threw her belongings into the case and fastened it.

He opened the door.

'A gipsy's curse on you, Modigliani. I hope you cough your lungs up.' Her boots clattered down the stairs. The street door slammed shut.

The rue Joseph-Bara was a tree-lined avenue off the rue Notre-Dame du Champs. Promptly at 11 am Amedeo rang the bell at No. 8. He was clean-shaven and was wearing his best cretonne shirt, scarlet sash and corduroy suit.

Leopold Zborowski greeted him like an eager spaniel and ushered him into an improvised studio with a stove, art materials and easel. Was there enough light? Enough oils?

Amedeo warmed to Leopold's shy charm and thoughtful brown eyes; he inspired trust and confidence. He looked round the studio, noting that the windows admitted plenty of light. It was fine, he said.

'Coffee before you begin?' Leopold enquired.

'I'd love some. Black and strong.'

Leopold disappeared, returning a few minutes later. With him was his wife, Hanka. She acknowledged Amedeo with a shy, almost formal manner. She was tall and carried herself with an almost regal bearing. Her hair was worn in the fashionable style of the day; her voice was well modulated, quietly authoritative.

Amedeo experimented with his palette until the colours corresponded with her delicate peach-coloured skin. She was indeed enchanting; it would be a pleasure to paint her.

She was immediately interested in Amedeo's Italian origins and questioned him intelligently.

'We are from Cracow,' she said. 'A city rich in architecture but, alas, lacking the sun of your country.'

'Cracow is a beautiful city, I'm told.'

'Beautiful, yes – but the winters are bitter. Leopold had rheumatic fever in childhood and his health is rather delicate. The Paris climate is kinder.' She told him of Leopold's early struggles in Paris. After graduating at Cracow University he had come to Paris to study French culture at the Sorbonne, but when the war with Germany broke out Leopold, as an alien, was sent to a prison camp. Fortunately after six months the French authorities relented and released all aliens.

'We've had a difficult time since,' Hanka went on. 'Leopold has worked day and night, hunting for rare books, lithographs, first editions – even addressing envelopes for five francs a hundred. On top of all that he writes poetry.'

'Ah, the music of the soul.'

'You like poetry?'

'I read nothing else.'

When Leopold rejoined them with coffee, they discussed poetry, quoting stanzas and comparing different poets' styles.

An hour sped by; the portrait was finished.* Leopold and Hanka were delighted.

'I knew the moment I saw the pastel in that old clothier's shop that you had a unique talent,' Leopold said, thrusting a fifty-franc note into Amedeo's reluctant hand. 'Please take it. I've just sold a Zola first edition. For a hundred francs.' Leopold glanced enquiringly at his wife, who nodded. 'I was wondering, m'sieur . . . that is, Hanka and I have a little proposition which might interest you.'

Amedeo waited. Leopold went on: 'What we wondered is . . . are you under contract to a dealer?'

'I was. But not any more.'

Leopold outlined the proposition. He would provide Amedeo with materials, a studio in which to work whenever he felt inclined; he would provide models, arrange advertising, exhibitions, brochures, and pay Amedeo a monthly allowance after deducting reasonable expenses and a small commission.

'I'm flattered you have so much confidence in me.'

'Then you agree?'

Amedeo held out his hand, laughing when the Pole pumped it vigorously.

'Hanka,' Leopold cried, 'our best vodka. A toast – to our future prosperity.'

* Called 'Anna', this painting hangs in the Galleria Nazionale d'Arte Moderna, Rome.

Six

America's President Wilson had declared in his presidential speech: 'Peace without victory.' The British Army was winning the third battle of Ypres. Soon, everyone thought, the war must end and Montparnasse would be just as it was in the old days.

Amedeo had much to be thankful for. He had met the girl of his dreams . . . Leopold had sold another portrait to Dr Alexandre . . . and the future looked less bleak.

What was this Dada movement in Switzerland everybody was talking about? It didn't seem any more original or revolutionary than what he, Chaim, Foujita, Maurice and the rest of the crowd had been painting for years. Only the Paris art critics, it seemed, did not appreciate that simple fact. They would. But, by then, it might be too late; for life for the artists who had not gone to war was hard. Somehow they struggled on, painting when they could afford to buy materials, discussing ideas and techniques when they could not. Somehow they kept their sanity.

'*Shalom*, Deo.' Chaim was at the zinc when Amedeo entered the Rotonde. 'There's an article about you in *L'Eventail.*'

'Ah, yes. It's by Francis Carco, the novelist.'

'*Sans blague*! That's a feather in your cap.'

Foujita and Fernande joined them.

'Beatrice Hastings is back in town,' Fernande said. 'What a nerve she's got. Fancy her showing her face in Montparnasse again!'

Beatrice, a militant feminist who wrote for several intellectual magazines in London, had lived in the rue Norvins before the war. Amedeo had known her for two years; but though her conversation had been stimulating, her artistic criticism beneficial, their relationship had been too stormy to be satisfactory to either of them.

'They say she's sponsoring a South American sculptor,' Fernande said.

'Sponsoring?' Amedeo said, grinning. 'Or devouring?'

Foujita said, 'How are sales, Deo? Leopold Zborowski seems to be in ten places at once.'

'Oh, so-so.'

'Have you read *L'Eventail*?' Chaim asked the others. 'Deo's becoming famous.'

Amedeo shrugged modestly, but secretly he was thrilled. Leopold had been so excited he had bought twelve copies and had stuck them on the walls of all the popular bars and cafés in Montparnasse.

'Tell me more,' Foujita said, delighted.

'Some of my drawings have been published in *L'Eventail* and *Cabaret*. It's Leopold's doing really.'

'How much will you get?' Fernande asked.

'*Chérie*,' Foujita said, 'this is prestige. Deo's work will be seen with Picasso's and Kandinsky's.'

'Perhaps they can afford to publish their work for nothing. Amedeo can't. Besides, I don't like Picasso. Nor Kandy-whatever-his-name-is. And if they're so great, why don't they help their friends?'

'An artist's work must speak for itself,' Foujita said.

'*Merde*.' Fernande spat. 'You're all crazy.'

'You're late,' Jeanne scolded smilingly when he met her in the Luxembourg Gardens. 'I thought you were never coming.'

'Wild horses couldn't stop me. Isn't André with you?' he asked, surprised.

'André's girl-friend is a milliner's daughter. Papa and the milliner aren't on speaking terms. André and I have an understanding: he sees his milliner – and I see you. And neither of us tells Papa. Am I very wicked?'

'Very,' he grinned. 'A Jezebel in the making. So where does your Papa think you are?'

'Meeting a girl-friend from art class. He doesn't approve of the Rotonde artists. "They're in league with the Devil",' she mimicked. 'Sometimes I could shake him, he's so narrow-minded! He won't accept that attitudes are changing. He still reads Pascal's *Pensées* to André and me every night after dinner, just as though we're children.'

'But there must be someone . . . special. Of whom he approves.'

She looked away.

'So there is!'

'It's not what you think. And I don't love him. His name's Pierre Poulenne and he's a clerk. His father's a friend of Papa's. Pierre's nice enough, but he's so boring. Boys of my own age just don't interest me. They're gauche, unimaginative and clumsy. They think I'm prudish – because I don't find their coarse jokes amusing.'

They walked on in silence a while.

'What did your Papa say when you told him you wanted to study at the Colarossi?'

'He was furious. He didn't speak to me for three whole days. Had it not been for *Maman*, he would have stopped me. Even now I'm only allowed to study as a preparation for the Ecole's entrance examination.'

'And if you don't pass?'

Jeanne shrugged. 'Papa wants me to learn dressmaking.'

Again Amedeo was aware of the resemblance of Jeanne to Ingres's portrait *Mademoiselle Rivière*; she had the same unfathomable eyes and haunting smile, virginal yet maternal, an inner serenity and wisdom beyond her years. Foujita had once said that all women were born a thousand years old.

'Is it true – you have girls up to your *atelier*, who pose . . . ' She turned away, blushing.

'In the nude?' he said with a roguish laugh. 'But of course! An artist must paint from life. What is more natural? Why, you draw nudes yourself at art school,' he reminded her.

'But we are thirty in a class. We don't speak to the models. Nor are we ever alone with them.'

He smiled. 'Do I detect a note of jealousy?'

They fell silent. Then, presently, Jeanne said, 'That actress, Elvira . . . does she still pose for you?'

'No.' He glanced askance at her. 'How did you hear about her?'

'She was your mistress, wasn't she?'

He shrugged. 'Yes.' There was no sense in denying it.

'Do you still see her?'

'No.'

He felt the warm pressure of her hand in his.

'Were you in love with her?'

'No.'

A strange expression lit her eyes. 'I'm glad.'

They lingered like all lovers. Then Jeanne said she had to leave.

Leaving the Gardens, he wandered through the streets, remembering her haunting smile, the way her nose wrinkled prettily when she laughed. He felt an emptiness that wasn't easy to explain.

He stopped outside the Rotonde, but for once he had no inclination to join the crowd.

He returned to the *atelier.* He lit the kerosene lamp, set up a new peice of canvas on his easel and began a portrait of Jeanne. He lost all track of time. Night fell. He went on painting, seeing Jeanne's face everywhere, in everything he did. He had a sudden desire to see her, talk to her, feel her warmth against him. He was impatient of the way in which they had to keep meeting; it meant inveigling André into deceiving Jeanne's parents, involving her in the deception too. What was he to do? Speak to her Papa? Explain that his growing friendship with her was not a mere peccadillo? 'Find a good woman, Deo,' Foujita was repeatedly telling him. 'Settle down.' Marriage? He wasn't ready to relinquish his freedom! An artist lived only for his work. And yet . . .

Thoughtfully, he put Jeanne's portrait aside to dry off and began to dab paint on to a fresh piece of canvas. 'Paint what the bourgeosie wants, Deo,' Foujita was always telling him. An emaciated kipper began to take shape. He prodded it with a stick to form its eyes. It seemed to stare at him balefully.

Dio mio, he wasn't a pavement artist! He could not lower his standards just to appease public taste.

He glanced at Carco's article which he had pinned up at the top of his easel . . . "Modigliani's art is several years ahead of its time. He has a unique gift, an inner vision which enables him to reveal the essential melancholy of the human soul . . . ' 'Ah, words. If only others could interpret the artist's message so easily. Degas had warned him, hadn't he? The old recluse had urged him to look within himself, deeper and deeper, until the ultimate truth was revealed. 'But don't expect the world to pat you on the back, *mon ami*,' Degas had said. 'Achievement must be your only reward. Self-knowledge. It's the only thing worth having in this crazy world.' Yes, Degas knew.

The next day Amedeo rose early and shaved carefully. Then he put on his red cretonne shirt and beige corduroy suit. He put the portrait of Jeanne in a wooden stretcher and wrapped it in paper. He left for Leopold's.

The Pole greeted him with some surprise: Amedeo wasn't usually so keen to make an early start.

'*Ecco*,' Amedeo said, thrusting the portrait into Leopold's hands.

Leopold stared at it for what seemed an eternity.

'Well? What do you think?'

'It's excellent,' Leopold murmured. He had not completely recovered from Amedeo's early arrival. 'One of the best you have done.'

'It's not for sale, you understand. I just wanted your opinion.'

'Of course,' Leopold murmured. 'Er, the model for today isn't due for another hour . . . I didn't expect you so soon.'

'No matter.' Amedeo lit a cigarette. 'I can wait. Go on with what you were doing. Don't let me disturb you.' He sat in an armchair and smiled at Leopold's bemused expression.

'Cheer up, Leopold. You look as though you expect the bailiffs at any minute! It's a beautiful morning. It would be sacrilege to stay in bed! Besides, I'm feeling on top of the world. Now, who's the model today?'

'Ruby Czechowska.'

Amedeo grimaced; she was a *grisette* who hung around the Rotonde. But beggars could not be choosers. Leopold had a living to earn, overheads to pay.

'I know you hate models like her,' Leopold apologized. 'But I have a buyer. A shopkeeper. He wants a nude for his summer-house – '

'Say no more, Leopold. I just hope you're charging him a fat fee.'

'I am, I am. Don't worry. Er, I'll get some coffee . . . '

'Relax, *mon ami*,' Amedeo said. 'Today I'm in love with the whole world.' Especially with Jeanne Hébuterne, he thought, and though he wanted to share his happiness with Leopold a sudden shyness made him reticent.

Ruby Czechowska arrived half an hour later. Amedeo had prepared his palette and was ready to begin. But the girl was in no hurry; she pretended to flirt with Leopold, who blushed and stammered, but her eyes never left Amedeo.

When Leopold left them on some pretext Ruby slipped off her coat, piqued that Amedeo had given her little more than a cursory glance.

'How do you wish me to pose?' she said petulantly.

'Nude. How else?'

'You're not very friendly today.'

'Let's start, shall we? Monsieur Zborowski wants the painting finished by midday.'

He was indifferent to her coquettishness and unmoved by her blatant sexuality; the sooner he finished, the better.

Ruby took off her clothes and faced him, bright-eyed with annoyance.

He began the portrait in silence, working quickly, in total absorption, emphasizing Ruby's rounded thighs which he knew would appeal to the shopkeeper.

'Are you still living near the Rotonde?'

He nodded.

'Not very talkative, are you? You never ask me to pose for you these days.' He's a handsome one, no mistake; strong, like a stallion. Those burning eyes and that hungry-looking mouth, the most exciting man in Montparnasse! 'I will. Willingly.'

Amedeo shrugged. 'There are plenty of models.' He didn't like the intense way she kept looking at him, devouring him with her eyes. Leopold should not have engaged her; she had an insatiable appetite for men. Given even the slightest encouragement she would dog his footsteps, pester him to let her stay with him. It didn't bear thinking about.

'I used to pose for Moise Kisling,' Ruby said. 'He thinks me *jolie*.'

'He's a fine painter.'

'He tried to make love to me,' she said archly.

He laughed. 'That's Moise all over.'

'Oh, I hate you. You never take me seriously.'

Whistling, he applied more paint.

'Moise thinks I have a great talent as a model,' she went on tartly.

Amedeo sipped the scalding coffee Leopold had brought. Why did every *grisette* in Montparnasse think they were irresistible? Didn't they know that modelling, in the professional sense, was an art? It was not simply a matter of undressing. He would sooner paint shopgirls, washerwomen, bakers, carpenters, milliners . . . people whose faces reflected the sadness and beauty of life.

'I'll go back to your *atelier* with you, if you want.'

'I have a regular model.'

'I wouldn't be a nuisance. I could clean for you, do your chores.'

Amedeo selected a coarse-haired brush and mixed a heavy yellow pigment. 'Lie back on the sofa, please.'

Ruby pouted, hardening the lines on a face which had already aged beyond its years. Her breasts had lost their youthful firmness, though she was not more than nineteen or twenty.

The morning wore on. Amedeo merely grunted and nodded as Ruby carried on a running commentary of her life and lovers. Thankfully, at noon, he had put the finishing touches to the painting. He set down his brushes and lit a cigarette.

'Tell the shopkeeper his canvas is ready,' he said when Leopold came in.

Leopold expressed some confusion at Ruby's state of half-undress.

'Pardon me, m'selle . . . I'll come back in a few minutes . . . '

Ruby paused from cupping her bosom into her brassière and stared at him in amazement. 'Never seen a girl undressed before, M'sieur Zborowski?'

Amedeo slipped on his jacket and picked up Jeanne's portrait. He had already forgotten Ruby.

'You're staying to lunch, Amedeo?'

'Sorry, Leopold. No time. I'm meeting Jeanne. Perhaps tomorrow. Give my regards to Hanka.'

'But your payment – '

Amedeo grinned. 'I trust you. *Ciao*.'

He walked down the rue Joseph-Bara and into the rue de la Grand-Chaumière. Some of the Colarossi students were already coming out for the midday break. Among them was Jeanne.

She stood on tip-toes to kiss him, slipping her hand into his and falling in step beside him.

He showed her the canvas. 'A present. For you.'

She looked at the portrait.

'Amedeo, you flatter me,' she said, pink spots colouring her cheeks.

'Don't you like it?'

'Oh, yes. You paint beautifully.' She was momentarily perplexed. 'But I can't accept it.'

'Why ever not?'

'Because – ' she began.

'Because what?'

'For a start it must be worth a lot of money.'

'So?'

'But I – '

'No buts. It's yours. I insist. Besides, I've been wanting to do a portrait of you for weeks.'

They sat at a table outside the Rotonde and Amedeo ordered two coffees. Presently he told her he would like to meet her father.

'You have no idea what he's like. He has a terrible temper. He may even throw you out.'

Jeanne studied his resolute face, thrilled he had proposed the confrontation. She felt the burning intensity of his deep brown eyes. How handsome he was! A twinge of jealousy went through her as she thought of the girls who had visited his *atelier*.

'I'll come to the house,' he said.

'No. I have another suggestion. On Sunday, after Mass, Papa is taking us for *café-crêmes*. It's supposed to be a family treat. I shall persuade him to take us to the Closerie des Lilas. You could meet us there.'

'But what if he won't go there, *cara*? You say he dislikes artists.'

'Don't they have poetry gatherings at the Closerie?'

'Yes. On Tuesdays. Max Jacob, Guillaume Appollinaire, and others. But never on Sundays.'

Jeanne smiled impishly, 'Papa doesn't know that. He has a passion for Pascal's *Pensées*. He'll agree.' She looked at him anxiously. 'You will be there?'

'I wouldn't miss it for anything.'

Amedeo escorted Jeanne back to the Colarossi and then returned to his studio. He felt as though walking on air, her voice echoing in his thoughts. Indoors, he lit the wood in the stove and put some coffee on to boil. Suddenly he remembered that Leopold had asked him to prepare his best canvases for an exhibition he was hoping to arrange at Mme Berthe Weill's gallery. It sounded promising: Berthe was renowned for her shrewdness and her ability for spotting new talent. He sorted through several piles of canvases . . . the laundry-girls, Gaby and Yvette; Elvira, Beatrice and Simone, 'La Canadienne', who taught the piano and, who Moise Kisling had declared, possessed the most beautiful décolletage in Paris.

Some of the paintings had gathered dust but, fortunately,

not enough to become ingrained; others, which he had propitiously covered with rice paper, were in excellent condition. Leopold had told him to prepare twenty or thirty; so he busied himself with the cleansing fluid, erasing the film of dust and dirt with meticulous care, as he had been taught to do at Micheli's, pleased when the thick impasto began to return to pristine condition.

How the Elviras glowed! The orange hues of the flesh tones seemed to radiate warmth and vitality. How Leopold had blushed when he had first seem them! '*Nom de Dieu*, I've never seen such colours. Such sensuality, such beauty! Why, they have the earthiness of Renoir, the sculpturing of Cézanne, the draughtsmanship of Rubens and your own rich texture. *Mon ami*, you are truly a great artist.'

He fixed the canvases round the walls, perusing them from a distance through half-closed eyes to observe the contrasts. Yes, they were worthy of showing. Surely success could not be far away. His years in Paris had been a bitter struggle against poverty and despair. But artists were destined to struggle. Van Gogh, Matisse, Degas, Cézanne, Gauguin, Seurat, Bonnard – they had all fought against prejudice and scorn. Yet they had triumphed. He would too. As Leopold repeatedly told him, it was just a matter of time.

That night he slept happily.

Sunday came at last. The moment he opened his eyes, squinting in the stream of sunlight which stabbed him, he thought of Jeanne. What would she be doing? Combing her hair at her dresser? Breakfasting with her family? It was ten o'clock. He had slept late. Move yourself. Up. Get dressed. There's no time to idle in bed!

Dressed in his best red cretonne shirt, beige corduroy suit pressed and brushed, he ate breakfast in the corner *brasserie*.

'*Bonjour, m'sieur*. You are bright this morning.'

He smiled at Mme Jardin, the plump *patrone*. 'Two important appointments.'

'On Sunday? *Alors*, an artist's work is never done, *hein*.'

He ate the freshly-baked croissants with relish; and sipped the strong, black coffee. The woolliness of sleep began to evaporate. Ah, but it was good to be alive.

'There was a woman in here last night, m'sieur. Asking for you.'

'Oh?' Jeanne? No, she would have left a note at his studio. 'Did she give her name?'

Mme Jardin's mountainous jowls wobbled as her brow creased in thought. 'Elinor? Something like that.'

'Elvira?'

'Ah, *mais oui*. I wasn't sure if you would want her to know . . . so I told her I hadn't seen you for some time. Should I have told her where to find you?'

'No, madame, you said the right thing.' *Dio mio*, would he never be rid of Elvira? 'If she comes in again, tell her I've left Paris. Gone back to Italy.' He paid for the coffee and croissants.

'*Au revoir, m'sieur*.' Ah, but he is a handsome devil; no wonder women are always chasing him. If she were twenty years younger . . .

Amedeo breathed deeply as he walked up the rue Joseph-Bara; the sun was warm on his skin. The *pâtisseries* were doing a lively trade. He went in the first one he came to. '*Du pain*. Two large.' He paid and resumed his stroll; the bread would save Hanka a journey to the *boulangerie*. He was whistling a Neapolitan love-song when he rang Leopold's doorbell.

Leopold appeared in his dressing-gown. '*Mais alors*, so early again. Are you not sleeping, *mon ami*?'

'Like a top. Here – ' he thrust the two loaves into Leopold's hands – 'your breakfast. How's Mme Zborowskai?'

'Well. Come in, come in. Hmm . . . the bread smells delicious. You'll have some breakfast with us?'

'No thanks. I've already eaten.' He was amused by Leopold's puzzled face. 'What's the matter?'

Leopold shook his head. 'Ach, there must be something behind it.'

Amedeo flung himself into a horse-hair chair, grinning.

'Can't you guess, *mon ami*?'

Leopold ruminated. 'A legacy?'

'Why, you lump of Polish ham, is there no romance in your soul? You, a poet – yet you think only of basics.'

Bemused, Leopold shuffled his feet.

'I'm in love, fathead! In *love*. Isn't it wonderful? I still can't believe it. It's everything Dante said it was, but more so. I feel as though I could paint a thousand portraits with one stroke. I, who didn't believe it was possible to have feelings like this. I, who thought love was just an illusion – for poets and dreamers.'

'But this is wonderful news, Amedeo. It calls for a celebration. Some vodka.'

'Later, Leopold. First, tell me about the exhibition. What did Mme Weill think of the Elvira nude you showed her?'

'She was impressed. The moment she set eyes on it, I knew we were in.'

'Bravo. When do we exhibit?'

'Not so fast,' Leopold said, smiling. 'Always you are like the wind. Like all dealers, *mon ami*, Mme Weill has to be cautious. You are still relatively unknown, by Parisian standards. So I suggested that if your work is acclaimed, as I'm sure it will be, she could say that she is your discoverer. It intrigued her all right.'

'So she will exhibit?' Amedeo said eagerly.

'Yes.'

'*Magnifico*, Leopold! You're a genius. What are her terms?'

'She has agreed to show your work exclusively for one month. She takes twenty per cent commission on everything sold.'

'We'll be rich, Leopold,' Amedeo cried, laughing. 'Think of it. A whole month in the rue Taitbout. All those wealthy connoisseurs of art spending thousands of francs! We're made, Leopold!' Suddenly he remembered the appointment at the Closerie des Lilas. 'The time, Leopold. What's the time?'

Leopold glanced at the clock. 'Almost half past eleven. Why? What's your hurry?'

'I'm meeting Jeanne's family at the Closerie.'

'Correction,' said Leopold firmly. '*We* are. What time are you due there?'

'Twelve.'

'*Mon Dieu*, why didn't you say so earlier?'

A few minutes before noon Amedeo and Leopold were sitting at a pavement table at the Closerie des Lilas Café, sipping coffee. One by one the tables began to fill. Amedeo drummed his fingers on the table-top. 'They should have been here by now. Mass finished at a quarter to twelve.'

'Perhaps Mass is a little late,' Leopold pacified.

Amedeo looked up the boulevard anxiously; Jeanne had been so certain her father would agree. Had something gone wrong?

'Relax, Amedeo. There's plenty of time.'

'They are coming. There – see? The girl with the chestnut hair.'

Achille Hébuterne was a stocky, florid-faced man with a spade-shaped beard, starched collar, frock coat and spats; the epitome of a provincial mayor. He ushered his wife, Jeanne and her brother André to a table, lifted his coat tails and sat down.

'I don't like the look of him,' Leopold murmured. 'He will need a lot of humouring.'

Jeanne's eyes searched the crowd, smiling when she found Amedeo. He waved to her surreptitiously and indicated that he'd brought his sketch-book.

'A flattering portrait will soften him up, Leopold.'

Amedeo began to draw the family group, oblivious of the harassed waiters who perspired from table to table with frozen smiles; the preening wives who paid lip-service to pompous husbands while trying to catch their lovers' eyes.

'How can you be so calm?' Leopold said. 'When I met Hanka's father I trembled so much he thought I had ague.'

Fascinated, Leopold watched Amedeo's dexterous pencil capture the very essence of Jeanne's wistful smile and the comfortable homeliness of Mme Hébuterne, a dainty woman with pretty features and hair beginning to grey attractively.

The drawings completed, Amedeo gulped his coffee. He rose.

'Don't forget,' Leopold said. 'Humour him – whatever he says.'

Amedeo winked, then approached the Hébuternes' table. '*Bonjour, m'sieur, madame*,' he said with a slight bow.

'Papa,' Jeanne said quickly, 'this is Monsieur Modigliani. The artist.'

Achille Hébuterne raised his bulbous eyes from his *café-crême*. He studied Amedeo at some length.

'So you're Modigliani. Quite the ladies' man, eh? Seeing you confirms what I've thought all along. That my daughter has been beguiled by your smooth tongue. Art for art's sake, etcetera.'

'Papa! It's not like that at all,' Jeanne began.

'In my opinion, m'sieur,' her father went on, 'artists are lazy good-for-nothings who can't earn a decent living any other way.'

'Monsieur Modigliani came because I asked him, Papa. He just wants to meet you.'

'Meet me? What could I possibly have in common with him?'

'But, Papa – '

'That's enough, Jeanne.' Her father glared at Amedeo. 'My daughter is at an impressionable age, m'sieur. She can't discriminate. Of course, I realize that it's fashionable for artists to scorn people who lead God-fearing, respectable lives – '

'On the contrary, m'sieur. My own family in Italy – '

'Furthermore, I won't have her mixing with arty rabble.'

Jeanne bit her lip. 'At least do him the courtesy of looking at his work, Papa.'

'Idle doodlings at a café table? You call that work?'

'He has great talent,' Jeanne cried, fighting back tears. 'Ask anybody in Montparnasse.'

'This is no time for hysteria, Jeanne.'

'*Maman* would like to see your drawings, Monsieur Modigliani,' Jeanne said. 'Wouldn't you, *Maman*?'

Amedeo hesitated, warning her with his eyes. The situation was turning to disaster. 'Perhaps another time, m'selle . . . '

'Now. I insist.' Jeanne took them from him.

Achille Hébuterne reddened. 'Jeanne! How dare you behave like this?'

Mme Hébuterne put a restraining hand on her husband's arm. 'The young man means no harm.'

'Let me be the judge of that, my dear.'

Jeanne showed the sketches to her mother. 'Look, *Maman* – our portraits. You see, Amedeo's style is unique.'

Her father gave them a cursory glance. 'Then why hasn't he drawn pupils in the eyes?'

'He doesn't put pupils in pencil portraits,' Jeanne countered. 'He doesn't think them essential.'

'Hah! These cafés are full of so-called artists. They all think they can draw like Leonardo da Vinci. But I'm not taken in. *I* know *art* when I see it. I've been to the Louvre.'

Leopold, poised timidly on the edge of the group, stepped forward, clearing his throat. 'Pardon the intrusion, m'sieur,' he addressed Achille Hébuterne. 'Perhaps I can explain . . . '

'Who the devil are you?'

'Leopold Zborowski, m'sieur. Dealer in fine arts. I'm Amedeo Modigliani's dealer.'

'Saints preserve us! I'm surrounded by wastrels!'

'But, Papa,' Jeanne began.

'Enough, Jeanne. We're leaving.'

Amedeo motioned to Jeanne to be patient a moment longer. To Mme Hébuterne he said: 'Would you please accept these drawings, with my compliments.'

Before Mme Hébuterne could reply, her husband seized them. Blood drained from Jeanne's face as her father screwed them up. Then he took out his wallet. 'Twenty francs, Modigliani. A more than generous sum.' He threw the note on the table.

'You disappoint me, m'sieur,' Amedeo replied, striking a match and holding the note in the flame, watching it burn. 'Your daughter's portrait is worth a thousand times more.'

Amedeo thumped Leopold's dining-room table. '*Dio mio*, but did you ever meet such a pompous ass? What right has he to sneer at artists, Leopold? And to humiliate Jeanne in public like that! Ah, the man's a menace.'

Leopold shrugged. 'It takes all kinds to make a world. Try to relax, *mon ami*; it aids the digestion. Wait until you taste Hanka's *kotletki*. To describe it as delicious does it an injustice. There's nothing like good food to cheer a man.'

Amedeo smiled. 'I should have humoured him, as you said. Is the situation irretrievable?'

'Perhaps. Perhaps not. He seems a very narrow-minded type.'

'Should I write a note of apology?'

'It would do no harm,' Leopold replied, nodding sagely. 'No harm.'

But, as he ate, Amedeo couldn't forget Achille Hébuterne's boorish behaviour; the more Leopold assured him that Jeanne's father would mellow with time, the more remote the possibility seemed. He should have realized that Jeanne's father would react the way he had. Like all the bourgeoisie, he condemned anything he didn't understand or approve of, was entirely without sympathy for artists. Admittedly, the crowd at the Rotonde were outspoken, boisterous, flamboyant . . . but they were hard-working, law-abiding and idealistic. If they sometimes uncorked their frustrations by drinking a little too much, was that a crime? They were the founders of a new liberalism, pioneering cavaliers in paint-scarred overalls who sought new horizons. Must they be scorned for refusing to stagnate?

Why, if it were left to the Achille Hébuternes, every ideology, every new mode of creative expression would be stifled at birth. Artists with a fresh approach would be ridiculed and ostracized. Only sycophantic society painters would flourish; originality and talent would die. But there was Jeanne to consider; he could not let her suffer because of what had happened. He would write a letter of apology. He raised his vodka glass.

'A toast. To Hanka . . . for her wonderful cooking. To

Leopold . . . for his friendship. Now, Leopold, to the studio: I'm going to paint your portrait.'

Amedeo worked with total absorption, sublimating his turbulent emotions, delighting in the anodyne of creation. Each stroke of the brush, every dab of pigment, every nuance of light and shade seemed to liberate his spirit.

Leopold sucked in his breath when he stared, spellbound, at the finished canvas.

Amedeo looked at him anxiously. 'You don't like it?'

'Don't like it? On the contrary . . . it's magnificent. You are truly a great artist.'

'Take it. It's yours.'

'Oh, but I couldn't; it must be worth – '

'No buts, Leopold. It's a gift. For your wife. For her beauty and charm.'

'You are too kind,' Leopold stammered. 'Hanka's in the kitchen. I'll take it to her right away.'

'Careful how you carry it; it's still wet.'

Leopold hurried out, holding the canvas as though it were a delicate piece of embroidery. Amedeo, smiling, lit a cigarette. Around the studio walls were hung portraits, Parisian scenes, a water-colour of Cracow University and a white-plaster church in Montmartre. The style was familiar. As he moved closer to examine it Leopold returned.

'My wife is delighted to accept. In fact, she's absolutely thrilled. But, please, you must let me pay for it – '

'Nonsense, my dear fellow. A gift is a gift.' He pointed to the painting of the church. 'You didn't tell me you were collecting Maurice Utrillo.'

'Yes. I like his work very much. I picked it up at the Flea Market. For ten francs.'

'A bargain. One day it will be worth thousands.'

'You know him, of course. I remember you telling me.'

'One of the first friends I made in Paris.' The painting had been done on a piece of stiff cardboard; obviously Maurice had been broke at the time. He observed Maurice's uncanny feeling for stucco, bricks and mortar; the pigment was encrusted with his friend's unmistakable white impasto.

'It's a fine example of his early white period. He probably traded it at some *brasserie* for the price of a drink. People dismiss him as a freak. They don't understand that he's tormented by nameless fears which he tries to drown in liquor. He's at the Villejuif Institution.'

'Taking the cure?'

Amedeo nodded. 'I'm going to visit him soon. They let him paint Montmartre scenes from postcards; the doctors call it occupational therapy. They say it's the latest thing in treating alcoholics.' He smiled. 'In the old days we used to sit among the crowd at Père Frèdé's café on the Butte. Everybody would be there: Picasso, Vlaminck, Derain, Van Dongen, La Goulue telling stories of Toulouse-Lautrec and the Moulin Rouge. While everybody talked and drank we'd be busy sketching them . . .' He paused, seeing Hanka Zborowska listening at the door. 'Ah, but I'm talking too much . . . '

Hanka entered the room. 'On the contrary, m'sieur. You are *simpatico*. Monsieur Utrillo must be very proud to have you as a friend.'

'But I'm no help to him, madame. I feel so helpless.'

'You have helped him, m'sieur . . . more than you know. I have an instinct for these things. Around you I see an aura: orange, like the afternoon sun. I see it now. Warm. Glowing.'

Amedeo realized he was looking at Hanka through a column of light from the studio window; it seemed to enshroud her in an almost mystical cloak.

'I think I understand. I have glimpsed something similar when I have been painting. But always it seemed vague . . . half-formed . . . somehow incomplete.'

Hanka smiled imperceptibly.

'Everybody has an aura,' she said. 'Only those whose eyes are truly open can see it.'

Seven

Sitting on a stool at the zinc in the Rotonde, Amedeo re-read Jeanne's letter. Almost a week had elapsed since his confrontation with Achille Hébuterne; every afternoon he had waited at the little café near the Colarossi, but Jeanne had not come. He had been unable to work and had been sleeping badly. He was disappointed that he had not received a reply to the letter he had sent her father.

At a nearby table Max Jacob, marijuana cigarette glowing and bright-eyed, was talking earnestly to Chagall and Soutine, hoping for some colourful quotes to his newspaper column. The English artist, Nina Hamnett, was introducing everybody to a pale, dark-haired young woman with sad eyes and a wan smile . . . 'I don't believe you've met the short story writer, Katherine Mansfield. From New Zealand . . . '

From another table fragments of conversations drifted across the café . . . 'Have you heard? Pavlova's leaving Diaghilev's *Ballets Russes.* Who will partner Nijinsky now?' . . . 'Isadora Duncan is marrying an American millionaire, they say. Heir to a sewing machine family' . . . 'Martinelli is taking over Caruso's rôle at the Met. They say he's burst a blood vessel in his throat' . . . 'The British troops are giving the Boches hell on the Somme. Terrible carnage, by all accounts. Worse than an abattoir . . . '

Amedeo returned the letter to his jacket pocket.' '*Please meet me in the Luxembourg Gardens on Sunday afternoon*,' she had written. '*I will explain everything when I see you. Jeanne.*'

Kiki and Nina Stein caught his eye. They waved to him; he returned their salutation.

'Amedeo,' Papa Libion called out. 'Telephone. A lady.'

Amedeo's heart fluttered like a bird. 'Did she give a name?'

Libion shrugged. '*Mon Dieu*, all this noise – '

Amedeo went to the cubicle behind the zinc and spoke into the phone.

'Jeanne?'

For a few moments the voice at the other end was blurred; then he recognized Maurice's mother, Suzanne Valadon. She told him Maurice could have visitors on Sunday; André couldn't get any more compassionate leave from the Army. Would he go with her?

'Of course, Suzanne. When?'

'Today.'

He visualized her distraught face and remembered the promise he had made; she needed a friend. He couldn't let her down. He would ask Leopold to keep his appointment with Jeanne; she would understand. It would take only a few minutes to call in at Leopold's on his way to the Métro.

'I'll come to the rue Cortot right away.'

Suzanne was wearing a rose madder dress with a lace bodice and ankle-length skirt; a small green hat set off her black hair flecked with grey. When she smiled it seemed to illuminate her whole person, resurrecting her youth at the Café Toubarin when she had been Renoir's favourite model, epitomizing the verve and *joie de vivre* of Montmartre's halcyon days.

Amedeo stared at the passing streets through the window of the bus they took to Villejuif, smiling to himself at the way Leopold's dreamy eyes had popped at the unexpected drama. He had shown Leopold Jeanne's letter, then explained about his promise to Suzanne. Leopold had readily agreed to go to the Luxembourg Gardens on his behalf. 'Tell her, Leopold, that the prince has found his princess.'

Suzanne was pale, but composed. 'The doctor says Maurice is very ill. But he has responded to treatment. How did I fail him? God knows, I did my best. I had a living to earn. Did I do wrong by keeping him with me, raising him myself? My mother wanted to take him to the country.' She shook her head. 'I just don't know.'

'We can only do what we think is best,' he murmured consolingly.

'He has a great talent. An instinctive ability. I gave him lessons, but he really taught himself. His art is the one thing which can save him.'

'Maurice will come through. You'll see.'

The bus rattled along the cobble-stoned street latticed with tram lines; hazy green foliage of limes and plane trees clawed at the bus's roof, slapping the windows as it moved past them . . . *tap, tap, tap . . .*

'On your feet, Utrillo. You too, Modigliani. Inspector Descartes wants to see you in his office.' Descartes, a short stocky man, wore his policeman's uniform like a suit of armour and swished at the air with his leather baton. 'Drunk and disorderly.' Swish. 'Causing a disturbance at the Lapin Agile.' Swish. 'You ought to know better. The third time this month.' Swish, swish. Maurice had said: 'It was the tourists, Inspector. Especially the Americans. They kept plying us with wine in return for sketches. They bring business to our city, n'est-ce pas? To have refused would have insulted them.' It had been 1910 and the Butte had been on the sight-seeing itinerary of every visitor to Paris. Where can we find Monsieur Toulouse-Lautrec's old atelier? Did he really do his drinking in the Lapin Agile? How much for a drawing, m'sieur? Do you actually know Degas and Rodin?

'Ah, the tourists. A necessary evil.' The baton swished again. 'Naturally you are both without funds; therefore unable to pay your fines.' Swish. 'You're lucky; the cells are already overcrowded, so I'm not pressing charges – but, mes amis, next time I won't be so lenient.' No, Inspector; many thanks, Inspector. 'One moment,' Descartes had said; fingering his handlebar moustache. 'This La Goulue who dances on the tables at the Lapin Agile. Is she really, ah, as voluptuous as they say?'

Tap, tap, tap went the branches on the bus roof . . .

'Maurice always talks about you,' Suzanne was saying. 'He says you understand why he drinks.'

They travelled the rest of the journey in an intimate silence, more effective than words.

The Institution, on the outskirts of the city, was a gloomy, grey-bricked mausoleum with grimy windows encased by iron grilles. The men at the gates wore expressions of grim suspicion, as though they viewed everybody as possible inmates.

Amedeo and Suzanne joined the visitors' queue at the main doors. People spoke little, and then only a few words in hushed tones. Everything about the place had a funereal air. Occasionally a wild-eyed face pressed itself against a barred window, staring curiously at the outside world.

Eventually they were shown into a tiny, airless cell. Maurice was at an easel crayoning a Montmartre street scene from a postcard pinned to the cartridge paper; the easel was the one concession allowed him by the asylum authorities.

'Maurice,' Suzanne's voice was a whisper. Her son's bloodshot eyes seemed to stare through her. Then his lips quivered; tears began to run down his cheeks.

'*Maman* . . . you came.'

Maurice's words began to tumble over each other in his eagerness. Amedeo could only guess at their meaning. He was shocked by Maurice's haunted eyes, twitching hands and emaciated body which seemed strangely disjointed and puppet-like in its movements. Between excited bursts of conversation a high-pitched squeal bubbled up in Maurice's throat and his pronounced Adam's apple jerked. His claw-like hands seized Amedeo's arm.

'Liquor, Deo. Did you bring the liquor?' His frightened eyes darted towards the door. 'They think I'm crazy. But we know different. Since I was fifteen I've known the *world* is crazy.' The claws felt Amedeo's pockets. 'Where is the bottle, *mon ami*? I've got a raging thirst.'

The words of Max Jacob echoed in Amedeo's ears . . . 'Utrillo is a *peintre maudit*; he's trying to turn alcohol into a religion.' He had defended his friend: 'I admit Maurice as a man is a failure; but as an artist he is a giant.'

Suzanne said querulously, 'I've had your painting *Rheims Cathedral in Flames* framed, Maurice. I'm going to show it at the Salon.'

For a moment Maurice's swimming eyes became lucid. 'Rheims Cathedral . . . my indictment of those German butchers.'

'I've seen it. It should be hung in the Louvre,' Amedeo said.

'Louvre, *merde*! You've got more talent in one finger than I have in both hands, Deo. Isn't that so, *Maman*?'

Suzanne smiled through impending tears. 'You both have a great talent.'

Maurice silently mouthed her words like an adoring child. '*Maman* always knows best, Deo,' he said eagerly, then, lowering his voice: 'Does La Goulue still do the can-can at the Lapin? Does she still ask about me?'

'All the time.' Amedeo was overcome by compassion. How Maurice had loved the Rabelaisian atmosphere of the Lapin Agile café, sketching furiously and crowing with delight whenever La Goulue relived nights at the Moulin Rouge, her wobbling mountainous body precariously balanced on a table, high kicking until she collapsed in a giggling heap on the floor. How Maurice had loved the exuberant way in which she would envelop him with her roly-poly arms and hug him to her voluminous bosom . . . '*Mais alors*, you're all skin and bones like Monsieur Toulouse. But La Goulue will fatten you up.'

An orderly coughed discreetly at the cell door. Amedeo took Suzanne's arm. The orderly advanced towards Maurice. 'Oh, yes, that's a pretty drawing. Doctor will be pleased. Now, it's time we had our little sleep . . . '

In the grey corridor they waited as the orderly locked Maurice's cell door.

'Don't upset yourself, madame. He's very much better, improving every day. When he came to us, why, we couldn't do anything with him. He accused us of trying to poison him; then he was convinced we were going to send him to the guillotine. *Mon Dieu*, what a time he gave us. I'm afraid we had to take his oils away, though. He kept eating them – ' he broke off when he caught Amedeo's signal, realizing his tactlessness. 'Don't you worry, madame. We'll soon have him well again.'

Amedeo accompanied Suzanne back to the rue Cortot. Neither spoke more than a few stilted words: the memory of

Maurice's bulbous eyes and symptoms of delerium tremens was an impenetrable barrier. They joined the Métro for Pigalle. Suzanne said anxiously, 'He will get better, won't he?' Amedeo murmured reassurances. He was still unable to reconcile that pathetic spectacle at the asylum with the jocular fun-loving Maurice he had known in his early Montmartre days.

'Thank you for coming,' she said. It was nothing, he said; he was sorry he hadn't been able to do more.

'You must come and have dinner with us. On André's next leave.'

He would love to.

Amedeo was waiting for Jeanne at the little café they had come to think of as theirs. Leopold had assured him that Jeanne had understood why he had not been able to keep their appointment. 'She couldn't conceal her disappointment, *mon ami*. She thinks the world of you.'

Now, the afternoon shadows were lengthening; the air was cool. From the distance he heard Louis-the-Madman's plaintive cries for rags and bones. He closed his eyes, the sun's sensuous rays warming his face, but he could visualize only gloomy corridors, bilious walls, imbecilic faces pressed against iron-barred windows, their mournful wailing like some diabolical chorus in Hades. Would Maurice always be a trembling, incoherent wreck? Suddenly he was aware of another's presence. He opened his eyes. Jeanne was standing at the table, face in silhouette, yellowing sunlight filtering through her hair; she seemed enshrouded by a golden aura.

'*Cara*.' He took her hand; it felt frail and vulnerable. Rarely had he seen her looking so madonna-like; his heart went out to her. She was the epitome of his dreams, the personification of Dante's immortal Beatrice. He buried his face in her hair with its jasmine fragrance, not trusting himself to speak as a surge of emotion constricted his throat.

He raised her face with his hand and looked into her eyes. He knew then he had been searching for her all his life. That strange urgency which had gripped him that first day in the Rotonde . . . that mysterious smile which had haunted him ever since. Suddenly he was impelled to put his feelings into words.

'I love you, Jeanne.'

No longer was love only for poets and librettists. It was incredibly, wonderfully, unbelievably true! Words that he had despaired of ever saying in absolute sincerity were now poignant and meaningful.

'I love you too,' she said. 'From that first day.'

'*Cara* . . . ' he began, groping for the words he wanted. Suddenly he was pouring out everything . . . his hopes, his frustrations, the visit to Villejuif, the shock at seeing Maurice so ill and pathetic. It seemed only weeks, not years, that he and Maurice had been carefree students, trading their talent with a pencil for a glass of wine in the cafés of Montmartre, loaning each other paints and brushes, praising each other's work, visiting Toulouse-Lautrec's old studio in the rue Caulaincourt. And dreaming of fame.

'Maurice and I were young and naïve. We thought Paris was ours for the taking.' He shrugged and smiled wryly. 'Ah, but what happened to our dreams . . . the sands of time. *Dio mio*, here I am, talking like a greybeard when I haven't even begun! What must you be thinking?'

'That I love you.'

He took her hands in his. 'I wanted it to be so different. The best champagne. Box at the Opera. A carriage through the Bois de Boulogne . . . '

'It's you I love. As you are.'

'But I will be a success,' he said passionately. 'I feel it in my bones.'

'I'm sure you will.'

'But enough of my problems. Are things any better at home? Has your Papa mentioned my letter to you?'

'He tore it up. He never even read it. And he's confiscated the portrait you did of me.'

'It's of no consequence, *cara*. I'll do another portrait of you. And another. And another – until you are sick to death of posing! We won't let anyone or anything come between us. Nothing can spoil what we feel for each other.'

'But Papa had no right . . '

'He has a father's right, *cara*. Give him time. He'll come round to our way of thinking.'

'Papa is too obstinate; he'll never change.'

'My father never wanted me to be an artist. "Over my dead body," he said. But here I am – an artist. And he's very proud of me.'

Oblivious to the people at the other tables he kissed her passionately. '*Carissima.* You are so beautiful I could gaze at you for ever.'

'Amedeo,' Jeanne protested through her happiness, 'not here – everybody's staring.'

'Let them.' He took her hand. 'You must be hungry. We must eat. A celebration. At *Henri's* in La Ruche. Or *Le Moulin*.' He still had most of the fifty francs Leopold had paid him; enough for a champagne dinner.

'Absolutely not,' Jeanne said. 'They're much too expensive.'

'But, *cara*, this calls for the best. Champagne, oysters – '

'Not at *Henri's* or *Le Moulin*,' she interrupted.

'But they are the best in Paris. And only the best is good enough.'

Everybody began to join in the playful argument. Jeanne, blushing, began to giggle.

Amedeo whispered, '*Henri's*?'

'Everybody's listening,' Jeanne giggled. 'Let's pay the bill.'

Laughing, in sheer high spirits, they left, hand in hand.

'One moment I'm telling you I love you.' He laughed. 'The next we are having our first tiff! Now, we must celebrate. First, some exquisite food and wine. I know just the place.'

'All right. But on one condition . . . '

'That is?'

'We go to the little restaurant in rue de la Campagne-Première. Where all the artists go.'

'Rosalie's?'

She nodded. 'I've heard so much about her. And they say

the food is traditional Italian, better than those fancy places in the Boulevard St. Germain.'

The moment they entered Chez Rosalie's the warm-hearted *patronne* sang a greeting and hugged them both, gabbling to them in a chaotic fusion of Italian, Yiddish and French, until they were reduced to tears of laughter. And Mama Rosalie laughed loudest of all.

'Luigi,' she cried. 'A bottle of chianti, pronto! The best in the house. Dedo has his *novia*.' She beamed at them. 'I will cook you the best spaghetti you ever tasted. What *are* you doing, Luigi? Picking the grapes? *Pronto, pronto*!'

Luigi came puffing up, a bottle all ready, and ushered them to a corner table. He lit the candle. 'We keep this one specially for courting couples,' he said coyly.

'Pour the wine, Luigi,' Rosalie scolded. 'Do you want them to die of thirst?'

'Sometimes I think you're completely *loco*,' she went on. 'Ah, but what a handsome pair you are. It reminds me of when my dear husband Giovanni was alive. He was a Tuscan.' She winked at Jeanne. 'Just like Amedeo. As handsome as a Michelangelo sculpture.' She began dabbing at her eyes with a polka-dot handkerchief. 'Ah, but I'm just a fat old fool.'

Amedeo and Jeanne stifled good-natured laughter as Rosalie waddled away to her kitchen, scolding Luigi and joking with her patrons.

'Isn't she wonderful?' he said. 'And she makes the best pastas in Paris.'

Jeanne was content just to be with Amedeo; she was too happy to speak.

Amedeo poured the wine. 'Ah, *frizzante*! Now's the time to drink it, *cara*, while it's prickly on the tongue. Come, drink up – why so quiet?'

'It's just as I imagined it. Chequered tablecloths. Candles in bottles. Oh, Amedeo, thank you for bringing me.'

'But you haven't eaten yet. Supposing you don't like Tuscany cooking? *Dio mio*, that will put me in the dog-house!'

'I'm sure I will.'

He held her hand across the table. 'Tonight, *cara*, Paris belongs to us.'

Suddenly the frustrations and disappointments seemed to slip away; he felt buoyant of spirit, as he had when he'd first set foot in Paris eleven years earlier. The difference in their ages suddenly didn't matter.

'I have been looking all my life for someone like you. And now here you are. Can you imagine what that means to me?'

Like all lovers, they told each other about family and childhood. Jeanne had been to a convent school where the nuns had maintained strict discipline. The pupils were not allowed to read any popular books or magazines; approved reading matter was Guy de Maupassant, Victor Hugo, Gustave Flaubert, Balzac, Racine and Voltaire.

'Not Dante?'

'Mother Superior forbade foreign writers.'

'Well, that's something I can put right. First thing tomorrow I'll get you a copy of the *Divine Comedy*.'

Rosalie came across, clucking like a mother hen.

'You lika da spaghetti?'

It was the best they had ever tasted.

'*Buon, buon*.' She ruffled Amedeo's thick, curling hair. 'You take care of Jeanne, you hear? She's good for you. I have an instinct in these matters.'

'I will, Momma Rosalie. I promise.'

Rosalie turned and beckoned to Luigi. '*Pronto, pronto*.' Luigi hurried to the table with two huge ice-creams decorated with chopped nuts and surrounded by slices of fresh peach and pears. '*Ecco. Cassata Neapolitan.* It's a special surprise. *Buon appetito*.'

'*Grazie*, Momma.'

Amedeo and Jeanne ate and talked and looked into each other's eyes. Amedeo had never been so happy.

'Modi, my old pal,' boomed Ortiz de Zarate, towering over them like an Amazonian chieftain. 'Who is your delightful companion?'

When Amedeo had made the introductions Ortiz called for mountains of spaghetti and buckets of chianti. He expounded his theories on art, ridiculed Dadaism, castigated the mercenary rue Laffitte dealers, ending the diatribe with some amusing gossip about the critic, Armand Avenne.

'We were just on our way,' Amedeo said, rising.

'So soon? But we must celebrate, *mes amis*! I insist.'

Beaming, Ortiz ordered even more chianti; he obviously intended making a night of the chance encounter.

'The party's just beginning!'

Hearing Amedeo's friendly protests, Rosalie bore down on their table, '*Basta, basta*,' she scolded the Chilean. 'Can't you see they want to be alone? You think they want to sit drinking with a bone-headed ox like you, eh?'

Ortiz roared with laughter. Then he leant forward and slapped Rosalie's rear. 'You and me, my Tuscany spaghetti-eater, we get drunk, no?'

Amedeo, laughing, guided Jeanne towards the door and blew Rosalie a kiss. '*Buona notte*, Mama. God bless you.'

They walked hand in hand along the Boul' Montparnasse, enjoying the balmy night air with its soft fragrance of begonias and jasmine, listening to the happy sounds of people in the cafés and the whispered conversations of young lovers. The city seemed breathless yet vibrant. A crowd of matelots spilled from a *brasserie*, laughing and singing snatches of ribald sea shanties; the *demi-mondaines*, nestling invitingly in shop doorways, flashing painted smiles at the reeling sailors. Artisans strolled arm in arm with their wives, nodding at friends and acquaintances; urchins with smudged faces and cheeky grins going from person to person: 'Spare a sou for my lame mother, m'sieur?'

Amedeo gave one of the urchins a handful of centimes.

'*Merci*, m'sieur. My mother will bless you.'

He laughed as the lad scampered off into the night. 'Don't spend it all on candies,' he shouted.

They sat on a bench beneath a hugh plane tree and indulged in that most Parisian of pastimes, watching the world go by.

'It's been a wonderful evening, Amedeo. I'd almost forgotten how to enjoy myself.'

'I'm pleased. Isn't Rosalie wonderful?'

'She's just as I imagined her.'

'And what a cook, *cara*! You won't get food like hers anywhere else in the city. Just the smell of it makes me homesick for Italy.'

'It means a lot to you, Italy.'

He squeezed her hand. 'One day you must come with me to Livorno. Then you will understand.'

He walked Jeanne home and then returned to his *atelier* in an elated mood. He was in love with a beautiful girl who felt the same about him! It was as though his Beatrice had been delivered to him . . . as if from a forgotten dream, a golden vision from a far country.

'Ah, Jeanne,' he said aloud as he lit the stove, 'you have given me a *raison d'etre*.'

The dry kindling wood began to crackle and spark; shadows danced and writhed on the studio walls like apache girls in a smoky cavern. The strange timelessness which had possessed him in Rosalie's imbued his every movement with a special emotional quality. Even the crackling of the coke stove captured his imagination. He must paint her from memory! Yes – there was no time to lose. The ecstatic impressions must be committed to canvas while they were still alive and crystal clear.

Eagerly he mixed the colours of his palette: dominant reds, browns and orange. Ah, what feelings they aroused within him! What tonal harmonies! What *chiaroscuro*! He searched for a fresh piece of canvas. But there was none. He half remembered Leopold mentioning that he had some fresh canvas at rue Joseph-Bara, but he had forgotten to collect it. *Dio mio*, how could he hope to be a great artist? He had a head like a sieve.

He sat by the stove, preoccupied with the colourful visions which crowded his mind. The urgency to paint Jeanne's portrait from memory became overpowering, almost a physical pain. He seized a canvas he had half worked days before. A baker's wife in the Boul' Montparnasse. He hacked away at it with a palette knife, removing the encrusted pigment.

He put the coffee pot on the stove, impatient for it to come to the boil. Eventually it began to bubble. He added a measure of cognac to the rich black liquid and tasted it. Ah, *bellisima*! Now he could work.

Quickly he affixed the canvas to his easel, dispensing with a stretcher in his eagerness to begin work. He felt the all-consuming urge flowing through him like a raging tide; always the desire to paint was like this: demanding, compulsive, agonizingly exciting. His body seemed to become an automaton, guided as though by an unseen hand. He gulped the coffee, scarcely aware that it splashed down his shirt. With urgent strokes of his brush he began to form an image, transluscent yet solid in form. Perspiration ran down his face. His throat felt dry; he drank more coffee, smiling to himself as he rememberd Leopold's alarm when the creative urge had come upon him. '*Mon Dieu*,' the Pole had gasped. 'You're like a man possessed.'

Even as a youth at Micheli's studio he had painted as though in a race against time. How his childhood friend, Oscar Ghiglia, used to chide him – 'Don't you think of anything but work, Deo? Come on, leave your easel. Everybody's going to the *bodega* tonight. There's a new girl singer. French. I'm told she's a beauty.' But he had always declined. Not that he didn't like drinking with his friends or flirting with the dark-eyed girls in the *bordellos*, but because he was driven by an insatiable desire to create, to learn, to develop his art. 'Painting is like the breath of life to me, Oscar,' he'd said. 'People like us have different rights, different values from other people. Don't forget we're artists. Our destiny is to create. Your duty is never to waste your talent. Your *real* duty is to save your dream.'

He stepped back from the easel and viewed the painting through narrowed eyes, pleased at the effect. Remembering that little speech he had made to Oscar – his credo – brought a half smile to his lips. The words seemed stilted now, vaguely unreal. Yet the truth of what he had said still applied. It *was* an artist's duty to preserve his vision of

Beauty. It *was* an artist's duty to raise himself above the ordinary, transcend the mundane and the conventional to reach new heights of human expression.

Jeanne Hébuterne. What unknown deity had sent her to him? Foujita was right; she had had an extraordinary effect on him, an unbelievable effect. He need no longer pay homage to Dante's Beatrice. He had found his own.

Never had he been more certain of his destiny.

Eight

Louis-the-Madman stepped down from his horse-drawn cart, describing an arc with his arm, evidently believing it to be the correct gesture when confronting men of the world. '*Bonjour, messieurs.*'

Amedeo and Leopold stared at the cart; they had never seen it so clean, it was absolutely spotless. Even more impressive was Louis's dress: polka-dot shirt, neckerchief and pressed velvet trousers, worn specially for the occasion. With an expansive smile he flicked the seat of the cart with a grubby handkerchief. '*Voilà, messieurs.*' Then he began to stack Amedeo's canvases in the back as though they were fragile china.

'Careful with those,' Leopold said, hurrying to Louis's elbow to supervise. 'They're valuable.'

'*Mais naturellement*,' Louis said, eyes popping. 'I understand about paintings, m'sieur. Ask anybody at the Flea Market if Louis doesn't know a bargain when he sees one. Once I posed for Degas. In the yard behind the Bal Tabarin.'

'You must pose for me,' Amedeo said. 'You have a fine face.'

'That's what Monsieur Degas said. Craggy, he said. Paid me ten francs.'

Finally Louis climbed up into the driving seat and snapped the reins. The piebald snorted and began a gentle trot up the street and into the Boul' Montparnasse. 'Where to, m'sieur?'

'Rue Taitbout,' Leopold said. 'Madame Weill's gallery.'

As they jogged through the streets Leopold brought Amedeo up to date with the news of his negotiations.

'The *vernissage* is to be at noon Sunday. Everybody who is anybody is coming. Civic dignitaries, government officials, art connoisseurs, businessmen. Madame Weill's clientèle have plenty of money to spend. The press have promised her a good write-up. André Salmon, Armand Avenne – '

Amedeo snorted. 'That parasite!'

'Armand Avenne has influence, Amedeo. If he mentions you in his column it's as good as a dozen sales.'

'Ah, my friend . . . always you're the eternal optimist. Don't forget how he treated Foujita and me at the Salon.'

'That was months ago. Besides, your reputation has grown since then.'

Suddenly the piebald reared and the cart lurched. Louis tugged on the reins. '*Merde*!' A mean-eyed mongrel yelped from beneath the cart, then shot across the road, tail between its legs, accompanied by motley curses and Louis's brandished fist. '*C'est fou, le chien.*' He got the piebald under control. 'A thousand pardons, *messieurs*.'

At Bertha's gallery Leopold paid Louis and thanked him. The gnarled old rag-and-bone man stared at the fifty-franc note; it was more than he took in a week at his own trade. 'M'sieur is most generous.' He tipped his forehead with a horny finger. '*Au revoir.*'

It took them an hour to hang the canvases. When the last one was in place Bertha, arms akimbo, began to peer at each through her thick-lensed spectacles. 'This model. She is a professional?'

'Not exactly,' Amedeo supplied. 'Her name's Elvira Lacrot. She's an actress.'

'I thought she wasn't a professional,' said Bertha shrewdly. 'She is completely natural. No artificiality in the way she poses. You have a true gift, m'sieur. Such pastiche! Such harmony of tone! Melancholy; and yet very moving. *C'est formidable*. Your flesh colours remind me somehow of Renoir's yet they have a hint of mystery. Colour is a matter of sensibility, of personal taste. But first an artist must have something to say, no? If he hasn't – *adieu*! He must love art before self, women, pleasures, even life itself. Art must be his life.'

She scrutinized the portraits again. 'A rare insight indeed. Almost as if you are looking into her soul . . . '

'I'm flattered, madame.'

'Don't be,' she snapped. 'When an artist allows himself to be flattered, he's lost.'

She took a document from a writing-bureau and handed it to Leopold. 'The contract, m'sieur. As we agreed. My expenses for print, advertising, food and drinks for the opening reception to be deducted from the gross. Agreed?'

'Agreed.'

'My gallery is also to have first option to stage Monsieur Modigliani's future exhibitions. Agreed?'

Leopold nodded.

'Ah, *bon*. Now, for the opening I have acceptances from Monsieur Simon, Minister for the Colonies; Madame Lefarge – she's a wealthy collector and sure to buy; Jean Cocteau; Gertrude Stein; Guillaume Appollinaire; Pablo Picasso; André Salmon; Fritz Sandahl; Francis Carco . . . Can you think of others? Celebrities will attract publicity and help sales.'

'Suzanne Valadon,' Amedeo said. 'I'm sure she'll come. Soutine, Foujita, too. And I could ask Degas.'

'Ah, *bon*. The more the merrier. You'll be there yourself of course.'

Amedeo stammered an apology; he had nothing in common with people who frequented galleries. 'True, they have money, madame. But in my experience they are completely lacking in artistic appreciation. They buy paintings in order to impress their friends. Or because a critic tells them to.'

Bertha sighed. 'You're an idealist. What does it matter what their reason is for buying? Your talent will be recognized; word will spread. That's the important thing.'

'I keep telling him the same thing,' Leopold said.

'Don't think I don't sympathize, m'sieur,' Bertha went on. 'I know how crass some of the so-called connoisseurs are. They talk of art and beauty, but half of them don't know the difference between a Picasso and a Pernod advertisement. They may not understand paintings, but the fact is they do buy them.'

'That's just the point, Madame Weill, everything I've been striving for . . . truth, beauty, artistic integrity. It's wasted on them. I might just as well have been a signwriter. I want people to buy my work because of what it arouses in them.'

Leopold shook his head sadly. How often he had heard Amedeo express those sentiments. How often he had pleaded with his protégé to swallow his pride, to bend with the wind. Amedeo's soul was that of a poet, concerned only with ideals and noble thoughts, the glory of art.

Bertha clicked her teeth. 'Artists! They are the most frustrating, exasperating – ' She met Amedeo's gaze; her eyes twinkled. 'I do understand your problems, m'sieur. But, as M. Zborowski said, does it really matter why people buy a painting so long as the artist can keep his independence? Surely that's the crux of the matter?'

'You're making it difficult for me to refuse,' Amedeo said, smiling.

'Then you'll come to the *vernissage*? People like to meet the artist at previews. And it does help sales. And the press will want to talk to you . . . '

Amedeo gave Leopold an appealing glance. He didn't wish to hurt Bertha's feelings, but . . .

'What Monsieur Modigliani is trying to say, Madame Weill,' Leopold explained, 'is that exhibitions make him nervous.'

'Ah, the artistic temperament? *Je comprends*. Marc Chagall and Georges Braque are just the same.' She tilted her head. 'Won't you change your mind, m'sieur? Just this once. Your presence really will make a difference.'

Amedeo found it impossible to resist her. 'For you, Madame Weill – I will.'

'*Bon*. Then it's settled. We meet here Sunday. Ten o'clock. We'll open the doors at eleven. Monsieur Zborowski tells me that you and Armand Avenne, the critic, don't see eye to eye.'

'That is putting it mildly,' Amedeo smiled.

'Well, don't worry. I haven't sent him an invitation,' she chuckled.

'You see, Amedeo – I told you she's one in a million.'

The topiary garden in the Avenue de l'Observatoire behind

the rue Notre-Dame des Champs was bathed in the tranquil sunlight of late afternoon. Amidst its sub-tropical shrubbery and exotic flowers, it was like being in a secret world.

Amedeo and Jeanne entered by the gate at the Fontaine, overlooked by Clinique Tarnier, enjoying the light breeze and bird-song. He told her about Bertha's gallery and the forthcoming exhibition. But he had mixed feelings about it: exhibitions had never been lucky for him. But Bertha and Leopold were so enthusiastic it was impossible not to be affected by their enthusiasm.

Jeanne squeezed his hand. 'You worry too much.'

'You see, Jeanne, ever since I was a boy I've had a vision. Call it a dream if you like. I knew if I kept searching I would find it. Now I think I have – ' he broke off. '*Mama mia*! You must think I'm a complete egoist. All I ever do when we're together is talk about my work.'

Jeanne smiled in that mysterious way of hers which always intrigued him. 'Aren't you surprised I came today?'

'Very.' He led her to a bench under the shade of a huge beech tree. 'Your papa has forbidden you to see me, you said in your last letter.'

They were silent a moment as a group of students sauntered past.

'Do you think it's wise, *cara*? To go against his wishes.'

'Papa has a stubborn streak. Once he has made up his mind on something – rightly or wrongly – he won't listen to reason. He's been like that ever since André and I were children. *Maman* means well, but she hasn't the strength of will to defy him. His word has always been law in our house.' She began to straighten the pleats of her skirt. Amedeo realized she was trying to tell him what the decision had cost her, emotionally, without his thinking her irresponsible.

'But I don't want you to think . . . ' she began, then hesitated. 'I'm old enough to decide things for myself. Papa's prejudiced because you're an artist and live in Montparnasse. To him all artists are idlers and wastrels. That's all he understands. Nothing will change him.' She smiled. 'Now it's my turn to say sorry. All I ever do is talk about Papa.'

He returned the pressure of her hand.

'I must seem very conventional,' she added, 'compared with the other girls you know.'

He kissed her lightly on the lips. 'You are absolutely adorable. And I love you. Why, haven't I spent the whole week painting your portrait from memory?'

'And what's wrong with the living model might I ask?'

'Why, nothing, but – '

'Amedeo Modigliani, I'm the only girl in Montparnasse who hasn't been invited to your *atelier*.'

'But – don't you know a girl throws her honour to the winds by accepting?'

'Now you sound like Papa.'

He gave her a questioning look.

She laughed. 'Do I have to force you at gun-point?'

At his *atelier* Amedeo was painfully aware of the gloomy hallway, flaking wallpaper and bare boards. He could only hope Jeanne wouldn't be too put off by it. He was glad he had asked Mme Velitch's maid to come in to change his linen and tidy up. He noticed, too, that the washing-up had been done. The dishes were neatly stacked on the rack above the sink. He stepped back from the door. '*Prego*.'

Jeanne went in. Anxiously, he watched her expression for the faintest sign of disappointment. There was none. She was fascinated by what she saw. Somehow she seemed to belong. Her eyes moved eagerly from portrait to portrait.

'It's just as I imagined it would be. Why, it's like the stage-set from *La Bohème*. 'It's exactly it – Rudolfo's attic!'

Amedeo smiled. How like her to be so tactful, to pretend his impoverished surroundings were romantic. He began to relax; it was going to be all right; he didn't have to pretend to be something he wasn't. She *understood*. That was everything.

Jeanne examined his paintbox, palette, brushes, canvases, drawings and carvings.

'Herr Schuler tells us "Beware Naples Yellow." ' She held

up the tube.

'He's right,' Amedeo agreed. 'A capricious colour. I rarely use it. Would you like coffee?'

She nodded.

As he lit the stove and prepared the coffee Jeanne studied the many canvases around the walls. One in particular caught her attention.

'I call that one *Girl in Blue*,' he said.

'She's sweet. But so sad. Who is she?'

'An orphan. I painted her when I was working at Cheron's.'

'You like children. I can tell.'

'They are such good subjects to paint, so natural, so expressive.'

He poured out the coffee. Jeanne sipped hers without taking her eyes off his paintings.

'One thing I've noticed,' she said. 'There isn't one still-life among your collection.'

'That's right. People are my forte.'

'Especially women,' she said, eyes twinkling.

His eyes flew to the Elvira nudes. He shrugged.

'Especially women, as you say. *Mama mia*, but I painted enough still-life at Cheron's to fill the Louvre!'

The afternoon sun was almost hidden by neighbouring roof-tops. The angular chimneys in silhouette resembled charred tree trunks in a petrified forest. The *atelier* became enshrouded in an orange glow, deepening to dark red.

Jeanne stood at the window watching the shadows encroaching into the warm hues. Her presence seemed to complement nature's colours; her tranquil spirit pervaded the room. Never had Amedeo experienced such an atmosphere of peace within the confines of his studio. He felt liberated, omnipotent. Visions of colours, shapes and designs unfurled in his mind's eye. Why, there was nothing he couldn't paint! Nothing he couldn't achieve! Creative energy seemed to burn in his veins like molten lava.

He selected a pencil with a razor-sharp point and opened a sketch-book. With rapid, unerring lines he drew Jeanne, his pulse quickening. A pale yellow aura had suddenly surrounded her.

'Paint me, Amedeo. From life.'

Her hands moved to her bodice; she began to undo the buttons.

'No,' he commanded gently.

'But I want you to.'

He shook his head. 'I'll paint you just as you are.'

For the first time in his life he experienced the emotion of possessiveness. To paint Jeanne nude would be to offer her to the world. Suddenly he knew he did not want to share her. Already he was beginning to think of her as *his*, a special person, to be seen by him alone. That other eyes might look upon her white dew-like innocence brought a surge of jealousy. Then and there he made a silent vow. He would never paint Jeanne nude.

'I won't be embarrassed,' Jeanne said.

'It's getting dark.' He lit the kerosene lamp. For a moment its soft hiss was the only sound in the room. Haltingly he put his thoughts into words.

'I understand,' she said simply.

'It would be an invasion of our privacy, Jeanne.'

She came towards him, smiling in that mysterious way which never failed to stir his emotions. She pressed her lips against his.

'That's one of the reasons I love you. Now paint me.'

Amedeo moved a chair by the window; he wanted the red-gold of the evening light to complement Jeanne's natural colouring. When he had seated her to his liking he viewed the effect through narrowed eyes. 'That's perfect, *cara*. Hold that pose.'

Amedeo plunged himself into his work. It was as though his hand were guided by an invisible force. Colour schemes throbbed in his mind's eye, vibrant, pulsating with urgency. The movement of brush to palette, to canvas, back to palette again seemed as one. The image on canvas unfurled. He had no idea of the time he had spent painting. So absorbed was he that he had hardly spoken a word to Jeanne.

'There. It's finished.'

Jeanne went up to the easel. Amedeo waited anxiously; it was not a conventional portrait. He had used the elliptical designs which, more and more, were characterizing his work. He had made Jeanne's head incline to one side, her expression wistful.

'Yes,' she said, her voice a whisper. 'You love me, I think you love me.'

Daylight thickened; the coke stove had burned low, emitting a dull red glow. They talked about everything; a new intimacy was growing between them.

Jeanne crossed to the bed. She began to undress as though it were the most natural thing in the world. Then she pulled back the covers and slipped between the sheets. 'Amedeo . . . it's cold.'

'Jeanne . . . '

'I'm *freezing*, darling.'

'But – ' His blood began to pound. 'You're sure? You are quite sure, Jeanne?'

'I was sure . . . that day at the Rotonde.'

'But you know so little about me. My work, my life . . . '

'I'm happy with you,' she said simply.

'But I put art before everything. It's my *raison d'être*. Art is a demanding mistress. I can't expect you to play second fiddle. You have the right to your lover's absolute devotion, Jeanne . . . not to have to share him with something so intangible.'

'What are you trying to tell me? That I mustn't expect too much of you? That you are too set in your ways to change? That you must feel free to express yourself in your work? I'm going into it with my eyes open. No girl lets herself be seduced unless she wants to be. For, in a way, this is a seduction, isn't it?' she added impishly.

Amedeo took her in his arms. There was something deliciously wicked in her tone. He was intoxicated by her fathomless blue eyes, her demure yet provocative smile which never failed to stir his emotions; she had a subtle fragrance which tantalized his senses.

He kissed her gently, then more ardently, feeling her move against him.

'Did I make you happy?' Her voice was anxious.

'Deliriously.'

'I was afraid you'd be disappointed. I'm not very experienced.'

He kissed her. '*Carissima*. You were absolutely perfect.'

The stove had burned low; the embers bathed the *atelier* a warm, intimate glow. Their love-making had transported his soul through mystical portals to the very realms of the gods. He took her hand and kissed it gently.

'I love you, Jeanne,' he said humbly. 'More than I can tell you.'

An intense emotion surged through him, stinging his eyes, choking his throat. 'Darling Jeanne . . . I feel reborne.'

She nestled against him.

'Happy?'

'Very. I'm a little sad, too.'

'But why?'

'Because you have to leave me soon.'

She smiled. 'I'll never leave you. I'm going to fetch my things.'

He could only stare at her.

'Don't you want me to be with you?' Her voice was a whisper.

'There's nothing I'd like more. But you don't know anything about me. Often I can't sleep and walk the streets till morning. I'm irritable and moody when work isn't going well. Sometimes I live on coffee and rolls for days on end – '

'Are you trying to tell me you don't love me enough?'

'I have never loved anyone else, *cara*.'

'Then there's nothing more to be said.'

Amedeo woke. Jeanne was beside him, looking at him.

'You snore.' She smiled, kissing the point of his chin. 'And already you are neglecting me.'

They lay in each other's arms; then Jeanne said: 'Who chose your name? Amedeo.'

'My mother. It means beloved of God.'

'Do they call you Amedeo at home?'

'No. By a childhood nickname – Dedo.'

'Day-doh. That's what I shall call you.'

As their love deepened, they became inseparable. They strolled through the lanes and along the boulevards and kissed under the linden trees by the Carrefour Raspail and saluted Balzac's statue. The Rotonde crowd took Jeanne to their hearts, but she and Amedeo preferred to slip away to their secret haunts. In him she had found a soul mate. And Amedeo had found his Beatrice.

But neither was fully prepared for the storm of abuse from Jeanne's father. She wrote him letter after letter, but he remained obdurate. He would never condone her behaviour, he said; her only salvation was to seek forgiveness within the Church.

'Papa has no right to criticize you like he does,' Jeanne said. 'He has no idea how hard you work. Or how precarious an artist's life is. He is threatening to make me made a ward of court.' 'We don't need his blessing, *cara*. If you feel as I do, we could be married at the Registrar's.'

'You're forgetting, I'm not yet twenty-one. I can't marry without parental consent.'

'But it's so unjust.'

'It's only two more years, Dedo. I'm willing to wait . . . if you are.'

'There's only one solution,' he said. 'I'll go to see your papa. Talk to him as man to man.' He looked for a sign of approval. 'I'm sure he'll meet us half-way.'

'He'll refuse to see you. I know him.'

'He might; but it's a risk worth taking.'

'If it were *Maman* I'd say yes, but Papa – '

'We must try, Jeanne. Maybe he will react exactly as you

say; but unless I go we'll never know.'

From the moment Amedeo arrived at the Hébuternes' fifth-floor apartment in the rue Tayot he sensed the tension in the air – just as though it were a physical presence. The maid blushed when he announced himself, and moved aside when he entered the reception hall as if she feared he might seduce her. Heaven only knew what she had overheard M. Hébuterne saying about him! Suddenly it all seemed hopeless; the house was permeated with prejudice and intolerance. He had been a fool to think that anything he could say would influence M. Hébuterne. How could he expect to break down generations of bigotry in one fell swoop? *Dio mio*, he had walked into a hornet's nest!

The maid returned. 'I'm afraid Monsieur Hébuterne does not wish to see you, m'sieur.'

He should have known as much.

'Tell him,' he said quietly but firmly, 'I shall not leave until he does.'

The maid smiled shyly, then she returned to the inner sanctum. From somewhere he heard the low rumble of voices. Silence. Presently the maid re-appeared. 'This way, m'sieur,' she said, blushing again when her eyes caught his.

He followed her down an airless corridor and into a large oak-panelled study with bookcases stretching up to the ceiling. The blinds were drawn; the only source of light was a tiffany lamp with a green shade. M. Hébuterne was sitting in a swivel chair at a leather-topped mahogany desk.

'Say what it is you've come to say, Modigliani, my time is precious.'

How smug, how self-righteous he was, Amedeo thought. He chose his words with care.

'This is as difficult for me as it is for you, Monsieur Hébuterne, but as men of the world – '

'I'm not a man of *your* world,' M. Hébuterne snapped. '*I'm* not a pavement artist. I believe in decency, accepted standards of behaviour – something you obviously scorn.'

Amedeo replied quietly: 'I came here to tell you, honestly and sincerely, that Jeanne and I love each other deeply.'

'Love? She's too young to know what it means. You inveigled her into living in sin in that den of iniquity you call an artist's studio. What would you know of love according to God's law? Drinking and womanizing in those, those . . . *vice dens*!'

Amedeo went on quietly: 'What do *you* know of a painter's life? Of how it really is?'

'Don't think I don't know what goes on in those studios. No decent person would set foot in them.'

'Have you any conception of how an artist suffers to express himself?'

'You talk to me of suffering? I, who have worked all my life to bring my family up as respectable, God-fearing citizens?'

'I respect that, m'sieur. But you know nothing of hunger, poverty, humiliation. An artist is exposed to all of these.'

'By choice, Modigliani. By choice. Remember that when you're starving in your attic.'

'It was my own choice, it's true. But the world would be a duller place if everybody chose security.'

'Security – which you seem to scorn – is very different from living in sin.'

'Is it a sin to love someone and be happy with them?'

'I didn't raise my daughter to let her throw herself away on a good-for-nothing artist. Why, I don't suppose you can keep yourself, let alone run a home. When I was your age I had risen to senior clerk. Now I am the manager. Why? Because I was hard-working, conscientious, ambitious. I didn't fritter away my opportunities At twenty I knew that if I worked at my book-keeping I would always earn a living wage. But I also realized that I'd need more than that before I could think of marrying.'

'I knew at sixteen that I wanted to paint. I could have had commercial success ten years ago had I wanted to be nothing more than a fashionable Salon painter.' Even as he was trying to explain Amedeo realized his efforts were futile. How could Achille Hébuterne, a man who had spent his working life buried in accounts ledgers, hope to understand intangibles, the abstract ideas with which the painter grappled daily? A sense of hopelessness overtook him.

'My daughter,' M. Hébuterne said, 'is not yet twenty-one. You are more than ten years her senior. Surely you must – ?'

'We've never been aware of an age difference; it has never bothered either of us.'

'I see. And the fact that you haven't a regular income . . . that doesn't bother you either?'

'Money's important, of course. But – '

'Ah,' M. Hébuterne cut in triumphantly, 'an admission. At last. Tell me, what do you earn at your so-called profession?'

'A hundred francs a month. Guaranteed by my dealer.'

'A pittance, m'sieur. And how often does he sell one of your masterpieces, *hein*?'

'Not often I admit. Sometimes it takes years for an artist to become established.'

'And you hope to support my daughter on that?'

'Yes – until my fortunes improve.'

'Jeanne has always had security, Modigliani. She isn't used to going without, making do.'

He looked Jeanne's father in the eye. 'Many couples have started married life on much less.' The words were said; for when he had made a pledge to Jeanne that he would marry her, he had meant it sincerely. Whatever her father said or did, he had promised her they would marry the very day she came of age, at twenty-one.

'Marriage? How dare you talk of marriage to my daughter? Why, you're not even a Catholic.'

'That's true, m'sieur. I take the point. My father – an orthodox Jew – was also a very religious man. But my mother was liberal-minded. She encouraged us to decide for ourselves. I follow no religion. If I have one at all – it is art.'

'How dare you force your way into my house like this? What right have you to demand my agreement over anything?'

'I love Jeanne. Nothing can change that fact.'

'Get out of my house, m'sieur.'

'Then you will not give us your blessing?'

'I'll see you damned first, Modigliani. I'm not a young man any more but if I have to throw you out, by heavens, I shall.'

Amedeo controlled his temper. How could he be angry with a man so riddled with prejudice? He felt only a deep compassion for him.

He turned to leave.

'And you can tell Jeanne from me that, so long as she associates with the likes of you and your gang of reprobates, she's no daughter of mine. I am disowning her until she comes to her senses.'

Amedeo went out into the corridor. There was an oppressive stillness; he could sense the undercurrents of suppressed emotion that filled the apartment. Somewhere a door opened. He heard the rustling of a woman's skirt. Mme Hébuterne was coming toward him.

'This way, Monsieur Modigliani.' Her voice was scarcely above a whisper.

He followed her to the stairs.

'He hasn't always been like that,' she said distantly. 'Try to find it in your heart to forgive him. He's not a well man.'

'I'm sorry. I didn't know.'

'He's very proud. And he means well, though it may not be apparent on the surface. But he's a good man.'

'I understand, Madame Hébuterne.'

'How is Jeanne?'

'We love each other very much. I will do everything I can to make her happy.'

'Yes, you will. I can tell. You will give her my love?'

'Of course.'

'*Au revoir*, Monsieur Modigliani.'

He took her bird-like hand in his. She smiled briefly, then she was gone, her dress rustling in the darkness of the long corridor.

Outside, he breathed deeply. He looked up at the windows on the fifth floor. The curtains were drawn. There was something forbidding about the apartment block. He felt he had to get away.

Nine

Suzanne Valadon was framing one of Maurice's scenes of Montmartre when Amedeo arrived at her studio in the rue Cortot. He was saddened by the lines of worry Maurice's alcoholism had etched into her proud face. But now, even in her early fifties, it was easy to see why Renoir had called her his favourite model: her cheeks still had the pinkness of youth and her figure, though a little plump, was pleasantly rounded. Maurice had never ceased to tell him of the debt of gratitude he owed her, and to his stepfather André Utter who had abandoned his own promising career as an artist to manage their affairs. Yet now, listening to her talk of art and painters' styles, it seemed impossible that she had supported her mother and herself when they had arrived in Paris from Limoges in the 1870s, hungry and penniless. Suzanne had become a trapeze artiste in the Molier Circus; but she had fallen during a performance and had almost died. She went into modelling and her face and figure soon brought her to the attention of Henri Toulouse-Lautrec, Degas and Renoir. But she revealed an artistic talent besides a talent as a model. The artists encouraged her . . . and her talent blossomed and matured.

He told her about the forthcoming exhibition at Bertha Weill's; could she possibly spare the time to attend the *vernissage* on Sunday? Just for an hour perhaps?

'Amedeo – this is wonderful news. You're on your way up. Why, all the successful artists have exhibited at Bertha's – Picasso, Rouault, Rousseau, Monet . . . '

'And Suzanne Valadon,' he reminded her proudly.

'Ah.' She shrugged. 'Just a few water-colours.'

'You do yourself an injustice, Suzanne. I know for a fact you showed *Nude With Striped Blanket* there. That alone has earned you a place in the Hall of Fame.'

She smiled. 'My career is over. Yours is just beginning. I'll try to come to the *vernissage*. But Sundays I always visit

Maurice at Villejuif.'

'Of course. How is Maurice?'

'Improving. Always he asks about you.'

'Give him my regards. And tell him I'll come to see him soon.'

'You've been a good friend to him. True friendship is as rare as honesty. You must come and visit me more often. And bring Jeanne; she's a wonderful girl from what you've told me.'

'I will.'

'It's lonely sometimes . . . without Maurice and André.' She brightened. 'But André's getting some Army leave soon; we must have an *atelier* party, just like old times. Ah, this accursed war! André says in his letters it could go on for another year. Sometimes I despair of my fellow men. How can they let all this killing go on and on?'

'Men have fought one another since time began; it's in their nature. Perhaps . . . some day when our children's children are grown up . . . men may learn to live in peace . . . '

'We're idealists, Amedeo. Perhaps God never intended us to know peace in this life. Perhaps we are simply deluding ourselves.'

He kissed her on both cheeks. 'You are a wonderful woman, Suzanne. Try not to worry too much about Maurice. He's tougher than we think. I'm sure he'll outlive us all!

Wintry sunshine, filtering through the cumulus sky, bathed the rue Cortot in a lemon-coloured glow; the street was barren, windswept, reminiscent of a Pissarro painting. Amedeo stood outside Suzanne's *atelier* a moment and reflected; it seemed so wrong, unjust, that this brave, talented woman had to endure such unhappiness. He thought of the empty-headed, self-satisfied wives of greedy merchants and shopkeepers for whom he had had to paint apples or flowers at Cheron's . . . idle, greedy, unfeeling. Suzanne was worth more than all of them put together.

* * *

Amedeo stopped outside Degas' house. The curtains were drawn; it looked deserted. He had been hoping Degas would be able to attend the *vernissage*.

He knocked at the door.

Presently it opened; a woman in a nurse's uniform stared at him.

'Would you tell Monsieur Degas that Amedeo Modigliani would like to see him.'

'Monsieur Degas is ill. He's not to have visitors.'

Ill? He had no idea! Quickly he explained he was an old friend and implored her to ask Degas if he would see him.

'Wait,' she said and disappeared.

When she returned, she said, 'M'sieur Degas will see you. But only for a minute, mind.'

Amedeo was shown into an airless bedroom. Heavy curtains were draped at the windows. A night-light burned on a table. Degas was propped up in bed. His face had lost its ruddiness; it was gaunt, strangely bloodless, but his eyes glowed and his voice retained its firm timbre.

'Amedeo . . . is it you?'

Amedeo shook the old artist's hand. 'Yes, *mon vieux*.'

Degas clicked his teeth. 'Don't be taken in by all this,' he growled, indicating the medicines on the bedside table. 'Damned fool of a doctor keeps telling me to stay in bed. Why, I can't imagine! Perhaps he thinks I'll go out and chase the girls.' He chuckled.

Amedeo laughed. 'Being ill seems to agree with you, *mon vieux*.'

'Ill? Who said I'm ill? That old biddy who let you in. *Mon Dieu*, but what a menace! She tittle-tattles to that damned doctor that I keep having nips of cognac. A man must have some pleasure.' He chuckled again. From under the pillow he produced a flask of brandy and filled two glasses on the bedside table. 'If she asks – ' he winked, – 'we'll tell her it's some medicine you've brought me. I've heard good reports about your work. Bertha Weill's showing it. That's good; very good. She has an appreciative eye. Good head for business too.'

Amedeo looked at him, amazed. 'But how did you hear?'

'Ah, there's nothing escapes old Degas, my boy. They say I'm in my dotage, on my last legs. Well, maybe they're right. But I'm damned if I'll go without a struggle. This derelict body of mine has a lot of fight left in it yet.'

The nurse came in. 'M'sieur Degas,' she scolded, 'you promised me. Only for a few minutes, you said.'

Amedeo said: 'I was just leaving, madame.'

'Leaving, be damned!' Degas boomed. 'You've only just arrived.'

'No visitors,' the nurse snapped. 'That's what Doctor Vernet said.'

'Woman,' Degas bawled, 'you'll be the death of me! What's the good of my having friends if I'm not allowed to see them?'

'I'm only repeating what Dr. Vernet – '

'Doctor Vernet, Doctor Vernet,' Degas mimicked. 'I'll show you I'm well enough to receive visitors.' Degas' hand, claw-like through arthritis, clutched at the bedpost. He began to haul up his emaciated body from the bed. 'Damn these old bones of mine!' The effort was too much for him; he collapsed back on to the pillows.

'Rest now, *mon vieux*,' Amedeo murmured. 'I'll come back. When you're well again.'

Degas' laboured breathing became calmer; he closed his eyes. 'Tired. It's so dark.' The nurse pulled the sheets up to the old man's chin, then joined Amedeo at the door. 'He's sleeping,' she said.

Degas' voice rasped at them. 'Oh no, he's not. *Nor* is he dead. So don't go sending for that damn fool doctor again.' He raised a gnarled hand to Amedeo. 'God bless you, Amedeo. Remember what I've told you. Seek within yourself. Find out what you have to give. The secret of being a painter is in the *emotion*.' His voice tailed off; he began to breathe with the slow regulated rhythm of sleep.

Bertha's gallery was lit by two yellow globes from the low

ceiling. Voices rumbled and reverberated; sherry glasses clinked; food plates rattled. Socialites with falsetto voices vied with the nasal whines of the professional art critics; lorgnettes were perched on prying noses; gregarious women fanned themselves with their catalogues.

Amedeo stood at the entrance with Leopold and Jeanne, hating every moment.

'Over there,' Leopold whispered. 'It's André Salmon. I think he wants to have a word with you. I know how you despise Armand Avenne and his crowd, Amedeo, but Monsieur Salmon is impartial. He's worth cultivating.'

'Butter won't melt in my mouth.' Amedeo winked at Jeanne.

Leopold kept smiling across at André Salmon who was trying to disengage himself from Mme Lefarge, a Parisienne hostess famous for her *soirées*, and her entourage. 'He's seen us,' Leopold said excitedly. 'Don't forget to say how much you admire his column.'

M. Salmon began to edge towards them. 'Monsieur Zborowski, Monsieur Modigliani,' he began.

That was the last they saw and heard of him. He was seized by Gustave Simon, the Colonial Minister, and his sycophantic aides. 'My dear Salmon,' they heard him say, 'don't forget we're invited to lunch with the Hertzogs. Terrible bores, but they have the finest *cuisine* in Paris. I have heard it said their chef was once in service with the Emperor Franz Joseph.'

Salmon's attempts to disengage himself were drowned as the minister's party made their exit. He threw Amedeo and Leopold a hopeless smile and shrugged with Gallic resignation . . . he was sorry, but they could see how it was.

'Our apologies, madame,' Simon said, shaking Bertha Weill's hand and smiling unctuously. 'Interesting exhibition. My regrets that we can't stay longer. A previous engagement.'

'Of course, Minister,' Bertha said dubiously.

'Another time perhaps,' Simon said, his thoughts occupied with gastronomic delights to come.

Amedeo, dismayed, smiled wryly at his friends. 'There goes my press mention.'

'But André Salmon promised us a good write-up,' Leopold said, furious. 'What right has that fat little buffoon Simon to drag him away? I'll write to every editor in Paris about it.'

'There's Max Jacob,' Jeanne said. 'I'm sure he'll write something in his magazine.'

'Oh, indubitably,' said the crestfallen Pole. 'But it has only a small circulation, barely five thousand a month. Salmon's column is read all over France.'

The *vernissage* had begun at 11 am. It was now noon. A huge crowd had gathered outside. Everybody was talking at once and pointing at the full-length nude of Elvira in the gallery window.

A hook-nosed crone was glaring at the nude. 'Disgusting.'

'Magnificent,' a man countered.

'Disgusting,' Hook-nose repeated, shaking her fist.

'Evidently, madame, your eye lacks an appreciation of true beauty. She's a goddess . . . and a witch. An Aphrodite and a Messalina . . . in one.'

'She's a trollop and no mistake,' Hook-nose sneered.

More people joined the crowd; they jostled and pushed, hoping for a closer look at the sensuous portrait. The street was packed.

'*Alors*, what a woman!'

The crowd began to take sides; tempers flared. Hook-nose's bird's-nest hat was knocked to the ground and trampled on. She began hitting out with her brolly. The crowd was turning into an angry mob.

'Help! Police.' Hook-nose screeched as she was borne along by the surging crowd. 'Don't you dare lay a hand on me.'

Two perspiring *gendarmes* forced their way into the mêlée. The arrival of law and order caused tempers to subside. One of the *gendarmes* took out his notebook. 'Now,' he addressed Hook-nose, 'perhaps you'd tell me who or what is the cause of this disturbance?'

She pointed at Bertha's window. 'That . . . that . . . brazen hussy!'

'Our children should be protected,' another woman shouted. 'They shouldn't be allowed to show such things in public. On a Sunday too!'

The two *gendarmes* stared wondrously at the Elvira nude. Then they remembered their duty and presented themselves to Bertha Weill, trying to register disapproval.

'That, er, painting in the window, madame. You'll have to remove it.'

Bertha gave them a withering glance. 'Why, might I ask?'

They fidgeted and cleared their throats. 'It's causing a disturbance outside. You'll have to remove it.'

'I'm sorry, but it's staying where it is. Good day to you.'

'Now be reasonable, Madame Weill. We know you run a respectable art gallery, but this, well . . . '

'What's the matter with the painting?'

'That's obvious to anybody with eyes.'

'Does the sight of a naked woman on canvas embarrass you then?'

The *gendarmes* blushed. The crowd began to titter.

'It's causing a breach of the peace. Take it down or we'll report the matter to our superiors.'

Jeanne stepped up to the two scarlet officers. 'That's the work of a great artist. You ought to be ashamed of yourselves.'

'You are acquainted with this Monsieur Modigliani?' said one, opening his notebook and wetting the point of his pencil.

'Yes,' she replied proudly.

'I see.' He cleared his throat. 'Your name, please?'

Amedeo stepped forward. 'Surely all this isn't necessary, officers.'

The *gendarme* drew himself up. 'An offence has been committed and it's my duty to make a report.'

'Offence?' Jeanne protested. 'What offence?'

Amedeo took her arm and gave the *gendarmes* a pacifying smile. 'Jeanne,' he murmured, 'let's leave well alone.'

'Name, young lady?' the *gendarme* persisted.

'Jeanne Hébuterne.'

The *gendarmes* exchanged glances. 'Are you by any chance related to Monsieur Hébuterne of Souchard's, the merchant bankers?' one of them asked.

'I'm his daughter.'

By now the entire street was packed; traffic had come to a standstill.

The *gendarme*, notebook at the ready, pushed through the crowd and entered the gallery. He addressed Bertha with the air of one entrusted with a vital mission. 'That painting must be taken out of your window at once, Madame Weill. I have just reported back to my superiors. My orders are to have it removed.'

'Over my dead body,' Bertha snapped.

'I must warn you, madame, that it's a serious offence to obstruct an officer in the course of his duty.'

'Don't threaten me, young man; I'm old enough to be your mother.'

'I have my orders,' he stammered, groping in his memory for the *gendarmerie* training manual's procedure for dealing with itinerant females.

Bertha snorted. '*Nom de Dieu*. They've taken our menfolk for the war . . . and left the boys for the police force.'

The *gendarme* blushed and licked the point of his pencil. 'The Commissioner himself will hear of this,' he said hotly. 'You full name, madame.'

'You'd better put that notebook away, young man, before I say something that will make your hair curl.'

Nonplussed, the constable appealed to Amedeo. 'If you refuse to remove it, m'sieur, my orders are to confiscate it.'

'You lay one finger on that painting,' Bertha said, 'and I'll swear more complaints against you than you've had coffee and croissants.'

The constable spread his hands. 'Please, m'sieur,' he appealed to Amedeo. 'Be reasonable.'

Amedeo approached the entrance to the window. He was trying to make light of the disappointment he felt; the exhibition had turned into a fiasco through no fault of anyone. It was simply bad luck. He looked at the painting. It had been acclaimed by his friends as the best nude he'd ever done. Now, Elvira's wanton eyes seemed to be gloating at him with mocking irony.

'You mustn't,' Jeanne cried. 'It's a wonderful painting. The police have no right to demand anything.'

The *gendarmes* exchanged more glances. Already the disturbance was assuming gigantic proportions in their minds; they were imagining themselves giving evidence in a sensational court drama . . . a Scarlet Woman posing naked . . . a strikingly handsome artist . . . the daughter of a well-to-do family . . . It justified all those gruelling months at the *gendarmerie* training college. Why, they might even be promoted.

'You are Monsieur Modigliani, the artist?' they chorused.

'I am.'

'And make sure you spell his name correctly,' Jeanne added. 'He's going to be famous.'

The crowd in the street had swelled. Amedeo's name was on everybody's lips. The rue Taitbout hadn't seen so much excitement in years. Word had spread to the distinguished guests inside. *Police*. It seemed to have a magical effect on them. Each suddenly remembered a previous engagement, an important business meeting, an aged relative they had promised to visit. The prospect of being involved in a scandal sent them scurrying for the door like frightened rabbits.

Mme Lefarge lost her lorgnette in the mad scramble. It was squashed underfoot by the fleeing connoisseurs of art.

'Help,' squeaked M. Demongeot, a stockbroker with artistic pretentions, 'let me get air. I suffer from claustrophobia.'

Tables were overturned in the stampede; plates were smashed; a coat-stand reeled like a drunken man.

The bourgeoisie's instinct for self-preservation was like an angry wave; the gallery rang with shrieks, curses and snarls. Bodies disgorged on to the pavement. A homburg rolled into the road. 'My hat,' wailed M. Demongeot. As he tried to retrieve it a workman kicked it into the crowd. Mme Lefarge, teetering precariously on high-heels, addressed the workman. 'You ruffian. I saw what you did.' She waved to the red-faced *gendarmes* trying to quell the riot. 'Officer. Arrest this ruffian.' Suddenly she found herself thrown into the hairy arms of a burly man in a butcher's apron.

'This is a bit sudden, isn't it?' he leered. 'But I'm happy to oblige, lady.' He kissed her roughly, laughing.

Mme Lefarge shrieked and beat her fists on his barrel chest.

'Ah, but you're a wild 'un! Well, I like a bit of spirit in a woman.' Roaring with laughter, he picked her up into his arms.

'Put me down – you beast.'

The crowd roared with laughter; this was better than the music-hall.

Amedeo stopped at the window. Jeanne was right; he had broken no law.

'The painting stays where it is,' he told the constable.

'Then you give me no alternative, m'sieur. I must impound these paintings and trouble you all to accompany me to the *gendarmerie*.'

The police commissioner's office was in a gloomy building in the Boulevard Haussmann. The flag of the Republic hung limply from a stunted flagpole over the entrance; the stucco walls were scarred and flaking.

Amedeo, Jeanne, Bertha and Leopold were escorted into an austere waiting-room.

The bored-looking desk sergeant perked up when he saw the two constables carrying Amedeo's canvases. 'The nudes?'

'Yes.'

The sergeant's bushy eyebrows quivered in anticipation. 'So these are what all the fuss has been about. *Mais alors*,' he gasped when he gazed at the Elviras. He crossed himself hurriedly.

They followed the sergeant and constables into a musty, airless office in which was a huge mahogany desk piled high with manila folders, filing trays and an assortment of brass paperweights. Behind it sat the commissioner. He stared at them myopically through thick-lensed spectacles, resembling a bewildered tortoise.

'Are you the head man?' Bertha demanded. He was. 'Then

how dare you send your menials to close my gallery. I'm a taxpayer. And I run a respectable business. They've ruined my carpets with their hobnailed boots. I'm sending in a bill for damages.'

The constables voiced a hot denial. Why, they had carried out the commissioner's orders at great personal risk! They had met nothing but opposition and abuse.

Bertha snorted. 'I've seen bulls in a china shop behave better.'

The commissioner banged a paperweight on the desk. 'This isn't a fish market. There is no necessity for everybody to shout. You are Madame Weill?'

'I am.'

'I see. You are the proprietor of the art gallery in the rue Taitbout?'

'I am. But I must say that in all the twenty years I've been in business I've never been subjected to such boorish behaviour by the Paris constabulary.'

The commissioner smiled thinly. 'Which one of you is the artist Modigliani?'

Amedeo stepped forward.

'And you, m'sieur?' the commissioner addressed Leopold.

'Leopold Zborowski, sir. Monsieur Modigliani's dealer.'

'And the young lady? How is she involved in this?'

'She isn't, m'sieur,' Amedeo cut in. 'She was a guest at the *vernissage* of my exhibition. If anyone's to blame, it's me. I ask that she be allowed to leave.'

'I'll decide whether she stays or leaves. She could be a material witness.'

'But this isn't a court of law,' Amedeo protested. 'We're not on trial.'

'True. It is, shall we say, merely an informal enquiry.'

'An enquiry into what?' Bertha demanded.

'This is just as difficult for me, madame, I assure you. I don't make the laws, but I have the job of seeing they are enforced. My constables inform me you have been displaying paintings – of nude women I believe – likely to corrupt young people.'

'That's a monstrous suggestion,' Jeanne interrupted. 'Their artistic merit is beyond question.'

'You have a testimonial to that effect, young woman?' he commented dryly.

'My name and reputation are testimonials in themselves,' Bertha said.

'That's as may be, madame. However, I must consider the facts of the matter. A number of respectable citizens have complained about your client's work – '

'To whom have they complained, m'sieur? Certainly not to me.'

'My immediate concern,' he went on obdurately, 'is whether or not charges should be brought.'

'What charges?'

'Displaying offensive material likely to corrupt . . . inciting a riot . . . causing a breach of the peace . . . causing a public disturbance . . . would you like me to go on?'

'Show me somebody who has been corrupted by these paintings,' Bertha retorted. 'Why, you haven't even seen them.'

The commissioner nodded to the sergeant. 'Have the paintings brought in. I wouldn't want Madame Weill to think I'm pre-judging the issue.'

The sergeant nodded to the constables. 'Jump to it; you heard what the commissioner said.'

The constables scurried out, returning with the canvases they had impounded. They held up the *Reclining Nude*. Elvira stared out at the commissioner in all her carnal glory, rich flesh colouring glowing sensuously.

His face turned a mottled purple; he appeared on the verge of an apopleptic fit.

'Why, this is scandalous,' he spluttered. 'I've never seen such depravity!'

Amedeo stared. Surely the man couldn't be serious?

'Why, she's showing . . . pubic hair!'

'What's so surprising about that?' Bertha asked. 'Isn't that the way Nature made woman?'

'*Mon Dieu*, are there no standards of decency left in Paris?'

'You talk of standards, m'sieur,' Jeanne cried. 'What standards permit your constables to seize an artist's work, destroy his livelihood, ruin his reputation?'

Bertha added: 'I've held many exhibitions – Picasso, Matisse, Renoir, Braque, Rodin. Nudes have always been the outstanding attraction. But never, never, has anyone ever tried to suppress them or have them banned.'

'How can you defend this sort of shameful titillation?' The commissioner poked an accusing finger at Elvira's groin. 'It's absolutely scandalous. It's pornographic. There are serious penalties for exhibiting pornographic material in public.'

'In that case,' Amedeo replied, 'why have Renoir's celebrated nudes been hanging in the Louvre for years?'

'That's not for me to say, m'sieur. I'm a policeman, not a judge. However, to assure you I'm being absolutely fair with you . . . earlier I telephoned one of Paris's most distinguished art critics. He's agreed to give us the benefit of his judgement in these matters.'

'Ah, Monsieur Salmon? Now perhaps we'll have some sanity.'

'M'sieur Salmon? I don't think I know the name. I telephoned M'sieur Armand Avenne.'

Amedeo looked at his friends in dismay. *Dio mio*, would he be for ever hounded by that obsequious sycophant, that toady who paid lip-service to wealthy patrons of the Salon d'Automne?

'Something the matter, m'sieur?' asked the commissioner. 'Surely I could not be fairer than that?'

Amedeo shrugged.

'Don't worry,' Jeanne whispered. 'We're not beaten yet.'

The sergeant disappeared and returned with Armand Avenne. The tall, cadaverous critic bowed to the commissioner and smirked at Amedeo; he had not forgotten the incident at the Salon d'Automne.

'M'sieur Avenne,' the commissioner began, 'you are, I believe, the art critic of *L'Art et la Mode* and *Les Echos*?'

'That's correct, m'sieur.' M. Avenne smiled ingratiatingly.

'And you are acknowledged to be one of the leading, if not

the leading, art critic in Paris?'

'I have that honour, m'sieur.'

'*Sans blague*,' Bertha snorted. 'Do you have a testimonial to that effect?' she mimicked the commissioner.

Jeanne stifled a giggle.

'Quiet, please,' the sergeant commanded.

The commissioner glowered at Bertha, then motioned to Armand Avenne. 'I'd be obliged if you'd give me your expert opinion, as a professional critic, as to whether these paintings are works of art, or whether you think them likely to corrupt the morals of decent citizens.'

Armand Avenne inserted a monocle. He peered at each of the canvases. Finally he removed the monocle and cleared his throat.

'In my considered opinion, m'sieur, they are the cheap, vulgar work of a typical Montparnasse pavement artist.'

'Shame on you,' Bertha snorted.

'Kindly control yourself, Madame Weill,' said the commissioner. He leaned forward. 'Your conclusions, M'seiur Avenne?'

'In my opinion, sir, these paintings are disgusting and deliberately sensational – and an insult to the upright artists of our city.'

'*Honi soit qui mal y pense*,' Bertha added.

The critic flushed. 'I didn't come here to be insulted, madame. I needn't remind you I've been a Salon critic for the past fifteen years.'

'Which probably explains,' Amedeo said, 'why so many mediocre paintings have found their way into the art galleries of Paris.'

Armand Avenne gestured to the commissioner. 'Must I endure the insults of such people, m'sieur? Why,' he added sneeringly, 'I'm told Monsieur Modigliani and his ilk get drunk every night in a verminous liquor den called the Rotonde.' His voice quivered with suppressed emotion. 'An establishment frequented by scurrilous artists and models who spawn this kind of filth.' He pointed at the Elvira nudes. 'Everybody can see she's a whore.'

'So,' Amedeo ridiculed, 'the status of an artist's model is your criterion for judging his work?'

'You have a glib tongue, Modigliani. But it can't change the truth.'

Bertha and Jeanne joined in the angry exchange. The office was a babel of voices. The commissioner rapped on his desk.

'We're not here to question M'sieur Avenne's reputation as an art critic.' He gave Amedeo a penetrating look. 'I have heard M'sieur Avenne's opinion; I have seen your work. Do you wish to say anything before I consider whether charges should be brought?'

Amedeo's gorge began to rise. He forced himself to remain calm. But it was a travesty of justice! The exhibition had been ruined, all chances of sales lost, and now he faced a possible fine and the confiscation of his best work.

'If, as Monsieur Avenne would have us believe, my paintings are likely to corrupt the good citizens of Paris . . . perhaps he would like to explain why the many famous nudes in the Louvre and the Musée National d'Art Moderne have not already corrupted everybody? Let me refresh your memory, M'sieur Avenne . . . for you yourself must have gazed many times at Goya's *Maja de Nuda* . . . Giorgione's *Sleeping Venus* . . . Suzanne Valadon's *Nude With Striped Blanket* . . . Titian's *Venus Awake* . . . Manet's *Wanton* and *Olympia* . . . Renoir's *The Nymphs* . . . '

'The saints preserve us,' Armand Avenne choked. 'The upstart dares to compare himself with the great masters. Why you're not qualified to mention their names, let alone have the temerity to place your work in the same category.'

'Go and peddle your prejudices at the Salon d'Automne, m'sieur,' Bertha snapped.

The commissioner interrupted; he had heard enough. Amedeo's words had impressed him more than he cared to admit. If he brought charges, a skilful defence lawyer would tear the prosecution's case to shreds; the entire constabulary would be made a laughing stock. Besides, he reflected, the nudes did stir the emotions in a very pleasing way . . .

'In the light of everything that's been said,' he announced, 'I've decided to return your client's canvases, Madame Weill.'

'*Merci*, m'sieur. I'm relieved common sense has prevailed.'

'However, I cannot permit them to remain on display. Whatever enlightened people like ourselves may feel in this matter, we cannot ignore the law.'

Jeanne squeezed Amedeo's hand. 'You see,' she whispered. 'I said we'd win.'

'What about my carpets?' Bertha asked, glaring at the sheepish-looking constables.

'Perhaps you'd send in a bill for cleaning, madame. I think the constabulary's funds could stand it,' he said with eyes twinkling.

Ten

'M'sieur Modigliani?' asked a carroty-haired youth in morning coat, starched collar and pin-stripes. 'I'm from *Le Figaro*. Would you like to tell the story behind the girl in your pictures?'

Amedeo, at the zinc in the Rotonde, waiting for Leopold, shook his head. *Dio Mio*, would they never leave him alone? All week he'd been pestered by reporters, art dealers and sensation-seekers wanting to know about the girl in the 'orange coloured nudes'.

'We have it on good authority,' the youth went on, 'that she's the daughter of a wealthy businessman rebelling against autocratic parents.'

'Sorry to disappoint you, my friend. There's no story. She's just an actress. Her name's Elvira Lacrot. And I've no idea where she's living. Now, if you'll excuse me . . . ' He waved to Leopold who had just entered.

The youth persisted, but Amedeo reiterated a polite refusal.

'Who was that?' Leopold asked as the youth left.

'Reporter.'

'He wanted an interview?' Leopold said eagerly.

'Yes. But I said no.' Amedeo signalled to Libion. 'Two coffees.'

'But why ever not? Everybody's talking about you. You can name your own price.'

'For painting titillation, yes. The police say my work is pornographic – *et voilà*! – I'm all the rage. Well, people are fickle; fashions change. Besides, they're interested only in a quick profit; they care nothing for what I'm trying to express on canvas.'

Leopold sighed. 'That's the trouble with having an idealist for a client.'

'Nobody knows more than I what you have done to promote my work. Like you I want recognition – but for the right reasons, not because my nudes stir up a hornet's nest. Say I'm reaching for the moon if you will . . . but I want to make people feel about life, give them a deeper insight into their fellow men. Idealism? Maybe. But ever since I learned to put paint to canvas I've sought to depict man's spiritual nobility. Am I striving for the impossible?'

'You're being true to yourself; more than that a man cannot do.'

'But you, Leopold . . . am I being fair to you? God knows how much of your life you've invested in me.'

'That's what a dealer's for. I've always believed in you, ever since we first met – in this very café. Call me a dreamer . . . but I have an instinct everything will work out; I feel it in my Slavic bones.'

'But you haven't had a holiday since I've known you. Didn't you say you'd like to show Hanka Heidelberg?'

'That can wait.'

Amedeo thought a moment. 'Remember the meat packer who wanted me to paint his *cocotte*? Do you still have his address?'

'Why yes,' Leopold said, puzzled, remembering how Amedeo had adamantly refused the assignment. He copied the address from his diary and gave it to Amedeo.

'Have you arranged for a model to come today?'

Leopold shook his head. 'Not until eleven o'clock tomorrow morning.'

As he made his way to the meat packer's *abattoir* Amedeo reflected on the debt of gratitude he owed Leopold. How else would he have survived through the lean months? Who else would have such unquestioning faith in him? On occasions Leopold even refused to take his commission. 'Pay me back when you're rich and famous,' he'd say. Lovable, head-in-the-clouds Leopold! A warm affection surged through him.

At the *abattoir* he sought out M. Carnelle, a corpulent man with a complexion like a beefsteak.

'M. Zborowski sent you?'

'Yes. He's my dealer.'

They haggled over the price.

'A hundred,' said M. Carnelle.

'And seventy-five.'

'A hundred and fifty,' M. Carnelle said obstinately.

'Agreed.'

M. Carnelle glanced furtively at his clerks. 'Rue Lipp,' he whispered. 'Number eighty-eight. Mme Pascale.'

Mme Pascale was fat, blowsy and running to seed. She gave Amedeo an appraising look when he explained his business.

'Claude's been urging me for months to sit,' she said. 'Last painter who came was an Armenian who pocketed my silver the moment my back was turned. But you I like,' she added, eyes moving over him like bailiffs taking inventory. 'When would you like to begin?'

'Just as soon as you're ready, madame,' he said, setting up his portable easel and mixing his palette.

She went into the bedroom.

She emerged, naked, voluptuous figure wobbling like a huge pink blancmange. 'Where would you like me to sit?'

'The *chaise-longue* will do fine.'

The stuffy room became permeated with her cloying perfume. When he asked if he could have a window open Mme Pascale replied that she was delicate and caught cold easily. He worked quickly, endeavouring to slim down the gargantuan folds of flesh without distorting reality too much.

Mme Pascale was looking at him speculatively.

'You married, M'sieur Modigliani?'

'Not yet.'

'You're wise. I was, once. To a lazy, good-for-nothing rogue who squandered every penny I earned. *Merde alors*, but what a disaster that was. Do you have a lady friend?'

'Yes.'

'She is special?'

'Very.'

'Ah.' She shrugged. 'You good-looking ones are always snapped up. Us older girls get landed with parsimonious types like Claude Carne. Still, he pays the rent.' She chuckled, 'And he's not so bad, as men go. How much is he paying you?'

'A hundred and fifty.'

'*Mon Dieu*,' she cackled, 'the old buzzard must be in love with me!'

The portrait finished, Amedeo collected up his things; he didn't like the expression in Mme Pascale's cow-like eyes; she was devouring him.

'What's your hurry . . . ?'

'Oh, another appointment.' He glanced at the time. Almost noon. M. Carnelle should be arriving soon.

'Couldn't it wait . . . say an hour or so? I promise you, *chéri*, you won't be disappointed . . . '

'Don't you want to see your portrait, madame?'

'Call me Marie; it's more intimate.' She poured herself off the *chaise-longue* and walked toward him, breasts thrust forward like a galleon's figurehead. 'Shy, *chéri*? There's no need . . . '

'M'sieur Carnelle will be here any minute. You wouldn't want to throw away everything, just for a moment's pleasure.' *Dio mio*, he thought, she's the worst kind of female predator, one who won't take no for an answer.

'It would be worth it with you,' she breathed.

Just at that moment the doorbell rang.

'Blast,' she growled and slipped into her négligée. 'The offer still stands, *chéri*. Any time.' She swept to the door. The meat packer beamed at her. 'Claude, how nice to see you!'

Next morning Amedeo thrust the money into Leopold's hand. 'Now you can take that trip to Heidelberg.'

The Pole blinked. 'But how? . . . Where?'

Amedeo told of his visit to Mme Pascale's apartment. 'That roly-poly meat packer was delighted. Said I'd made her look like Madame de Pompadour. *Chacun à son goût*,' he added, smiling.

'But it's yours,' Leopold protested. 'I can't accept.'

'Oh yes, you can. I insist. Now, who's the model this morning?'

The model, Nina, was a milliner's assistant; this was her day off. She was a pretty gamine-faced girl with a retroussé nose and cheeky grin and she posed well. Amedeo had finished a nude study when Leopold brought them coffee.

The Pole blushed scarlet when he set eyes on Nina. Amedeo threw her a wrap, amused by Leopold's embarrassment; in another man it would have been ludicrous, but Leopold's innocence and painful shyness were the very qualities that endeared him to Amedeo.

'Ah, just how I like it,' Amedeo said, gulping his coffee as though it were an elixir. 'Stygian black and exactly the right thickness.' It was like a drug to him; stimulating him when his energy flagged.

Nina screwed up her face. 'Ugh. How can you drink it so strong, m'sieur?'

Amedeo smiled. 'Some artists drink, Nina. Others take hashish. My vice is coffee.'

Nina peered at the canvas. 'That's really lovely, m'sieur. If I could paint like that I'd soon tell that old battle-axe at the shop, Frau Zimmerman, what she could do with her hats. But I daren't tell Philippe, my young man, I'm posing for you – he'd throw me out!'

He laughed.

'You're like a zephyr, Nina. The goddess Nike would be proud of you.'

She giggled. 'M'sieur talks in riddles.'

'Off you go. And don't give Philippe all your earnings.'

After Nina had left, Leopold expressed surprise that he should be so enthusiastic about a milliner's assistant. He was never usually so laudatory about semi-professional models.

Amedeo searched for words to describe the strange sensation he'd felt while painting. 'It was like nothing I've ever known. My brushes felt as though they were guided by a hand . . . but not my own.'

Leopold gave him a bemused smile. First Amedeo had given him 150 francs, then he eulogized an ordinary shop-girl, and now he talked of an unseen hand. *Hein*, but would he ever understand him?

'Don't look so alarmed, I'm not losing my reason. Sometimes an artist must throw caution to the wind . . . otherwise his imagination atrophies. Now, go and tell Hanka about Heidelberg. I'm told the *bier kellers* alone are worth the trip.'

The weeks passed. Now, with Jeanne relieving him of domestic necessities, he began to work like a demon. He painted Max Jacob, Jacques Lipchitz, Ortis de Zarate, Fernand Léger, Mois Kisling, Mac Orlan, Diego Rivera, Marie Wassilief, Leon Bakst, Brancusi, Blaise Cendrars . . . and Jeanne, at every opportunity. When he was overcome by fatigue, he catnapped; when he ran out of oils, he used pastels. There seemed no end to the creative flow; yet never was he satisfied, convinced he had not yet reached his nirvana. An inner compulsion drove him harder and harder. But what he was seeking, the quintessence of the human soul, always seemed tantalizingly out of reach. How to project emotion on canvas? he asked himself. Colour wasn't enough; nor composition, nor form. Somehow he must combine all three to achieve the ultimate *sensation*. Only then would he be lifted to the realms of the gods.

He pounded the streets, painting anybody who aroused compassion . . . a scrubbing woman at her tub of ley, a mother suckling her child, a vagrant delving into a dustbin, a cheeky midinette outside a hosier's.

At the studio of Chaim Soutine, in the damp, verminous bowels of Cité Falguiere, Amedeo drank the White Russian's potent vodka as he painted the gangling, lank-haired artist. Like some strange troglodyte of the Steppes, Chaim thrived amidst the chaos and stench of mouldering carcasses hanging from the rafters of his cave.

'Good God, Chaim, how can you bear this awful smell?'

Chaim shrugged. 'After a while you become immune.'

Amedeo poked a maggoty fowl with a stick. 'How can you stand looking at this day after day?'

'But see the reds, blues and purples. Where else will you

see such colours?'

Amedeo marvelled at Chaim's canvases. It was incredible that such colour schemes had been conceived by a tow-headed peasant who could barely read or write. Art collectors dismissed him as a *peintre maudit*. But Amedeo had no doubt his friend had genius. Time would prove him right, he thought.

'Clasp your hands in front of you.' Amedeo squinted to gauge tonal harmony. 'That's fine.'

'You like the vodka, Deo?'

'Raw. But it certainly keeps out the cold!'

'I made it from seed potatoes and corn. Just like the real thing, eh?'

The raw spirit burned its way down Amedeo's throat. If he could survive Chaim's vodka, he thought, he could survive anything. He completed the background of the portrait: a sombre sea-green motif with dark and light patches, the essence of Chaim's *maladie du pays*.

The Russian stared at the finished portrait.*

'It's me – but I don't look ugly.' He peered in a cracked mirror. 'You really don't see me as ugly, Deo?'

'Of course not.'

'That waitress in Marie Wassilief's *cantina* says I am.'

'That's her way of saying she likes you.'

Beaming, Chaim refilled Amedeo's glass.

At the communal wash in the Cité Falguieres, Amedeo was captivated by the washerwomen as they squeezed, rinsed, rubbed, gossiped and cursed their 'idle, good-for-nothing' menfolk. Their exuberance stirred his inherent compassion. He made sketch after sketch. They were the spirit of Paris.

On his way home he stopped in at Madame Jardin's café. As he drank black coffee he was suddenly aware of how tired he felt. He caught a glimpse of himself in the mirror behind the counter. *Dio mio*, he was wearing fatigue like a mask. He

* National Gallery of Art, Washington, D.C.

was pushing himself too hard, but he knew he could no more quell his inner driving force than halt the flow of the Seine.

Later, at his *atelier*, he studied the drawings. He was creating a unique style; he was looking at the world in a way which no one had ever done before.

'The last few years seem to have counted for nothing,' he told Jeanne. 'There's still so much to discover, so much to achieve. I'm only just beginning to find myself. There's something inside me, telling me I'm near to the key.'

'Don't you think you should sleep? You look so tired.'

'You're right. A man cannot live for his work alone. Especially when he has someone as beautiful as you to care for.'

'Action speaks louder than words, Dedo,' she said, kissing him.

'You're a wicked cat.' He laughed, as Jeanne purred.

Much later, in the darkness, he lay listening to Jeanne's regular breathing next to him. The urge to be up and working began to take possession of him. Why wouldn't it leave him alone? Colours danced before his eyes. His brain was teeming with ideas, questions, imponderables, weird shapes.

Often, in his Montmartre period, he had roamed the streets of the Butte, experiencing a strange affinity with the sights and sounds of nocturnal Paris; it had anaesthetized the violent tumult of his imagination. Tonight, the demon would deny him the merciful oblivion of sleep. He got up and sat at the window; the air was cool.

'Dedo,' Jeanne said. 'What's wrong, darling?'

'I couldn't sleep. I'm waiting for dawn to break. It's always an awe-inspiring sight, no matter how many times one sees it. But you, *cara*, you should be asleep.'

'I'll make some coffee. We'll see the dawn together.'

Watching her prepare coffee he noticed a difference in her; a wistfulness, a preoccupation. For some days now she had been unusually withdrawn and given to moody silences. That she felt the family rift deeply he knew only too well; but it had never affected her so profoundly as it appeared to be doing now. When he had tried to discover what was preying on her mind, she dismissed it as his imagination.

She was humming a haunting melody; he couldn't quite place it, yet he knew it well.

'What's that piece of music?'

'Chopin. One of the *Nocturnes*.'

'Of course. The music of the night.'

He remembered she had had a letter the day before; postmarked Montparnasse. Usually she told him about her letters; this time she'd said nothing.

'Who was your letter from, *cara*?'

'From *Maman*; just the news from home.'

'How are they?' He curbed the cold fury that flowed through him as he remembered his meeting with Achille Hébuterne. He was being unreasonable, he told himself, but hard though he tried to see her father's point of view, he couldn't forget M. Hébuterne's attitude. He had tried to meet the man half-way, but all he had received was abuse.

'*Maman's* well,' she said, forcing a smile. 'André has passed his accountancy exams.'

Her smile was too bright, he thought.

'And your father . . . no word?'

'None.'

'*Cara* . . . something's troubling you.'

Jeanne didn't answer.

'It's your father, isn't it? He's threatened you with something.'

'Oh no, no . . . ' He saw she was close to tears.

'Darling Jeanne.' He took her in his arms, feeling her trembling against him.

'Oh Dedo, tell me you love me.'

'More than anything in the world. Remember that very first night together . . . how we promised we'd never have any secrets from each other? You spoke from the heart then . . . '

Jeanne pressed her face against his chest. Presently she said softly: 'The other week, when I was late coming home and told you I'd met some of the girls, from the Colarossi . . . '

'You had a drink with them; there's no harm in that, *cara*.'

'But I didn't meet them, Dedo. I lied to you.'

'Ah,' he teased, 'what a terrible crime.'

'I went to see a doctor. Dr Devraigne.'

'A doctor? But you haven't had a day's illness since I've known you.'

'It wasn't that I went to see him about . . . '

Suddenly he understood. *Dio mio,* but how could he have been so unperceptive, so thoughtless, so absorbed in work? Since their first night together they had loved passionately whenever the mood took them.

'You're . . . ?'

She nodded.

'But . . . how long?'

'Nearly three months?'

'But why on earth didn't you tell me earlier?'

'I was afraid you'd be angry . . . think I was trying to trap you into marrying me.'

He laughed. 'Angry?' He waltzed her round. '*Mama mia*, I'm thrilled to bits. A baby! But this studio won't be big enough for the three of us. We must think of a name . . . Gianni? Vittorio? Carlo? Which do you prefer?'

Jeanne laughed through tears of happiness. 'There is just a remote possibility that *he* will be a *she*.'

'Then we'll call her Jeanne. After her beautiful mother.'

The Artists' Quarter was delighted by the news of Jeanne's pregnancy. Foujita threw a champagne party and everybody crowded into the *atelier*. Rosalie closed up her restaurant for the night and arrived with her son Luigi. 'My little Jeanne,' she cried, Tuscany eyes moist with memories. 'The first *bambino* is always the worst; after that they come as easy as peeling potatoes.' Amedeo gave everybody a cigar and spent the evening in dazed wonder.

Their happiness was marred only by Jeanne's parents who remained as intractible as ever. As the weeks passed Jeanne blossomed. Amedeo showed her off at the Rotonde at the slightest excuse. 'There's no prettier sight than a woman with child,' he told everyone.

One April evening, as Amedeo and Jeanne were dining, André Hébuterne called on them. He looked round the *atelier* with glowing eyes, envying Jeanne her independence and happiness. How often he had dreamed of breaking away from their father's tyranny; but he lacked his sister's courage. He had wanted to be apprenticed to a firm of picture restorers, but had bowed to his father's wishes that he study accountancy.

'I bought one of your paintings,' he told Amedeo, shyly. 'I keep it hidden in my wardrobe.'

When he took his leave he kissed Jeanne and said, 'Can I give *Maman* a message?'

'Tell her Amedeo and I are very happy . . . that we wish Father well . . . that we hope one day we can settle our differences.'

The art market, depressed by the war, plummeted to an all-time low. Even established painters were finding themselves on hard times. Picasso had moved to the Pyrenean village of Ceret, where the living was cheap; others had gone to the Brittany fishing village of Pont-Aven to revive the Breton School begun by Gauguin nearly twenty years before.

Food prices soared. The café *patrones* laid off waiters. 'The accursed war!' they moaned to anyone with half an ear. 'It is ruining us.'

Paris was in the grip of an austerity it had not known since the Revolution of 1830 when the monarchy had been overthrown.

The war dragged on into early summer. General Haig's break-through with tanks to Cambrai was halted, not by German resistance but because of his troops' exhaustion. Ludendorff launched a counter-attack which threatened to split the Anglo-French armies under the command of France's General Foch. But Foch's counter-offensive began to push the Germans back.

Jeanne was nearing her time. Amedeo was worried about their draughty, damp *atelier* with three flights of narrow stairs that would be difficult for Jeanne with a baby. But finding another studio was almost an impossibility for, ironically, the growing vogue of the Artists' Quarter had caused rents to rise far above the 100 francs he paid. Soon there would be doctor's bills, hospital fees . . .

He awoke next morning bathed in perspiration. He stared at his ashen face in the mirror. But he refused to let Jeanne send for Dr Devraigne.

'It's just *la grippe*. A few days' rest will put me right.'

The influenza bout was worse than he cared to admit and he was ill for three weeks. During his convalescence he promised Leopold that as soon as he was well he would take Jeanne to Nice for the holiday Leopold had been urging him to take for months.

'Think of it as a new phase in your career, *mon ami*. I'm told Provence is a painter's paradise. I'll send your monthly allowance on to you. And Dr Devraigne will write to the hospital in Nice – '

'But the *atelier* . . . who's going to look after it, pay the rent?'

'It's all been taken care of. Jacques Netter has bought ten paintings. For five hundred francs. And Dr Alexandre has bought two . . . for two hundred francs each. Fernande has agreed to look in once a week. So there's nothing to keep you in Paris.'

Eleven

The cherry trees were in blossom when they left for Nice; but the newspapers spread gloom and despondency about the war. Many predicted another year's carnage in the trenches; already the senseless toll of life had claimed thousands, among them the poet, Rupert Brooke, and the brilliant young sculptor, Henri Gaudier-Brzeska.

Amedeo had a strange prognosis that their sojourn in the Midi would see a turning point in the war. The politicians had declared in 1914 that "hostilities will be over in months"; it was now in its fourth bloodstained year.

He was eager to see the sunflower fields and gnarled olive trees and Vincent Van Gogh's tortured cypresses. As their train steamed through the Rhone Valley he made notes for portraits and mulled over Foujita's advice as to how to adjust his palette to the harsh light of the Midi. Micheli had demonstrated changing light values on white cartridge paper pinned to his studio walls. During the day he would show his students how the reflected light had changed subtly in hue; it had been a valuable lesson.

'What are you thinking about, Dedo?'

He smiled. 'Of when I take you to Italy to meet Mama and Papa, brothers Giuseppe, Umberto and Emanuele and old friends from Micheli's studio – Georgio, Oscar, Anselmo, Gianni. They'll flirt with you, of course, and I'll be like every other jealous lover. I'll show you our cathedral, the art gallery which has paintings by Titian, Caraveggio and Murillo . . . ' He closed his eyes at the memory, then went on: 'Then, in the evenings, we'll stroll through the cobbled streets where the English poet Shelley wrote his verse . . . see the statue of Ferdinand the First, who saved our town from the Barbary pirates. And the old port where I used to sketch the fishermen. From the harbour on a clear day you can see the islands of Elba, Gorgona and Alexandre Dumas' Monte Cristo, shimmering like emeralds in the Mediterranean.'

'It sounds wonderful.'

'I dream of entering Livorno like Radames, bearing gold and jewels . . . with you as my Aida.'

'You *are* a success now, Dedo. We can go to Italy whenever you want.'

He groped for words to explain what he felt deep inside, but he was suddenly confused, unsure. His boyhood dream of achieving the stature of the Italian masters . . . Leonardo da Vinci, Michelangelo, Bellini, Titian, Giorgione . . . seemed presumptuous, arrogant. To achieve true greatness, he reflected, one must have humility; yet, polemically, he wanted to return to Livorno with all the trappings of fame, to repay his mother's unfailing devotion and faith, to glorify the family name. And there was Leopold – and the artists who had befriended him when poverty and privation had been his constant companions. 'I want to repay the debt of gratitude I owe them, Jeanne.'

'I know you do. That's why I love you so much.'

The cottage Leopold had rented for them at Cagnes-sur-Mer was on a hillside blanketed with lavender and thyme. From their bedroom window they could see the sea across fields of maize and sunflowers. Amedeo was intoxicated by the rich landscape, peach-coloured sky of early morning, swaying carobs and cypresses, red-tiled stone-built houses with pepper-pot chimneys. After breakfasting, and before the sun rose to its zenith, he'd paint in the kitchen garden; in the heat of the afternoon they would *siesta* until the cool breeze of early evening.

But the fierce sun began to sap his vitality after the relatively mild Paris climate; the solution was to paint indoors or under the grape-vine trellis. Little wonder, he thought, the residents of Arles had thought Vincent van Gogh mad, setting out as he had from his yellow house every morning, easel strapped to his back, to stand in the cornfields painting in the fierce heat. Little wonder Vincent had become disorientated and eccentric, to be locked away in the asylum at St Remy where he finally shot himself.

But, once Amedeo adjusted to the heat and organized a working routine, he began to send two or three canvases a week to Leopold.

On sultry evenings they went into Nice and strolled beneath the rustling palms along the promenade, drinking *café-crême* at a little bistro overlooking the Baie des Anges.

It was an idyllic existence. Lulled by the hot, drowsy afternoons it seemed almost as though Paris had belonged to another life.

Summer mellowed into autumn. A letter from Leopold said the paintings were selling and there was no reason why they should not remain in Cagnes until the baby was born. Dr Devraigne had arranged a bed in Saint-Roche Hospital and he, Leopold, was taking care of the financial arrangements.

'And,' Amedeo read aloud to Jeanne, 'Chaim Soutine and Fernande and Foujita are coming for a few weeks' holiday. There's room for them here with us. Why, it will be just like old times!' Eagerly he thumbed through the Baedeker guidebook. 'We must plan some excursions for them, *cara*!'

He broke off, alarmed, when Jeanne winced and held her abdomen. '*Cara*, what's wrong?'

'It's nothing; just the baby.' She smiled. 'He's strong, like his father.'

He laughed; soon they would be a family.

Fernande, Foujita and Chaim Soutine arrived at Cagnes in fine spirits. Amedeo ushered them into the nearest bistro, bought *fine* champagne and plied them with questions about the Artists' Quarter. He listened, rapt, as they brought him up to date with the news; he hadn't realized how much he had missed Montparnasse. Now, hearing the gossip, triumphs, heartaches, affairs, he felt homesick for city-life.

Foujita and Fernande were accommodated at the cottage; Chaim found a room in the village. Each day they met for a swim and Jeanne and Fernande shared the cooking; in the evenings they discussed everything from Jung's theories to the price of hog's-hair brushes.

One day they were visited by Amedeo's old friend, Leopold Survage, and his mistress, Germaine Meyer. When Survage saw the cottage had a piano he insisted Germaine play. As she played Ravel's *Ma Mère l'Oye*, Amedeo did a portrait and presented it to her. Survage was delighted and bought Veuve Clicquot champagne and reminded Amedeo of the portrait he had done of him years before. 'I treasure it still. It's the eyes,' he explained. 'Deo has painted my left eye normal, but the right is just one colour with no pupil. The effect is quite extraordinary.' Amedeo remembered the occasion vividly. 'With one eye you look outside,' he'd told Survage at the time, 'with the other you look inside.'

One golden afternoon on the beach Chaim kept them amused by scrubbing himself with soap and plunging into the waves; he had never seen the sea before in his life. And when Amedeo bought him a tooth-brush and demonstrated how to use it, the wiry Russian had brushed his teeth for hours on end until they glowed like pearls.

A mist over the sea evoked in Amedeo the subdued tones of the streets of Paris. He set up his easel and began to paint; but he could raise no more enthusiasm for seascapes than he had for landscapes; people were his *métier*. 'Why waste my time on seascapes?' he told Jeanne, whose yellow maternity smock emphasized her opaline features and russet hair. 'Much better to leave them to painters like Turner and Canaletto who are the masters.'

At the bistro, that night, Amedeo joined in his friends' affectionate badinage, but his thoughts kept returning to the Paris boulevards . . . the waifs, Apaches, gipsies, washer-women, midinettes, demi-mondaines, beggars, servant girls; he wasn't a *plein air* painter, his genre was people. In them he saw a poignant beauty and universal truth. The insistent voice within him kept saying, 'Paris, Paris, Paris!' He could see the flowering chestnuts in the Luxembourg Gardens, red braziers outside the Moulin de la Galette, leaves swirling along the Boulevard Raspail, coffee grinders' shops, wine-stained café floorboards . . . the browns, russets and yellow ochres; low-key colours, melancholy yet hauntingly beautiful.

He said nothing to Jeanne; but, as they lay in each other's arms, the mistral whining and rattling the cottage shutters, she said: 'You miss Paris, don't you?'

'We are happy here.'

'You'd be happier in Paris. It's in your blood.'

He made a token protest, but he knew there was no deceiving her. She seemed to know his every thought; since his friends had arrived he had thought of little else. Something in the city satisfied a strange hunger. The bright light of the Midi was giving him headaches and he longed for the subdued greens and browns of rainswept boulevards.

'We'll go back, Dedo; just as soon as the baby is born.'

'You really won't mind?'

'Fernande knows a *pouponnière* where the baby will be cared for . . . just until we get on our feet.'

A mist tinged with green swirled around him. He was groping along a dark alley, a terrible weight pressing down on him. Faces loomed out of the putrescent haze, faces ravaged by age and suffering . . . La Goulue high-kicking and shrieking to the raucous frenzy of the can-can . . . 'Fancy a night with me?' she cackled. Where was he? He caught glimpses of Montmartre, but it was distorted as though he were viewing it through warped glass. '. . . looking for a model, Amedeo?' said a scarlet *grisette*. She was a montage of all the models he had ever known. Now he was at the ticket barrier at the Gare de Lyon, carrying two leather suitcases and the paintbox Aunt Laura had given him when he had left Livorno more than a decade earlier. A manly hug from Uncle Garsin . . . 'Do what you feel you must, boy; there's nothing you can't achieve if you want it hard enough.' . . . '*Cocher, cocher*!' 'Where to, m'sieur?' 'A good hotel. But first, show me the sights of the city' . . . Arc de Triomphe . . . Notre-Dame . . . Place du Tertre . . . Les Tuileries . . . Pont-Neuf . . . Les Invalides . . . Eiffel Tower . . . Les Halles . . . rue de Rivoli . . . Ile St-Louis . . . Place de la Bastille . . . the swaying motion of the horse-drawn *fiacre* lulled him to sleep . . . 'Hotel Madeleine, m'sieur.' 'Ah, *grazie, cocher*!' A month's rent paid in advance for a studio room . . . a three-coloured lithograph of Carpaccio's *Two Courtesans* pinned over his bed . . . a letter to his mother Eugenia . . . 'Paris is everything I dreamed it would be, Mama; the light is less bright, but I shall soon adjust to it . . . ' Tapered candles flickering, high-vaulted ceilings, ornate stone pillars, an eerie silence, incense . . . a choir singing somewhere above . . . faces half-remembered emerged from the dark recesses of his mind . . . crones and beggar women from the shanty huts behind the Moulin de la Galette . . . crumbling moss-covered gravestones in the Cimetière de Montmartre . . . a young man in a blue suit, spats, opera cloak, carrying a silver-topped cane . . . a vision of himself in his early twenties. But there was something odd about his features . . . the skin was stretched tight, like a fleshless mask . . .

He jerked up in bed, bathed in perspiration, heart pounding. He saw the familiar white-washed cottage walls, oak beams and water pitcher on the table in the corner. Jeanne was bending over him.

'Dedo, you frightened me. You were shouting. Gasping for breath . . . '

'Just a silly nightmare, *cara*. I've probably been out in the sun too much.' He breathed deeply. His palpitating heart slowed to a steady rhythmic beat. He remembered the half-finished portrait of the baker's assistant at the village *boulangerie*; but, for once, he lacked the urge to paint.

'Let's take the bus into Grasse, Jeanne. We can have a picnic. Just the two of us. I'm told the town is full of exotic flowers at this time of year.'

They spent an enjoyable day in the little hill town, picnicking in a poppy field. They talked of the future, of the child Jeanne was soon to have, but his cheerful mood couldn't dispel an inner anxiety.

That night, long after Jeanne was asleep, he lay staring into the darkness . . . seeing again the vision in the dream . . .

The October countryside was a deep russet. Two weeks had passed since Foujita, Fernande and Chaim had returned to Paris. The latest letter from Leopold was full of reassurances of better things to come, but it was hard to conceal his disappointment; he was producing some of his finest work, earning the admiration of artist friends, yet the public remained indifferent. Only other artists, it seemed, knew what he was trying to say on canvas. *Mama mia*, was he now reduced to wallowing in self-pity? If the fools were blind, he must work even harder to make them see!

He immediately wrote to Leopold, thanking him for the money he'd sent, that he was slaving away and would soon be sending five more portraits, his best wishes to Hanka and 'my warmest affection to you.'

November came.

'Monsieur Modigliani, please be patient!'

'But all this waiting, nurse . . . it's killing me. You are sure there's no sign yet . . . ?' Underfoot he squashed a half-smoked cigarette and lit another. 'Is there no message? You are sure she's all right?'

The dumpy nurse raised her eyes heavenwards. *Mon Dieu*, she thought she had seen every kind of anxious father-to-be, but he was a revelation to her. He burned up more nervous energy than ten men; and those deep brown eyes! He was so attractive he made her feel weak at the knees.

'There's nothing to worry about, m'sieur. Your wife is in good hands.'

'*Grazie, molto grazie*.' He paced back and forth. How he had laughed when other men had told him what an ordeal the waiting had been! But, *Dio mio*, it was worse than anything he could have imagined!

The nurse smiled. 'I'll let you know the moment the baby arrives.'

Amedeo stared out of the waiting-room window. He was vaguely aware of a noise in the distance; people singing . . . the *Marsellaise*! What did it mean?

Suddenly the whole hospital was in a state of excitement. An orderly burst in shouting, '*Vive la France*!'

He caught the man's arm. 'What is it? What's happened?'

'The war, *mon ami* . . . haven't you heard?'

'What?'

'It's over; they've just announced it on the wireless. The Boches have signed the Armistice. *Vive la France*!'

The hospital was in an uproar. Amedeo had never seen so many people rushing about in different directions. People were laughing and crying and thanking God. He asked about Jeanne, but it was impossible to make himself heard. Someone was pulling at his sleeve. 'M'sieur Modigliani.' The dumpy nurse was beaming up at him. 'Don't you want to see your daughter?'

Daughter? In a daze he followed her into the maternity ward. He hardly recognized Jeanne: ashen-faced, eyes dulled by the aftermath of pain. She smiled bravely. 'Dedo . . . I'm sorry I took so long . . . '

'*Carissima*.' He knelt by the bed and covered her with kisses. He looked at the baby, too overcome to speak.

'Little Jeanne,' he whispered, smiling.

From the adjoining wards came the joyous *Marsellaise*.

Jeanne frowned. 'What's all that singing about?'

'*Madonna mia*. I'm so proud to be a papa I forget to tell you. The war's over.'

'Thank God,' Jeanne said, smiling through her tears. 'Now I know we are going to be happy. The three of us.' She closed her eyes.

How long he knelt beside the bed he had no idea; he looked at the baby in awe. He felt suddenly cold. His elation began to fade. The hospital ward was claustrophobic. The smell of the antiseptic . . . the ether . . . the white walls and stark lights. Were they a harbinger of the future?

A hand touched him lightly on the shoulder. It was the night nurse. 'M'sieur Modigliani, *s'il vous plaît*. She's sleeping.'

'*Pardonnez-moi*. I was forgetting . . . '

The nurse smiled sympathetically. 'Don't worry. She'll be

home with the baby in a few days. All she needs is rest.'

'You'll take good care of her – '

'Of course.'

He was sitting outside a seafront bar. It was hours since he had left the hospital but he had been unable to shake off his depression. He stared morosely across the Baie des Anges. He tossed back a glass of *marc* and ordered another. There was a pile of saucers on his table. He saw the waiter's hesitation.

'I've got the money,' he said recklessly. 'Here ' he added, pulling out a handful of notes. 'Take what you need.'

He had lost count of the number of drinks he had had. All he could think of was Jeanne's expression when she had said they would be happy together. But how could he tell her about the man in the corridor who haunted him day and night? The raw brandy began to steady his nerves. It was stupid to drink himself into a stupor. So what? he thought. In his Montmartre days hadn't he always boasted that he wanted *une vie brève mais intense*? He was fighting a losing battle. The nameless demons were too strong; there was nothing for it but to seek oblivion in alcohol. For a few hours he would have respite from the appalling burden of his tormented soul. Why couldn't he be simple and uncomplicated? Why was he driven by this strange compulsion? Where was it going to end? Why could he never find peace of mind?

'Waiter.' He fumbled in his pockets for more money.

'M'sieur?'

'*Marc*. Bring the bottle.'

The waiter scooped the money off the table with superb Gallic indifference. A customer wanted to drink himself silly; it happened all the time. Life was like that.

'Fifty francs, m'sieur,' he said when he returned with the bottle. 'You gave me forty-five.'

'Ah, yes . . . ' Amedeo produced another coin. Wasn't that just like the French? Get the money first. Then let the customer go to the devil.

'*Merci*, m'sieur.' The waiter disappeared inside again.

Amedeo poured out a glass and gulped it without a break. That was the last of his monthly allowance from Leopold. But what the hell – it was a celebration. The war was over; he was a father.

'So let's drink to that,' he said aloud, pouring another glassful. But, deep down, he knew that wasn't the reason. Most of the previous month's allowance had gone on drink. He had wired Leopold for more money. Putting *marc* in his coffee had done the trick, he thought. Didn't leave an odour on the breath. He had become so adept at holding his liquor that Jeanne had never suspected.

The night air, coming off the sea, was turning cooler. He shivered and started coughing.

From the door the waiter said, 'You ought to go inside, m'sieur. The sea breeze is deceptive.'

'You're right,' he muttered, holding a handkerchief over his mouth. He moved inside and sat at a table by the door. He didn't like the café's dark recesses. He drank the last of the *marc*. Out of the corner of his eye he saw him. At a corner table. A ghoul with hollow eyes, bloodless lips and clawlike hands. He closed his eyes. When he looked again the table was empty.

'That man – '

The waiter, hovering nearby, stared to where Amedeo was pointing. 'M'sieur?'

'He was sitting at that table. You must have seen him.'

The waiter started to humour him. 'That table has been unoccupied all evening, m'sieur. You must have seen someone else.' He glanced at the *patrone* behind the zinc and raised his eyes to the roof.

'It was him,' Amedeo said, coughing into his handkerchief. He held it up in front of him. There it was, the all-too-familiar sign; that damnable red stain.

He dragged himself to his feet, feeling himself breaking out in a cold sweat, and lurched blindly into the night.

Twelve

The wave of euphoria created by the Armistice in November rushed on into 1919. Paris had become a teeming cauldron, a Saturnalia for pleasure-seekers of every nationality. Brothels, cellar *boîtes* and *chansonniers* sprang up at every turning and girls poured in from every conceivable town . . . Rennes, Nancy, Lille, Orléans, Poitiers, Tours, Cherbourg, Grenoble . . . the city was an irresistible magnet, a Mecca for every provincial working girl. They arrived with battered cases, wide-eyed, hopeful, gullible, dreaming of a stage career; but, small of talent, the dreams soon crumbled and many found it too easy to drift into the netherworld, to graft a living before their looks faded.

Mistinguett's famous legs and singing of the legendary *Mon Homme* was the rage of the *Folies-Bergère* . . . Ponselle and Martinelli thrilled Paris Opéra audiences with duets from *Aida* . . . flame-haired Yvette Guilbert became the toast of the Opéra Comique . . . Nijinsky and Pavlova were the sensation of Diaghilev's *Ballets Russes* . . . champagne flowed like water as Parisians embarked on an orgy of self-indulgence as though there was no tomorrow.

At the Rotonde, tables groaned under the weight of food and drink. '*Mon Dieu*,' Libion exclaimed, welcoming Amedeo and Jeanne, 'but you've come back to a city that's gone insane!'

Amedeo bought everybody cigars and boasted: 'I'm a father now, *mes amis*. I'm getting fat and becoming a respectable citizen.'

'You, a father?' Blaise Cendrars said. 'I can't believe it.'

'Two years ago I wouldn't have believed it myself.'

They settled into the *atelier* again. He began to work under pressure; for now there was an extra mouth to feed, a wet nurse to be paid. On Sundays they visited little Jeanne at the nursery at Chaville, near Versailles, where she was being cared for by a nurse, from Loiret, named Marie. Amedeo would arrive with an armful of toys and play with his daughter on the lawn. 'Isn't she beautiful, *cara*? Now we have two madonnas in the family.'

Back in his old haunts and surrounded by his friends he painted some of his finest canvases, wonderful studies of artists, children, beggars, servant girls, midinettes; but his favourite model, as always, was Jeanne. He never tired of painting her . . . *Jeanne In A Pullover . . . From The Front Seated . . . With Blue Eyes . . . With Arm Raised . . . In Chemise . . . Full Face . . . Leaning Against A Chair . . .*

'Stay exactly as you are, Jeanne. Don't move an inch; that's perfect.' His brushes flew over the canvas; it was a declaration of his love. 'I'm going to call it *In Profile, Seated*.'

She smiled. 'Don't you get tired of painting me, Dedo? Wouldn't you rather be painting a new model?'

'I'll paint you for as long as I can hold a brush.'

'But the *atelier's* full of my portraits.'

'Precisely what Leopold keeps telling me. He can't understand why I won't offer them for sale. Well, I tell him, "Leonardo da Vinci refused to part with the *Mona Lisa*; it was a personal testament to a woman who was very special to him. These are my testaments. One day they'll be worth thousands of francs." And when I'm dead and buried,' he smiled, 'you'll be a wealthy widow.'

'You frighten me when you say things like that.'

He laughed, but he was aware that she seemed to be reading his innermost thoughts.

'Your cough isn't any better; you promised you'd see a doctor if it didn't clear up.'

'A touch of bronchitis. I always get it in winter. It's a legacy from childhood.'

She put her arms around his neck and looked deeply into his eyes. 'If anything happened to you my life would be over.'

'Nothing's going to happen to me.' He kissed the tip of her nose. '*Cara bellisima . . . ti voglio bene*.'

The morning air was crisp. Along the Boulevard Raspail a tramp, cocooned in old copies of *Le Figaro*, yawned and swung his legs off the wooden bench; it was time to think about sustenance; another day had to be lived.

'*Bonjour*,' Amedeo said, opening his sketch-book.

'*Bonjour*, young fellow. *Merde alors*, these creaking old bones of mine!'

The old man watched Amedeo sketching. He looked at the finished drawing. 'Wish I had your talent, m'sieur. I wouldn't be rotting away on a street bench, I can tell you.'

'Here. Take it. It's yours.'

'I've no money, m'sieur.'

'An artist's reward isn't always monetary, *mon vieux*.'

'*Merci*. But I'm damned if I know where I'm going to put it. This bench, as you can see, is the only home I've got.'

'Then use it to keep out the cold.'

Church bells rang nearby; the old man rose. 'Time I was off. That's the nuns' bell: they're serving soup.'

'Is it good soup?'

'Prosper Montagne wouldn't include it in his gourmet's guide, but to a man like myself who hasn't tasted a square meal in months – excellent.'

'May I join you?'

'*Allons*!'

Amedeo had long planned a series of drawings of Paris's under-privileged. Leopold had been enthusiastic when he'd outlined the idea; it would be a record for posterity, a glimpse of a Paris tourists never saw. The editor of *L'Eventail* had expressed interest and had the first option to publish them. This seemed an ideal opportunity to begin it.

At the Couvent de la Visitation the down-and-outs were gathering . . . beggars, cripples, vagrants, alcoholics, drug addicts, veterans of the Franco-Prussian War and assorted flotsam with the hopeless air of defeat. They were queueing outside the kitchen, each holding an earthenware bowl. The doors opened. A Sister came out, followed by two nuns wheeling a trolley on which was a huge urn of steaming broth. Each man held out his bowl, murmuring, 'Bless you, Sister.'

Amedeo made sketch after sketch. This was exactly what

he had been looking for: life in the raw, the grass roots of survival. His sketch-book full, he dropped a handful of coins into the Couvent poor-box, pleased with the morning's work. With his few remaining francs he bought a litre of *Lachryma Christi* on his way home; it was Jeanne's favourite wine.

At the *atelier* Jeanne was working at her easel, completing a view from their window which she had begun the day before. He admired her bold use of colour. 'Herr Schuler's right, *cara*. You have a feeling for colour.'

She demurred; he was the artist in the family; she painted only to pass the time while he was out. He sat at the table, his overcoat wrapped round his shoulders, black felt hat pulled down and read *Les Chants de Maldoror* which he often called 'my Bible'. So absorbed was he that he scarcely noticed Jeanne sketching him.

She showed him the finished drawing. He studied it at length. 'Sometimes, *cara*, I think you know me better than I know myself.'

'*Dio mio*, Jeanne, when will we ever be free of debts and bills?' He waved a letter from their landlord. 'The rent's going up. From next January.'

He thrust it into a drawer full of other creditors' letters; he would settle them when he received his next allowance from Leopold. But though dealers were expressing interest in the work of Foujita, Soutine, Kisling, Lipchitz, and especially his own, there was never enough money for their growing needs. Besides canvas, turpentine, oils and brushes, there was food, baby clothes, new furniture, the slate at Libion's; it was a vicious circle. But he enjoyed his growing reputation as 'the handsome Italian with the burning eyes.' More and more his name was mentioned in the galleries and salons. *Paris-Soir* featured him in an article about 'the Bohemian artists of Montparnasse'. Life became a carnival of fancy dress balls in the rue Huysmans, dinner parties at Paul Fort's studio, *vernissages* in the rue Lafitte, social evenings at Foujita's or Kisling's, talking, eating, sleeping and painting.

When Jeanne suggested he relax he merely laughed and threw himself harder into his work, ignoring the fatigue which had become a daily companion. His inner compulsion grew more and more demanding; sometimes even he was alarmed by its all-consuming intensity. He kept himself going on black, glutinous coffee laced with cognac . . . until he fell asleep at his easel. Often he would be woken by Jeanne in the morning, unable to remember what effect he had been trying to achieve on canvas the night before. Shopgirls, bakers' wives, flower-sellers, washerwomen, gipsies, waitresses, seamstresses . . . more canvas, more oils, more turpentine! Hissing gas lamps in the streets at night, sitting on a boulevard bench at dawn, trips to Chaville to see their daughter, sentimental evenings at Chez Rosalie's . . .

In May Jeanne became pregnant again.

'*Mama mia*! Soon we'll be four,' he laughed. 'Is it possible?'

They attended the opening night of the ballet *Parade* at the Châtelet Theatre, with music by Erik Satie, book by Jean Cocteau, sets and costumes by Picasso.

On a *café-terrasse* he told Foujita about Jeanne's pregnancy. The little Japanese slapped him on the back and bought him a cigar. 'Incentive, Deo. That's what you needed. You'll paint better than you've ever done.'

He shrugged. 'If only hard work was enough, Foujita . . . '

'The writer, Jules Renard, put it in a nutshell, Deo. "*To be talented is not to write a single page; it is to write three hundred pages. There is not a story that an ordinary intelligence cannot conceive. The strong do not hesitate*" . . . you see, I know it by heart . . . "*They go to their table and they sweat and stick at it until the end. That alone differentiates them, the men of talent, from the feeble who never begin.*" 'That's how it is with you, Deo. You sweat blood to put on canvas the visions you see in your head. *Mais alors*, but what a bloody life we artists lead! Come on, let's have a cognac.'

'Is that the whole story, Foujita? Sweat and toil . . . is that the artist's destiny?'

'For the great, yes.'

One July morning he woke and realized it was his thirty-fifth birthday. He stared at his reflection. Gone was the deep tan from Provence. Now it was pale and drawn. He complimented Jeanne on her ripening figure: to him a woman was at her most beautiful when she was with child. He put on his hat and coat.

'Must you go to Leopold's today?'

He shrugged. 'We need the money. We still owe little Jeanne's wet nurse for last month, remember?' He coughed. Somehow he stifled it before it turned into a spasm.

'Stay home today, Dedo. One day won't make any difference.'

'I can't.'

'I found this this morning.' She was pointing to a dark red stain on his pyjama jacket.

'So?' he said hotly. 'It's paint. What's so strange about that? This place is covered in paint stains.'

'It isn't paint.'

He hid his alarm. 'We need money, Jeanne. We're behind with the rent. We owe for groceries. And I'm sick of being cross-examined.' He strode out, slamming the door. He knew he was trying to sublimate fear by giving vent to anger. He stopped on the stairs, ashamed of himself. He retraced his steps and opened the door. For a few moments they looked at each other. Then he said, 'I'm sorry I shouted.'

'And I'm sorry I went on at you.'

'You were right about the stain. It isn't paint. It's this cough. It must have torn a little blood vessel in my throat.'

Jeanne kissed him lightly. 'Let's forget about it. Don't work too long. I'll cook you a nice dinner tonight.'

Her eyes were so full of love, so trusting, he couldn't bear to look at them.

He walked along the rue de la Grande-Chaumière and turned into the rue Notre-Dame du Champs. He stopped in his stride. He was rooted to the spot by a skull-splitting pain.

He clutched at the wall to steady himself. Lights danced before his eyes. Nausea ran through him like acid. The spasm passed as suddenly as it had come. It left him weak and trembling.

'Something the matter, m'sieur?' a voice said.

Amedeo looked at the man's worried face. His pounding heart began to subside.

'It's nothing,' he said. 'Just a dizzy spell.'

'But you're as white as a sheet. Shall I send for a doctor? The café across the road has a phone.'

'No. I'm all right now. Thank you, *mon vieux*.' He waved and continued on his way. He had had headaches before – but nothing so blinding. He thrust it out of his mind as he turned into the rue Joseph-Bara, his step firmer. He rang Leopold's bell. The Pole's welcoming smile was like a sanctuary. 'Come in, come in.' Leopold dropped his voice. 'That collector I told you about. He's here. With his wife. He's *formidable*. But the wife . . . she's the one to go for. Very coquettish. All you need do is smile at her. Flirt a little maybe . . . '

Amedeo smiled. Leopold was becoming a wily old bird.

'I'll be a Casanova.'

'We shouldn't resort to such subterfuge,' Leopold smiled. 'But we've got to live, *hein*?'

He followed Leopold into the studio. The Pole made the introductions. M. Curtois, it turned out, was a jobber on the Paris Bourse. Yes, he knew all about Gauguin being a successful stockbroker before turning to painting. He'd been encouraged to invest in up-and-coming artists by his colleagues. 'Inflation plays havoc with the franc, *mon ami*; so invest your money in art.' Madame Curtois wore an ostentatious brocade dress, numerous bangles and bracelets and had her hair up in the fashionable minaret style. She wouldn't know a pavement artist's doodle from a Michelangelo, Amedeo thought. To her a painting was something she could show off about.

'You're from Italy,' she said, fluttering enormous false eyelashes at Amedeo. He nodded.

'Are its artists as good as its wines?'

'Better,' he said, smiling. Ah well, would it hurt for once to suffer a fool gladly? He kept smiling as Leopold and M. Curtois discussed a price.

Mme Curtois's eyes never left Amedeo for a moment. 'That one, M'sieur Modigliani, does it have a title?' She was pointing to the canvas of a lad he had painted in the yard behind the Cité Falguiere. How well he remembered the boy's pride in being painted! He had given him a ten-franc piece and told him to keep it in his hand until he got to the *pâtisserie*. Jeanne thought it was one of his best works; it seemed a shame to be parting with it. But he had to live.

'*Boy In Blue Jacket*,*' he said.

'It's delightful. Really charming. And so lifelike. Pierre, Look at this boy. We must have it for our sitting room.'

M. Curtois took out his wallet. 'You did say one hundred francs, M. Zborowski?' Leopold nodded. M. Curtois peeled off a hundred-franc note. 'It's subject to an affidavit of course. It's not that I doubt your integrity, m'sieur. But one hears so many stories about forgeries. One can't be too careful.'

'Indeed not, M'sieur Curtois.' Leopold drew up the certificate. He and Amedeo signed it.

Mme Curtois peered at another canvas. 'What a lovely girl. Who is she?'

'A gypsy girl,' Amedeo said, remembering the occasion when he and Jeanne had been in the Midi. The woman had been begging outside a bar. He had persuaded her to pose for him for twenty francs; even when he had handed her the money she was still suspicious of his motives. Money for sitting still for half an hour? She couldn't believe one got money so easily.

M. Curtois peeled off another hundred-franc note. Another affidavit was signed.

When the Curtoises had gone Leopold got out his best vodka. 'It's from the Kielce district, Deo. The best, *Salute*.

*Guggenheim Museum Collection, New York.

You've earned it. Especially as the art market is so depressed. Vollard's have closed one of their showrooms. Rosenburgs are laying off salesmen. Picasso can't even sell his Cubist work. Soutine is existing on potato stew. I tell you, *mon ami*, things are in a bad way.'

Amedeo shrugged. The art market was always in a state of flux.

'Do you have a model coming to day?'

'Nina Stein.'

He nodded; she was a good model, a professional.

'And I'm arranging an exhibition. In London.' Leopold paused to see how Amedeo would react to the news. Nobody in the Artists' Quarter had ever exhibited outside France. It had happened purely by chance. An English collector, Sacheverell Sitwell, had been in Paris on business; he had made enquiries in the Rotonde about the new-wave artists. Someone had given Leopold's address.

'London? But who do we know in London? Why, you've never even been there.'

Leopold told him of the meeting with Sitwell. 'His family are very influential in cultural circles. He wants to stage it at Mansard's in Bond Street. He showed considerable interest in your work, Chaim's and Foujita's.'

'It's flattering news, Leopold. But are we well enough known in London?'

'Oh, indubitably.' From a leather briefcase Leopold produced some newspaper clippings with a conjuror's flourish. 'They're in English, of course, but see – there's your name, mentioned several times. If you're a success, your name will be made. Your Paris market value will double, treble.'

'Aren't you jumping to conclusions, *mon ami*? Remember what happened at Bertha Weill's?'

'But this is London. Monsieur Sitwell thinks buyers will be falling over themselves to buy your nudes. English collectors aren't so prudish.'

'That's not what I've heard. Pious, hypocritical lot by all accounts.'

Later, as he painted Nina Stein, he reflected on what Leopold had said. A successful showing in London would certainly cause a stir in Paris among discerning collectors and cognoscenti. First thing tomorrow he would sort out some suitable canvases; and the series of drawings he'd done at the Couvent de la Visitation; it would be an ideal opportunity to see how well they were received.

Nina's portrait was finished within the hour; he felt quite light-headed from the sustained effort. To his surprise he saw he had drunk a whole litre jug of black coffee.

Leopold studied the painting. 'Your work gets better. Each new canvas you do I think to myself, "He has reached his apogee." Then you confound me by painting an even better one. But one thing worries me, Amedeo. You drive yourself so hard; art isn't a race against time, my friend. Hanka's worried about you too.'

'Jeanne is always telling me the same thing. But you know how women love to dramatize and exaggerate; it's their nature.' He gave the Pole a playful punch. 'I'm working on something special. A portrait of Jeanne. Like nothing I've ever done before. I think you'll be impressed.'

How could he begin to explain that he didn't fully understand the strange forces that drove him to new heights of self-expression, or the bizarre dreams, or the compulsion to lose himself in the streets . . . seeking what? The nirvana of the night? He didn't know.

On his way home he stopped at a *café-terrasse* in the rue Notre-Dame du Champs; the euphoria of the vodka and news of the London exhibition had evaporated. He was sitting in the sun, but he felt cold. He ordered strong black coffee. He sipped it, idly, as the sun sank behind the monolithic chimney-stacks of the Splendide laundry. He looked along the avenue. A man with a curious gait, arms and legs going like pistons, was shouting, 'Deo!'

Maurice? Could it be? Surely he was still in the sanatorium?

'Deo, *mon ami*,' Maurice panted, collapsing into a chair. 'I knew I'd find you here.' He was grinning like a schoolboy playing truant. 'Hardly recognize me, eh? I'm a walking bag of bones, but I'll soon put that right; we'll go on a binge to end all binges.'

Amedeo was shocked by his friend's emaciated appearance; his breathing was like a death rattle; sweat ran down his hollow cheeks like rancid fat; his bones were almost poking through his skin.

'But how – ?'

'When did they let me out? That's the whole joke, Deo. They didn't. I've escaped. The *flics* will be searching all over Montmartre; but I'm in Montparnasse. Clever, eh?' He groped in his pockets. 'Here – a hundred francs. Suzanne gave it me on visiting day. Sold some of my paintings. Know how I did them? From postcards. I copied them, but made them bigger. The plebeians won't know the difference, eh?'

'Do Suzanne and André know you've cut loose?'

'No.' An emaciated hand gripped Amedeo's arm. 'Don't tell André. He'll have me sent back. He doesn't like me being at Suzanne's.'

'But what about treatment?'

'*Merde*. What do I need with treatment? Those doctors and their mumbo-jumbo. I swear they're mad – all of them. I'm not off my head, Deo. You know that. I only get funny when I've been drinking.' He clutched his throat. '*Mais alors*. I've got such a thirst. I'm like a dying man in the Sahara. Come on, let's find a bar with a *patron* who hasn't got a cash-till for a heart.'

Amedeo thought about Jeanne at home. He was already late. 'Some other time, Maurice.'

'Deo.' Maurice looked hurt, 'You're my pal. Just a few *marcs*, eh, for old times' sake? What do you say? Then I'll go back to Villejuif. I promise.' He searched Amedeo's face for a glimmer of hope. 'You can't let me down, Deo. Not your old friend Maurice. Who gave you oils and brushes when you were broke? Who talked Laura Wylda into putting your paintings in her shop window? Who used to go drinking with you in the Lapin Agile?'

'All right. Just a few. For old times' sake.'

'Now you're talking. Come on – I know just the place. *Le Chat Qui Fume*. It's a little bistro where the Colarossi students go.' He grinned. 'I know all about your girl, you dark horse. Suzanne told me. She's got chestnut hair and a face like a Botticelli angel. And all the time you told me you were a confirmed bachelor.'

Maurice suddenly looked over Amedeo's shoulder. 'The *flics*.'

Amedeo turned. Two uniformed policemen were sauntering along in their direction.

Maurice dropped on his hands and knees and scurried into the café. From inside the door he whispered, 'Stay where you are, Deo. They may be looking for me.'

The two policemen walked by, engrossed in each other's conversation. When they had gone Maurice reappeared, a shade paler.

'Let's go,' he said anxiously. Amedeo followed Maurice through the alleys to the bistro. Maurice strode up to the zinc and ordered cognac.

'Wine's cheaper, Maurice.' On wine Maurice would stay reasonably sober.

'Cognac,' Maurice repeated. 'This is a reunion, Deo. The best in the house, *patron*.' The *patron* produced a Napoleon 1914.

'Ah, Emperor's brew! Excellent, excellent!'

Maurice poured out two glasses, pushed one towards Amedeo, gulped his own with a flick of the wrist. '*Mon Dieu*, but it's been weeks since I've tasted cognac.' He poured another and tossed it back.

Ten years ago, Amedeo thought, hell-raising in Montmartre had seemed fun; they had been full of *joie de vivre*, trading pastel portraits for drinks. Maurice's inventiveness for wheedling wine from stone-hearted *patrons* had borne the stamp of genius; when one ruse had failed, he had produced another and another until they either got a carafe or were thrown out. Few understood the demon inside Maurice which drove him to drink himself into oblivion; when drunk he was his own worst enemy: self-destructive, surly, inarticulate. But he painted with true inspiration and had a genius for evoking the melancholy atmosphere of the poorer districts of Paris. Because of that, Amedeo thought, Maurice could be forgiven his craving for liquor.

A crowd of students had gathered at the zinc. One addressed Amedeo, shyly at first, then became emboldened by the envious expressions of his companions.

'There's only one artist in Paris who wears a wide-brimmed black hat like yours, m'sieur – Amedeo Modigliani.'

Amedeo smiled and nodded. Three autograph books were thrust under his nose.

'You're wasting your time, *mes amis*. It's Maurice Utrillo's autograph you should be after. He's one of France's greatest painters.'

Maurice snorted. '*Merde*. You've got more talent in your little finger than I've got in the whole of my body. Ask him to do you a drawing, boys, and you'll see technique no art school could ever teach you.'

Amedeo's protests were drowned by a chorus of eager voices. The whole thing was student nonsense, he thought, but there was no harm in it. He called for pencil and paper. With bold strokes he caught a good likeness of a carroty-headed youth. He signed it. 'With my compliments,' he said, handing it over.

The youth produced a handful of change. Amedeo shook his head. The youth pushed it across the zinc. 'A carafe of Bordeaux, *patron*. For my distinguished friends.'

The *patron* raised an eyebrow; he couldn't see anything distinguished about a crowd of revellers. But their money was good.

Maurice cackled. 'This takes me back to the Lapin Agile, Deo. Remember La Goulue?'

At the mention of the can-can dancer's name the students' eyes lit up. Did he really know her?

Maurice gave them a scornful glance. 'One didn't *know* La Goulue, *mes infants*. One worshipped her. But in a way you'd never understand.'

'At our academy they've got some posters of her. At the

Moulin Rouge. Toulouse-Lautrec did them. She's a legend.'

'Legend, my arse,' Maurice said. 'She was a fat old cow with the morals of an alley cat. And she could drink the likes of you lot under the table without as much as a belch.' He gulped his wine. 'La Goulue, the glutton. Do you know she once threw the Prince of Wales her garter; laughed like a drain he did.'

Maurice, Amedeo could see, was beginning to warm to his worshipping audience. He endeavoured to lead his friend away, but the youths felt they had a proprietary interest in the artist with the face of a gargoyle. They clustered around him, fascinated by his capacity for liquor; this was something to tell their friends at the academy. Anecdotes of the notorious Moulin Rouge dance hall poured from Maurice, each one more extravagant than the one before.

Seeing Maurice borne along by the crowd of sycophantic students brought back memories of that Indian summer of 1914 when he and Maurice had been companions in Montmartre. The Butte had teemed with fakirs, mystics, Wandering Jews with the stigmata, Trotskyites playing chess with Lenin, children frolicking with balloons and paper windmills, *cocottes-de-luxe* parading along the Boulevard de Clichy. The cafés had hummed with gossip and rumour about the war, *agents provocateurs* had eavesdropped at every zinc . . . 'A fat old Archduke Ferdinand assassinated at Sarajevo? *Mais alors*, whatever next!' . . . 'The Emperor Franz Joseph turning senile? *Tant pis*! The Habsburgs need some new blood' . . . 'There's a Russian monk named Rasputin; he's the Tsarina's favourite, but they say he has the evil eye . . . ' Maurice had been carefree, exuberant, full of youthful bravado; now he was ravaged by liquor, a pathetic scarecrow who seemed one foot away from the grave.

Somehow Amedeo got him outside. But the students followed them into the street; they began to sing a drinking song from a popular operetta. Maurice joined in and brought a coughing fit on himself. He stumbled against a plane tree and sank to the pavement. He pointed to a white-washed wall across the street. 'My White Period. Don't want to go back to

Villejuif . . . I'm not crazy like they say.' He closed his eyes and began to snore.

The students lifted him up. '*Vive* Maurice Utrillo!' Maurice responded by waving an arm. The crowd began to surge along the street with Maurice aloft, singing and shouting.

Amedeo was in a daze; he hadn't been aware of how much wine he had drunk. The street lamps were swaying; he could see two of everything. He leaned against a wall, powerless to stop Maurice from being borne away.

He wandered through labyrinthine alleys behind the Boulevard Montparnasse, oddly comforted by the hissing gas-lamps and creaking shutters, chipped stucco and stubbly cobblestones: it was the quintessential patina of Paris from which he absorbed an almost spiritual nourishment. A church clock struck 3 am. He had an odd presentiment he would never see Maurice again.

Jeanne was waiting up when he got home. He stood, swaying, in the middle of the room. He could sense her disapproval just as though it were a physical thing. She was sitting in the rocking chair, sewing a blouse, her ovaline face unusually pale in the light of the kerosene lamp.

'All right,' he said thickly. 'It's late. And I'm drunk.'

She said nothing.

He flung off his hat and sat on the divan.

'Go on. Say what you're thinking. I've squandered all our allowance from Leopold. There's nothing to eat in the house.'

Without raising her eyes, Jeanne said: 'You don't have to make excuses. You're your own master.'

'Don't you want to know who I was with?'

She didn't answer.

'Maurice Utrillo. That's who. He's run off from Villejuif. He came looking for me because he needed a friend. I just couldn't turn my back on him.' The effect of walking home had begun to sober him up. As his mind started to become clearer he began to see himself as he must appear to Jeanne. 'All right. I know what you must be thinking. What your father said is coming true. Starving in an attic studio. Me getting drunk. Say it, why don't you? It's written all over your face. Remember I warned you when you moved in with me? Nobody forced you. You came of your own free will.'

He regretted it the moment he uttered it. He was beginning to feel sorry for himself. Nobody had forced him to get drunk either. He was responsible for his own actions. It was boorish of him – and heartless – to vent his growing disillusionment and frustration on Jeanne. She believed in him, stood by him, loved him. He went across to her and knelt down. Emotion constricting his throat, he kissed her tenderly. '*Mea culpa*, *cara*. Can you forgive me?'

'Oh, Dedo . . . ' Her face began to crumple.

He took her in his arms. 'Darling Jeanne, what have I done to you?'

'Why must you drink like you do? With Maurice of all people.'

He collected his thoughts. The time for white lies was over. But how could he tell her of the hellish nightmares that assailed him in those black moods of depression? It wasn't fair to burden her with it; it was something he alone had to live with. And the man in the corridor? How could he even begin to explain something he did not understand himself? Perhaps he really was what people said . . . a *peintre maudit*, cursed by the gods, fated? The critics called his work *morbidenza*. But what did those parasites know? They were devoid of insight.

'Leopold stopped by earlier.'

'Ah, the Cracow poet. What glad tidings did the Polish prophet bring? Nobody wants my paintings? He can't afford to pay us an allowance next month?'

'He came to see how we both were.'

'I know, I know. He's our one true friend. He feeds us, clothes us, believes in us, prays for us – '

'Stop it. It's not worthy of you.'

He dropped his eyes, ashamed. 'I know. I'm sorry.'

'I didn't think he looked well. He's lost a lot of weight.'

'He's always been a bit sickly-looking. I don't think it's anything serious.' Leopold had looked unusually pale, he thought. But the Pole had never had much colour in his cheeks.

'I'll make you some coffee,' Jeanne said.

'*Grazie*. Strong and black.'

She lit the stove and put the coffee pan on to boil. She realized that nothing she could do or say would change him. To try would only alienate him from her. He was an artist. A great artist. He was destined to sacrifice all for his art, to drive himself harder and harder. From the beginning she had realized it would be like this; she had known there would be a part of him she could never possess. And she had long since resigned herself to it. Fernande had once said, 'You love a man for what he is, warts and all. And if he's an artist he'll have more warts than most. But we go on loving them.' Was she expecting too much of him? She thought of the time she had met her mother in the Luxembourg Gardens; Amedeo had been at Leopold's, working.

'Your father doesn't know I'm here,' she said, smiling nervously beneath her net-veil. 'How are you keeping?'

'Fine, Maman. We're both fine.'

'Is there anything you need?'

'Nothing.'

'I want to do what's right, Jeanne. But I just don't know which way to turn. Your father loses his temper if I as much as mention Amedeo's name.' She dabbed her eyes with a lace handkerchief. 'You've no idea what I've had to put up with . . .'

'Please don't upset yourself on our account. We're quite all right. Really we are.'

'Your old room is just as you left it. We haven't touched a thing. If you should ever think of . . . '

'Yes, Maman. I understand. But how can I ever forgive Father for what he's said about Amedeo? He makes no effort whatever to understand him. He has no conception of what it's like to be constantly humiliated by critics and dealers.'

'Don't judge him too harshly, Jeanne. He's a proud, God-fearing man. All he needs is time. He's been a good father to you and your brother; always remember that.'

'Oh yes, Maman. We had material comforts, everything . . . except love and forgiveness. His heart is cold. He is ruled by his head.'

'Men are weak, Jeanne. They're selfish and stubborn. We women always make the mistake of expecting too much from them. God knows I've tried to make him see both sides . . . '

'You've done all you can, Maman. We all have. If things are going to change, it's Father who will have to change them.'

'I'll try, Jeanne. I'll try. How is the baby?'

'She's fine, Maman. She'll be walking soon. Just as soon as we can afford a bigger studio we'll have her with us.' Was it true? Of late Amedeo had shown less and less interest in the baby; he rarely talked of visiting her.

'I feel so helpless sometimes, Jeanne. You're my only daughter and I do nothing . . . '

'But you do, Maman. Your letters mean a lot to me. Please don't worry about us. We're going to be all right. It's just a question of time.'

'Dedo?' She could see the pain in his eyes.

'*Cara*.'

'I love you.'

'*Mea culpa*, Jeanne. You deserve someone better. You've got your whole life ahead of you – '

She placed her finger on his lips.

'I will never want anyone else, Dedo. You are my whole life.'

Thirteen

December was a black month of winds, ice and snow. Plumbing froze. Pipes burst. Tramps died under the bridges of the Seine. War widows were turned on to the street by landlords greedy for higher rents. Nuns at the Couvent Dames de la Visitation fed the destitutes. A dray horse deposited a pile of manure at the foot of Balzac's statue in the Carrefour Raspail. A Tsarist emigré shot himself in a backstreet hotel when he read of Bolshevik reprisals. Puffy-faced merchants gazed in awe at Nina Stein's décolleté, Aicha Goblet's gossamer dresses and Ruby Czechowska's pear-shaped *derrière.* Nina Hamnett, the water-colour painter from London, acted as mother confessor to penniless artists. The *grisettes*, the phosphorescent bats of the netherworld, made eyes at any man who had the price of a demi-carafe. And the Rotonde crowd tightened their belts and prayed for spring.

At the studio of Moise Kisling the artist colony were drinking rum punch to keep out the cold. Everybody was there: Moise's parties were famous.

'Leopold in London?' the Polish sculptor cried. 'What on earth is he doing in that nation of shopkeepers? Can you imagine those Londoners buying anything other than Turner, Sickert and Constable?'

Max Jacob drawled, 'Such an unimaginative lot, the English. We gave them Impressionism. They gave us the Wellington boot.'

Foujita, his hands full of Ardennes ham sandwiches, was saying to the model, Kiki '. . . you've never heard of Dadaism? Impossible.'

'What is it?' she asked, tossing her long black hair. 'A new kind of drink?'

The dapper Japanese rolled his eyes up to the ceiling. '*Mon Dieu*, the bitch doesn't know Dada from a daiquiri.'

'It's the new wave of painting,' Amedeo elucidated. 'They say it will have a greater impact than Cubism.'

Max Jacob drew on a marijuana cigarette. 'Its leaders are Max Ernst, Marcel Duchamps and Hans Arp. You can find Duchamps in the Café du Dome. He plays chess all day long. And paints all through the night.'

The vodka flowed. Moise replenished the rum punch. And everybody drank too much. Ortiz de Zarate stretched his huge bulk out on the floor. 'Try to step over me, *mes amis*, and remember – all that matters for an artist is what comes from his heart.'

'You're drunk,' Marc Chagall said. 'An artist must also use his head.' The wiry little Russian was famous for his meticulously painted canvases.

'Paint only what's in your soul,' Férnand Léger said.

'Paint rotting meat,' Chaim Soutine muttered just before passing out, his gnarled face a beatitude of contentment.

The party became rowdier. Fernande did a traditional Moselle folk dance. Moise sang a Poznan lullaby and wept copiously. 'Us Poles are a sentimental lot.'

Amedeo whispered in Jeanne's ear, 'Let's slip away.

She squeezed his hand in acquiescence; it was like ice.

As they walked along the Boulevard Raspail Jeanne felt her baby kicking. She was reminded that they hadn't visited little Jeanne for a fortnight. Amedeo had been too busy trying to sell his work; she hadn't wanted to add to his worries. The doctor said the baby was due in February. She had no one to turn to. If she mentioned it to Amedeo he would become moody and change the subject. Rosalie had made light of it. 'The first is the worst, child. After that they come as easy as shelling peas.' But she couldn't stop herself fretting about the future.

They sat on a bench. Amedeo stared into space, saying nothing. The night air began to aggravate his cough. He held a handkerchief over his mouth. He rose unsteadily.

'It's time we went home.'

He was sketching a young couple in the Rotonde. A voice

said over his shoulder, 'Do you remember me, Monsieur Amedeo Modigliani?'

He looked up. It was a girl. He put her at no more than her twenties but she looked prematurely old. Her eyes were dulled by heroin.

'Don't you remember? I posed for you once.'

He stared at her closely. Could it be? The hair was dyed, the figure fuller, the face ravaged . . . yet was it her?

'I was *très jolie* then. Now I am ugly. Gaby, the laundry girl.'

'Of course, Mademoiselle Gaby. But you are still *jolie*.'

Something flickered briefly in her eyes; then faded.

'I'm an old crone. I haven't looked in a mirror for six months. But I was pretty once, wasn't I? I had a good figure.'

'You did indeed.' He was appalled at the deterioration in her. She bore no resemblance to the flaxen-haired, pert-faced girl who had posed for him. He had arranged some modelling work for her at the Colarossi but she had vanished from Montparnasse. He had heard she had gone off with a circus juggler.

'I live in La Ruche nowadays. See that man over there? The one with the check shirt.' He saw a rat-faced cullion talking animatedly to an American tourist at the zinc. 'He's my protector. He's good to me. He only beats me if I don't earn much money. Underneath he's a baby. He needs me.'

The American, who was wearing a carnival sombrero and a floral shirt, pushed his way through the crowd. He touched his hat at Gaby and smiled beerily. 'Mademoiselle Gaby?'

She went into weary pretence of coquetry; but her eyes were dead.

'Your brother back there said you was in need of a little company.'

She gave him a mechanical smile. 'Before we go, honey, would you buy a drawing of me?'

'Yeah, sure. But – ' He saw Amedeo's sketch-pad and he broke into a broad grin. 'Sure, Gaby. You just sit on this stool and look pretty.'

Amedeo sketched her as she had been when she had first

posed for him. He signed it and handed it to her.

'Say, Gaby, that's damned good. How much do we owe you, young fella?'

'Five francs.'

'Here's ten. *Bon soir*. We gotta go now.' He dragged Gaby away.

'*Adieu*, Amedeo,' she called over her shoulder. '*Les marches aux modèles*, if you ever want me. Corner of the rue Vavin.'

He watched her disappear into the crowd. He felt a great sadness for her. He closed his sketch-book. It was late. Jeanne would be wondering where he'd got to. He buttoned his coat and went out into the night. *Dio mio*, but how time had flown. Soon it would be the New Year, yet it didn't seem more than a few weeks since they had left Paris for Provence. The old newspaper-seller on the corner of the rue de la Grand-Chaumière had long since gone home but her news-board was still there. He glanced at the torn poster flapping in the wind. DEGAS EST MORT. He was stunned. In his mind's eye he saw the old warrior's defiant eyes; he had given the grim reaper a run for his money. It was a hollow victory. The reaper had claimed Degas. But his paintings would assure him immortality. 'God be with you, *mon vieux*,' he murmured. He was filled with an overwhelming sadness.

From the shadows a girl emerged. '*Bon soir*. You looking for a little company?'

Blindly he walked on.

'Twenty francs, m'sieur,' she called after him.

He stopped by the *brasserie*, and drank a large *marc*; his depression did not lift. He paid and left. Slowly he climbed the stairs to the *atelier*. Degas dead. He was filled with a cold fury. Indoors, he told Jeanne.

'It's such a waste, Jeanne,' he said, slumping into a chair. 'Life's so futile. You spend your whole life battling for survival. Then – *phut*! – you are no more.'

'Shall we not go to church tonight?'

He had forgotten. He'd promised to go with her to Midnight Mass. He sprang up. 'I'll wash and change.'

'If you'd rather not . . . '

He kissed her. 'I promised, remember?'

'But, Dedo . . . ' Jeanne held her stomach. 'Will it matter . . . me looking like this?'

He laughed. 'Who could object to a woman with child? It is the time she is most beautiful.'

The Church of the Nativity was a flickering mirage of candles. Amedeo gazed at the ornate architecture, built during Louis XIV's reign, three hundred years earlier. Somewhere a choir was singing a Bach chorale. He experienced a spiritual affinity with Jeanne as she knelt beside him in prayer. He admired the church's magnificent cupola with its intricately sculptured decoration done by the Anguier brothers; and Mignard's wonderful fresco of St. Louis and St. Anne.

After the service they walked back through the Observatory Gardens. The wind had dropped; the air was still, the night sky a rash of stars.

'Soon it will be the New Year,' Jeanne said.

'We'll go to Italy. In the summer. The fields will be red with poppies – ' The ground moved under him and the world spun.

'Dedo – what's wrong?'

'Faintness . . . perhaps lack of air in the church.'

'You're shaking. And feverish.'

'Just the cold. I must be coming down with flu; it's the time of the year for *la grippe*.'

As they walked to the rue de la Grand-Chaumière, he talked of Italy, of his apprenticeship at Micheli's, of the School of Fine Arts at Venice, of childhood experiences, half-forgotten, buried beneath the strata of years in Paris.

'Micheli still has his studio at Livorno. Of course his hand won't be so steady and his beard's probably grey . . . but he's a wonderful character. I'm sure you'll like him . . . '

At the *atelier* the coke stove was still hot; its coals glowed red beneath the layers of ash. Jeanne raked it and fed logs and coke; it snapped and crackled and showered sparks across the floor.

'Like Lucifer's breath,' Amedeo said. 'Warmth, *cara*. That's what I need. Burn, stove!' He felt curiously light-headed. He lay on the bed; the room was spinning. He closed his eyes. He sat up when he heard Jeanne opening the door.

'Where are you going?'

'Mme Velitch has a phone. I'll send for Dr Devraigne.'

'No doctors, *cara*. They prescribe balsam or some patent medicine and charge the earth.' He fell back, sweat breaking out. He was immediately sorry he had spoken so vehemently. 'Stay here with me, Jeanne.'

'But you're ill – '

'Just flu. Besides, we can't afford doctors. We're going to need every sou when our child is born.'

'Father would lend us money.'

'I'll not beg or ask for charity. That would give him the excuse he's been looking for . . . to say "I told you so".'

'But this is an emergency, Dedo. He'll listen to reason.'

'*Pazzienza, cara*. Leopold will be back from London soon; then we'll have money to burn.' Was he trying to reassure Jeanne . . . or himself? But Leopold *had* been optimistic; his last letter from London had eulogized the Mansard Gallery, rhapsodized about the Sitwells and the promised visit of the novelist, Arnold Bennett. But the warm-hearted Pole was a romantic, easily swayed, gullible to the point of exasperation. Poor Leopold; lovable Leopold. If the exhibition were not a success, it would be Leopold who would be heart-broken.

'You're like ice,' Jeanne said, slipping into bed beside him. 'Hold me close.'

Amedeo woke; the sun's rays were streaming in through the window. It was late afternoon. The space beside him was empty. Then he heard Jeanne moving about in the kitchen; he savoured the moment as the smell of bacon and eggs wafted into the room. Mama Modigliani . . . chopping up courgettes and wishing him *buon appetito*; Papa reading Spinoza in an imperious voice while he and his brothers had pulled faces and stifled laughter. Papa, a proud die-hard who ran the family business as though it were the only one of its kind in Italy. Something had died inside Papa when the Stock Exchange collapsed in the 1880s and he awoke one morning to find himself bankrupt. They had been forced to move from their fine house on the fashionable Via Roma to a modest apartment in the Via delle Ville. In his humiliation his Papa had avoided his old haunts and friends, but kept alive his dream of re-establishing the family business. His commercial traveller's job paid little and it had been a constant struggle to keep his family fed and clothed. Their fortunes had plummeted. Papa fell ill. The bailiffs were knocking at the door and Mama Modigliani was pregnant with Amedeo. Under an old Italian law bailiffs could not impound a bed in which a woman was about to give birth. Papa had piled the family heirlooms and valuables on the bed, thus saving them. Eugenia went into labour an hour after the bailiffs had left. Nobody could shake her faith in the divine providence of Amedeo's birth; she believed he was destined for greatness. In her diary, when he was two years old, she'd written '. . . Dedo is moody and spoiled, but *joli comme un coeur*.'

Amedeo pulled back the sheets and stood up; his head swam and throbbed. He saw Jeanne had used up the last of the wood and coke: fuel was the first priority. He searched his pockets: fifteen francs. So little!

Hearing him moving about Jeanne came into the bedroom; she tried to persuade him to go back to bed, but she knew once his mind was made up there was no changing it. But she couldn't bear the thought of him hawking his drawings around the cafés.

'Couldn't you ask Hanka for an advance on next month's allowance?'

He reflected a moment; sometimes one had to swallow one's pride. He kissed her forehead and promised he would return soon.

The streets were almost deserted; the city had a Siberian bleakness about it. As he was passing the shop of Adolphe Basler he heard raised voices. Through the grimy window he saw the dealer talking to an elderly woman with a sad but proud face. Basler caught his eye through the glass and shot outside. He produced his most ingratiating smile and pleaded for a few minutes of Amedeo's valuable time.

Amedeo was about to tell Basler to go to blazes when he was moved by the woman's expression.

'She's got a painting,' Basler whined. 'A still-life; she says it's one of yours. But everybody knows you only paint portraits.'

Amedeo approached the woman. 'May I see the signature, Mother?'

She indicated Basler. 'That robber offered me twenty francs. But it's worth twice that.'

Amedeo studied the painting: a bowl of fruit on a table with a chequered cloth. He didn't recall it. Had he done it at Cheron's? He couldn't remember; it was his own signature all right. Yes, some months earlier . . . a young artist from the Alsace who hadn't even the price of a plateful of spaghetti at Rosalie's. He'd signed the canvas to increase the young man's chances of selling it.

'My late husband bought it, m'sieur. At an exhibition in the rue Huysmans. He paid forty francs.'

Basler sneered: 'You were cheated. This isn't a Modigliani.'

'Oh, but it is, Basler. The lady speaks the truth. It's from my Montmartre period,' Amedeo lied. 'And worth considerably more now.'

'How much more?' Basler said craftily.

'Oh . . . at least seventy-five francs, I'd say.'

'*Mon Dieu*, do you want to ruin me? Sixty.'

'I'm surprised at you, Basler! Cheating a poor widow. What would they think on the rue Lafitte if it got around – ?'

'You – you wouldn't dare!'

'Oh, but I would.'

Basler bit his lip and hopped from one foot to another as though afflicted by St Vitus Dance. 'Sixty-five. My final offer.'

Amedeo took the woman's arm. 'Let's go, Mother. We are wasting our time.' He was enjoying himself, watching the parsimonious dealer's expression. How soon would the man's business instincts overcome his meanness?

'Seventy then.'

'Seventy-five, Basler.'

'You've got a stone for a heart, Modigliani. You know I'll never find a buyer.'

'Rubbish. You'll get twice that from one of your moribund customers.' He smiled as he watched Basler counting the money into the woman's hand; if only the old miser had known what he was really buying . . .

Outside, the woman shook Amedeo's hand. 'God bless you, m'sieur. May Dame Fortune smile on you.'

'It was nothing.'

'Tell me the truth now . . . did you really paint it?'

He smiled. 'Use the money wisely, Mother; some questions are best left unanswered.'

He raised his hat and walked in the direction of the rue Joseph-Bara.

Hanka welcomed him but he sensed something was wrong. She told him she had had a letter from Leopold; the exhibition was arousing a lot of interest. He made small-talk; somehow he couldn't bring himself to broach the subject of his monthly allowance. He picked up his hat and began to make his excuses for leaving.

'What's on your mind, Amedeo?'

'Nothing. I'd better be going.' He was disturbed by the bitterness in her voice.

'Is it money? Yes. It's always money, isn't it? Leopold doesn't have it to give you. We've been living on haricot beans for a fortnight. He had to sell some of his books to pay his fare to London.'

A cold knot tightened in the pit of his stomach. She had every right to be bitter; she must think of me as a millstone round Leopold's neck, he thought. At this very moment Leopold is probably huddling in some run-down boarding house, existing on rolls and coffee. No wonder Jeanne had thought Leopold had looked thin. The Pole had been denying himself so that he, Amedeo, should not go without. *Dio mio*, but how could he have been so blind? He felt ashamed that he had never enquired into Leopold's finances. He had always taken his monthly allowance without question. As his right. It had never occurred to him that the money wasn't coming from the sale of his paintings. All the time he had been buying drinks for the gang at the Rotonde Leopold and Hanka had been living on beans . . .

'I have a few francs,' Hanka said, 'if it will help.'

He shook his head. He groped for the words to express his shame. 'I just don't know what to say, Madame Zborowski. You must think I'm – ' He broke off; words were not enough. The thought of Leopold's impoverished circumstances and Jeanne sitting alone at home made him realize the hopelessness of his dreams and ideals. He had sacrificed everything in the pursuit of the Absolute. Perhaps, all along, it had been an impossible dream.

'Don't write to Leopold that I came about money, Madame Zborowski. He has worried on my account long enough.'

He turned and left. How far he walked he had no idea. Café followed café. Whenever he sold a drawing he drank a glass of *marc*. The raw spirit was the only thing that was keeping him going. He had a wild notion that it could somehow burn out whatever it was that was gnawing his lungs. The more he coughed, the more he drank. Night wrapped its protective cloak around him. He heard footsteps. He looked over his shoulder. Nothing but the shadows. But he's there, he thought. The man in the hallway has always been there, dogging my footsteps. It is inevitable we should one day come face to face. He had had an appointment with him ever since he had come to Paris. Why not hasten the inexorable conclusion?

He walked along the rue des Fauillantines, past the Abbey of Val-de-Grace, across the rue Pierre Nicole, into the rue Henri Barbusse. It was only a short distance now to the rue Notre-Dame du Champs and home. There was something he had to finish.

As he climbed the stairs he went through his pockets.

Thank God he still had a few francs. He counted them. Twenty-five. Yes, it was enough to say Hanka had given him a small advance. He could not bring himself to tell Jeanne what he had learned. She had enough to worry about with the baby.

'Dedo, you look frozen. Where have you been? It's nearly midnight.'

'I'm sorry, *cara*. I didn't realize.' He thrust the money into her hand. 'I ran into Blaise Cendrars. You remember him: he lost an arm in the war. We had a few drinks. I just didn't realize the time had gone so quickly. Then, walking home, I had the urge to paint you.' He tore his jacket off. 'I'll get a canvas ready.'

'Now? But it's so late, Dedo. You're tired out of your mind.'

'I feel it here, Jeanne.' He put a hand on his chest. 'It's bursting to come out. It won't take long. I promise. You don't have to change. Sit for me just as you are.' He mixed his colours feverishly. He would paint the very beauty of her soul: serene yet wistful, innocent yet mysterious. It would be the epitome of his dreams.

Jeanne sat on the bed. A feeling of hopelessness came over her. It was impossible to penetrate his stubborn streak. She must let it run its course.

'That's fine, Jeanne. No, perhaps you'd better wear a hat. Here, this one. Ah, yes, that's perfect. Now, tilt your head to one side. *Bella, bella*. Now put your forefinger under the tip of your chin. Perfect. Hold that while I get some coffee.'

He went into the kitchen. The bottle of *marc* was where he had hidden it behind a pile of canvases. He poured it into the coffee jug. A few weeks earlier a glassful had been enough to calm his overwrought nerves. But he was becoming immune to it. Now he needed a whole bottle at a time to satisfy the craving. In the cafés he bullied people into accepting a drawing in return for a drink. If they refused he became belligerent. Often he would catch a glimpse of his face in a shop window; it was surly and haunted. Sometimes he would cough up the liquor before he could swallow it. He began to feel the phantoms of the night were drawing their net tighter. The moment he smelt liquor all his good intentions were swept aside. It was as though his will had snapped. The self-destructive force which had lain dormant for years now took possession of him. He drank from the jug, gratified by the burning sensation in his throat.

He carried the jug into the bedroom and put it by his easel. 'Stay exactly as you are, Jeanne. You look lovely.'

He squeezed oils on to the canvas and attacked it like a man possessed, his dark eyes glowing with feverish intensity. He cross-hatched with quick, bold strokes. This was what he had been seeking: a portrait like no other he had ever done. Fatigue buffeted him in ever-increasing waves. He gulped more *marc* and threw himself back into his painting. Within half an hour it was finished. He stood back: it was a final testament.

'What do you think, Jeanne?' The room was swaying; his body felt leaden.

Jeanne's eyes swam as she looked at the portrait.*

'Dedo . . . it's – ' She broke off as he suddenly lurched forward, coughing. With a low moan he ran to the kitchen, clutching his mouth with both hands.

'Dedo – what is it?'

He bent over the sink. His throat was filled with a fiery red ball. He remembered no more.

It was an endless nightmare of fitful sleep and tortured visions. Night and day became one long delirium. In the dark corners of his mind he could still see the violent stain in the sink.

He opened his eyes. He was in bed in the *atelier*. Jeanne was sitting in a chair by his side.

'How long have I been ill?'

'Nearly a week. Don't try to talk.'

'It was the cough, wasn't it? It brought on a haemorrhage.

* *With A Hat*. Private collection, Berne, Switzerland

All I needed was a few days' rest. I'll be all right now.'

Jeanne bathed his forehead.

'You didn't send for the doctor . . . ?'

'No,' she lied, remembering Dr Devraigne's grim expression. Remembering him saying that Amedeo needed warmth and sun.

'Thank God. I can't stand their mournful faces.'

'Try to sleep now.'

He looked out of the window at the rooftops bathed in the yellow ochre of wintry sunlight and the blue of the cirrus sky thinned by January's starkness. It reminded him of one of Maurice's Montmartre scenes.

He studied his face in the mirror. His cheeks were hollowed, his eyes sunken and bright. Too bright. He looked like a fugitive from Emile Zola's *Nana*, a ravaged dissolute from Hugo's *Les Misérables*. Such a strange brilliance in the eye. Was it really his own face or an amalgam of Frédéric Chopin's, Oscar Wilde's and Eugène Delacroix's? Ah, Goethe, Schopenhauer, Heine, Spinoza, Baudelaire, Mallarmé . . . where was their divine vision? Were artists simply prisoners of their talent, stumbling through the darkness?

Rain was beating on the windows; the air was oppressive. He raised himself up. His head swam, then cleared. On the easel he saw the portrait. Yes, it was finished. There was nothing left to keep him. He had formed a plan. He had only to bide his time . . .

Jeanne wrapped her shawl round her shoulders. Dedo was sleeping. She let herself out quietly and went down the stairs to Mme Velitch's apartment and asked to use her phone.

'*D'accord*, Madame Modigliani. How is your husband?'

'Much better, thank you.' Everybody in the district thought of them as being married. She asked for the number.

'Doctor Devraigne? Madame Modigliani. You told me to phone the moment the fever left him . . . Yes, Doctor . . . Yes . . . He is sleeping now . . . You will call in later tonight? *Merci*.'

Mme Velitch had made some tea. They sat talking for a while. Jeanne gave her a franc for the phone, thanked her for the tea, then went back upstairs.

Amedeo's clothes had gone. The bed was empty.

The rain on his face was oddly comforting. His overcoat was saturated but he was only concerned about keeping his sketch-book dry. The streets had the greyness of dusk. Waiters on the *terrasses* were changing the tablecloths. He felt curiously light-headed as though he were floating. A feverish excitement ran through him.

He went in the first bar he came to.

'*Marc*. Large.'

The patron poured it out. 'Five francs.'

He riffled through his pockets; two francs. He took out his sketch-pad and pencil. 'Your portrait for the drink.'

The man shrugged dubiously. But he was impressed with the drawing; the likeness was uncanny. He pushed the glass towards Amedeo.

The demons began to creep out of their hiding places. Dark shadows began to surround him. He was hardly aware of what he was saying. Words poured from him. 'I've given my soul to Art, *mes amis*,' he said to the curious bystanders. 'There's nothing left to do but die. When the man in the corridor points the finger at you . . . that's when you make your will.'

He was outside. Rain. Merciful night. Had to earn money. Jeanne and the baby. Leopold and Hanka. He stumbled against a lamp-post. Café names danced in front of him like marionettes . . . Select . . . Café du Dome . . . Closerie des Lilas . . . Le Coupole . . . Les Trianons . . . Bal Bullier . . . Lavenue . . . Deux Magots . . .

He crossed a bridge over the Seine, gazing up at the stars, devouring the mysterious night. He was seized with an urge to see Maurice. He staggered down alleys, lurched along cobbled lanes. He felt comforted by his old Montmartre haunts. In the Lapin Agile he sold some sketches. He banged on the zinc, demanding brandy. People had become blurred images.

'Get out.' A hand sent him spinning through the street door. But he only found it amusing. It was like old times.

He suddenly recognized the rue Cortot. He found Suzanne's studio and rang the bell. He felt the half-bottle of cognac in his pocket. Maurice would no doubt be in need of a drink. A light came on. The door opened. André Utter appeared in his nightrobe.

'Good Lord, Modi, is it you? You're soaked to the skin. Come in, come in.'

'Want to have a drink with Maurice.' He threw himself into a chair. 'I gave them a fright in the Lapin Agile, André. They thought I was a ghost. *Dio mio*, it's like Siberia in here. Where's Maurice?'

'He isn't here, Modi. We haven't seen him for days. Look, let me take your coat – '

'There's no time, André. Hear this damned cough of mine? It's killing me. In the hallway there's a man bearing me a deadly grudge. He dogs my footsteps. There's no escape. He always knows where to find me.'

'Stay there. I'll fetch Suzanne. You need something on your stomach. I bet you haven't eaten anything all day.'

'Don't need food, André. Got to go.' A coughing spasm made him bend forward. He hauled himself to his feet and made for the door.

'Modi, wait – '

The night embraced him like an old friend. The rain on his burning face was like manna. He lost himself in the streets, unable to distinguish reality from fantasy. Stabbing pains in his chest made him catch his breath. He couldn't move. A burning lava filled his throat. The ground erupted beneath him. He fell headlong into the abyss.

Globules of white hovered over him. Everything was cocooned in a grey mist. What was that sickly, cloying odour? Hospital ether.

'Jeanne . . . is that you?'

'Yes, Dedo.'

'Where is this?'

'Don't try to talk.'

He was so tired. In his mind's eye he saw himself at fifteen riding in a farm cart across the rolling fields of Tuscany. The cart was being pulled by two oxen. The farmer had been impressed at the sketches he had done. '*Bello, piccolo*. So you're going to be an artist, *si*?' Indeed he was, he had said with youthful pride.

'*Cara Italia*,' he said.

The pain was ebbing. It was so peaceful now. A warm glow stole over him. A *fata morgana* beckoned . . .

The white globules began to go dark.

He had no fear.

Fourteen

Her bedroom was exactly as she remembered it. The same white-washed walls and gauze curtains, the same chequered bedspread and walnut dressing table. In the cupboard were her convent school books and teddy bear her mother had kept out of sentiment. There was her very first portrait on enrolling at the Académie Colarossi – a charcoal sketch of her brother André – and the pastel scene which had earned her a seal of merit. There were her student sketch-books and, hidden between the pages, the caricature she had done of Amedeo.

She began to comb out her waist-length chestnut hair; then she started to plait it in the style Amedeo had loved so much. 'It makes you look like a Bellini madonna, *cara*.'

The initial shock of the terrible nightmare at the Hôpital de la Charité had worn off; now, she was tranquil, serene, able to think of the night Amedeo's friends had found him lying in front of Balzac's statue, soaked to the skin and delirious. She had feared the worst the moment they carried him indoors. '*On le voyait finir*,' she had said; she had seen him wasting away. She remembered the very first time he had read Lautreamont's *Les Chants de Maldoror* to her; how moved she had been. The Comte de Lautreamont, he had told her, had been a man of vision who had died young, neglected, his talents unsung. Fame had come to him only in death.

She recalled the Roumanian sculptor, Constantin Brancusi, once saying, 'Fame doesn't give a damn about artists when they chase her but the moment they turn their backs on her she runs behind them.'

Again she found herself reliving the nightmare at the Hôpital de la Charité. For days his life had hung in the balance. Once, he had rallied briefly and spoke her name. But his illness had gone too far. He sank into a coma. The end had come on the night of January 24th. The Sisters of Mercy and Dr Devraigne, whom Leopold had called in, had tried to comfort her. 'If only we'd got him to hospital earlier . . . but he has burned himself out. He must have suffered for many weeks. He was a brave man . . . and now he is at peace . . . '

Poor Leopold; what a shock it had been. He had arrived back from London so excited. 'I sold almost everything, Jeanne. Everyone wanted to know about him. The tide has turned at last.'

But Amedeo had not heard the good news: he was keeping his final rendezvous with the man in the corridor . . . And how the carrion crows had gathered as the news of Amedeo's collapse went through Montparnasse; she could still see them in her mind's eye, waving their cheque-books, and haunting the studio.

She opened the copy of Pascal's *Pensées* her mother had given her on her sixteenth birthday; she turned the pages, coming to the passage she had marked . . . *The heart has its reasons that the mind knows nothing of* . . .

Closing the book, she went to the wardrobe and changed into the skirt and high-collared blouse she had been wearing the first time she set eyes on Amedeo.

There was a knock at the door. 'May I come in, Jeanne?'

'Yes, Father.'

He opened the door and came in hesitantly. 'You should try to sleep, Jeanne; it's late – '

'I'm not tired.'

'I know how you must feel but it's best that it ended when it did. He was a dying man, Jeanne; you had no future with him.'

'Will you go to the funeral, Father – at Père Lachaise Cemetery?'

'You know my feelings in this matter, Jeanne.'

'Yes. You've always judged him harshly. Just as you have me. But it is you, Father, who should ask forgiveness for what you have done.'

'Your bitterness towards me is to be expected. But the fact re – '

'People are beginning to say what his friends have always

known,' she interrupted, accusingly. 'That he was touched by the hand of genius. One day the whole world will recognize his art.'

He avoided her eyes. 'Your mother and I are thinking of your future now, Jeanne. And the baby's. You know we will do anything we can to help.' He hesitated. 'You must leave Paris.'

'I shall never leave Paris, Father. Amedeo is to be buried here.'

'You must leave Paris as soon as you're well enough. We've made all the arrangements. Some friends of ours . . . in the country . . . are willing to take you and the child.'

'I've given you my answer, Father.'

'Jeanne, I have my reputation to consider. My superiors do not know about . . . ' He tailed off. 'I'm sure you understand what I am trying to say, Jeanne. This is just as painful for me.'

'Of course, Father.' Her thoughts were elsewhere.

'You may not think it now, but one day you will be able to put all this behind you, make a fresh start in life.'

'There is no other life, Father. Amedeo was my life.'

M. Hébuterne cleared his throat with difficulty. 'I've asked Monsieur Lavall, of Rosenburg's Gallery, to value the paintings at Modigliani's attic – '

'You had no right, Father. The studio is locked. And I have signed all Amedeo's canvases over to Monsieur Zborowski. He is Amedeo's dealer. We do not need anyone else.'

'But, child, you're going to need money.'

'I have made all the necessary arrangements, Father. There is nothing for you to do. Everything has been taken care of.'

'You're in an overwrought state, child. You don't know what you're saying. Everything will look different in the morning.' He went to the door. 'Good night, Jeanne.'

'Good night, Father.'

He looked at her, then closed the door behind him.

The dawn light crept over the grey rooftops. Jeanne was standing at the window. She remembered the solemn promise she had made to Amedeo. Their life together had been brief, she thought; but their love would be eternal.

She opened the window and stepped on to the narrow balcony. The air was crisp; she shivered and gripped the wrought-iron railing. Pastel yellow rays of early-morning sunlight lay like lattice-work over the cobbled street below. She looked up at the clear sky. The world was suddenly a glorious collage of colour.

Her hand let go of the railing.

A crowd gathered around the cumpled body. They stared at the plaited hair and pale oval face: it was beautiful even in death. She was just twenty-one years old. Somewhere in the distance an angelus bell began to ring.

The sun rose. Paris began to wake.